ON THE SLY

ON THE SLY

A Sylvia Wilson Mystery

WENDY L. KOENIG

1

The door to my bar wouldn't open. It had unlocked fine, but wouldn't move, as if it had a hidden bolt. I glared at the sign on the door: "Smugglers, Sylvia Wilson proprietor".

I am Sylvia Wilson. This was my bar.

It was 3 PM. Time to open; people would want a cold beverage while they waited out the soon-to-be rush hour traffic.

This first Monday of September in St. Louis felt like early August. Shimmers from the triple digit heat rolled across the sidewalk and street. Rivers of sweat coursed down my forehead and face, soaking the neck of my tee-shirt, a new sleeveless I'd bought when visiting the Arch a week ago. It featured the famous landmark on a soft green background, and I hoped it wouldn't stain.

Shaking my head did nothing to help with the sweat. I balanced my groceries on my knee and rubbed the burn out of my eyes with the dry hem of my shirt. A car honked on its way past. I blindly turned and lifted my chin by way of greeting.

Midwest politics.

Or maybe I was flashing everyone.

I shifted my three bags of food higher. The handle of my fourth bag had broken at the store, shattering a bottle of orange juice in the parking space next to mine. I'd picked up the glass shards, swore a lot, and piled the remaining groceries into the other three bags, making it impossible to carry them by the handles. Hence, I now had all three bags in my arms.

First the orange juice, and now the door of my bar. My day was cursed before it even began. I yelled at the door, "Come on! You're killing me, here!"

The metal of the door was burning hot when I shoved all my weight against it. It didn't budge. It was, of course, at that precise moment that my bladder chose to remind me of the seven samples of pumpkin-pie-spice latte I'd pinched from the barista at the grocery store. The whole reason for my parking in front in the first place. It would have been a straight line in the front door, past the bar where I could have dropped my three bags of groceries. Then down the hall, detour to the alarm for the split second it would take to turn it off, and into the bathroom.

Growling my frustration at my bladder and the cursed day, I kicked the bottom of the door, collected my keys from the lock, and headed around the corner, glancing in the barred windows, though it was too dark to see anything inside. I rounded the second corner, nearly jogging toward the back door, gravel crunching under my feet. I should have parked back there and come in that way, instead of worrying about the few extra seconds it would take to double back after depositing the groceries on the bar. Just the exercise of the walk around the building drenched me. And I'd brought no spare clothes. At least the bar would be cool.

I slid my key into the back door, only to discover it wasn't locked. I'd definitely locked it when I closed. Someone had been in my bar. I shoved open the door, noting the alarm was disabled. Not bothering to turn on the back hall light nor shut the door behind me, I walked down the streak of light from the open door and dropped the groceries on the corner of the bar.

Smugglers had always been like a secret lover to me, pulling me into its embrace. Yet today it felt… off. Silent. Sullen, almost. On a quick glance, I didn't see anyone. I traveled back down the hall, did my bathroom business, came out, flicked on the hall light, shut the door, and turned up the air-conditioner. My gaze traveled down the hall, past the bathroom, past the wide open register, past the celery falling out of the wilted grocery bags onto the bar, to the dark open area beyond. Even from where I stood, looking through the dimness of that room, I could see something large blocking the front door. As I approached, I detoured briefly to the freezer to put away my newly purchased ice cream.

Then I turned on the lights to the front room and saw a body jammed against the front door. And blood. Lots and lots of blood. In a lake on the floor. All over the door, the pool table, the wall. On the nearest tall tables and chairs. I couldn't honestly see a single clean space within fifteen feet of the door.

"Well, shit." I shook my head and pressed my lips together. There would be no opening the bar today. Maybe not for the week.

The body was lying on its side, facing the interior of the room. Beneath the ski mask, the neck was sliced wide open. Bulging eyes stared at me. For just a moment I froze and stared back. Even though I'd seen dead people before – my parents and grandparents – it had been at funeral homes. It was a whole different thing, staring me in the face.

The heavy, coppery odor of blood hit me. Only so much more than just a cut finger. I swallowed hard a few times as my stomach seized at the smell.

The dead person was most likely a man, judging by the size. He was big, somewhere around 180 lbs, but thick fleshy forearms didn't really make me think of a body builder. There was no way he could possibly be alive, what with his larynx hanging out and all, but I watched his chest for movement anyway. I wanted to be able to say to any nightmares that might visit that there was nothing to be done. The chest was absolutely still; he was definitely dead.

The lessons my father and brother had taught me kicked in. Better late than never. Glancing around again for anyone lurking in the shadows, I forced myself to walk calmly past the emptied register to the far end of the bar, where I kept my safe. I didn't need any still-hiding killer getting jumpy just because I rushed for my gun. Took out the Ruger .357, just in case someone was still there. I also pulled my cellphone out of my pocket and hit the first number on my speed dial.

While waiting for my call to be answered, I began a circuitous route around the room. Though the building was rectangular, the patron portion was built like an L, with the longest part going the full front of the facility. It had three tall tables, a pool table, a couple video games, a jukebox, a rarely used dart board, and five booths. The walls were filled with photos of cops in uniform, doing vacation type stuff. Mostly fishing, but some other sports, too. These were all signed by the participants. There were two TVs mounted in optimal places. I'd put a giant flat screen with six more booths and the two gender-neutral bathrooms down the side. Behind the bar was a locked storeroom.

First, I checked the storeroom was still locked. Next, I peeked into the bathrooms. Finally, I looked into all the booths for anyone hidden. I was careful to stay near the wall so as to not contaminate the scene too badly.

Finally, after about the nine hundredth ring, my brother, Aaron, answered, a bit exasperated and more than a little tired. "Syl, I worked a midnight —"

"There's a body in my bar."

"…What?" The grogginess was suddenly gone from his voice.

"A body. In Smugglers."

"I'm coming. Tell me you called the cops before you called me." A sudden flurry of motion sounded from his end of the line. I thought I heard a feminine voice in the background.

"You're a cop. I called you."

He swore, and I hung up. He'd call it in.

I'd moved fast around the room and had reached the edges of the blood swamp surrounding the body. There was no way anyone could get close to it without getting in the slick. I studied the man, taking in more details. Caucasian. Grey razor stubble stuck out from the sliver of exposed chin and, likewise, salt and pepper chest hair peeked out from beneath the collar of the undershirt. I guessed he was somewhere between 45 and 55.

Unbidden, the memory of my father's body rose to the surface again. Beside his, my mother's. I'd barely recognized them, as broken as their faces had been. We'd had to have a closed casket service. They'd been about the same age as this man when they'd been killed walking beside an Iowa country road. The driver was so drunk that he never even noticed he'd mowed down two people and destroyed the lives of their teenaged children. A dull weight settled into me, replacing the image. Though it had been eight years, again I felt adrift.

I took a deep breath, shook away the fog, and focused once more on the victim in front of me. Over his tee, he wore a buttoned designer-type shirt, though the blood had saturated it so much that I had no idea the color. The newish khaki pants were the kind that came from a cheap department store. There were a lot of creases and stretch marks from sitting and growing bigger. He hadn't seemed quite old enough to be retired. Close though.

Heavy biker gloves with fingertips intact, but knuckles cut out, covered the man's hands. He'd definitely come here for a robbery. I glanced around the room. The thieves had all the time in the world to rob the place. The till was empty, but all three TVs, including the giant flatscreen, were still there.

Either this guy had an argument with the killer, or he'd been duped by him. No matter which way, this robbery was really a murder.

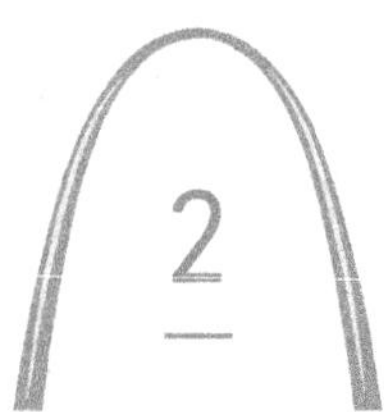

I returned my gun to the safe. Then pulled a stool from in front of the bar around to the back, settled on my perch, and concentrated on not thinking about the death of my parents. I was thankful, now, that I had parked out front. There would be plenty of responder vehicles, and I didn't want my Jeep to get hemmed in.

I tried to ignore the deep odor of blood. Despite my best efforts, the smell got to me and my stomach started rolling again. I rose and opened the back door for some fresh air. The heat of the afternoon almost made me stagger back, and instant sweat sprang up on my skin again, despite the air conditioner at my back. I shaded my eyes and peered around the small lot. Parked in the back left corner was an ugly beige Toyota Corolla. 2007, or so. I wasn't surprised. It wasn't unusual for a stray vehicle to be left behind from a late night hookup or someone too drunk to drive.

Besides the deep layer of dust, the Corolla was rust pocked and both front tires were balding on the inside. Totally fitting with a retired guy wearing rumpled khakis. I went to the car and looked through the driver's side window. The door locks were up, so using the hem of my shirt, I gave the door a try. A belch of overhot air blasted me with the stench of rancid french fry grease and soured milkshakes. My stomach gave a long, long roll of unhappiness, but ended when I stepped away and took deep breaths through pursed lips.

Oil stained wrappers and fast food bags littered the floor. Stains covered both front seats. Another thick layer of dust blanketed the dash and instrument panel. Smudged finger marks had cleared away the dust over the gas gauge. The back seats were no different than the front, except the pile of trash reached epic proportions. I'd have to burn my new shirt.

My cellphone chirped and I pulled it out of my pocket to see Peaches's name and number. She was my Uncle Tripp's second wife. A much younger and bustier woman than his first. She was beautiful with bright highlights in her naturally blond hair. And she was a good person. When Aaron and I'd arrived to live on their ranch in Texas, Peaches was oh-so-aching to be maternal to the two of us, when all we wanted was to be left alone. We were teenagers and we made her life as difficult as we could, especially me. She took it in stride. Even built us a firing range so we could keep up with what our Dad had taught us. Helped me win expert marksman at the local gun club every year. Eventually, Aaron and I had grown to love her.

But, that very moment wasn't a good time for a chat. I dropped the unanswered phone back into my pocket. The cops would be arriving any second; there was already a siren headed my way.

I didn't have much time, so I gladly abandoned the trash piles and focused elsewhere. Spying a disgusting paper towel on the floor of the passenger's side, I snatched it up. The central console was filled with CDs exclusively. The registration in the glove compartment was for Martin Degere, the Bureau of Investigations Chief for the Metropolitan Police. I was familiar with him from a couple shop parties I'd visited with Aaron.

He was a tall, thick-set, Black man, earning himself the nickname 'Bear' when he was a patrolman. Then he'd risen in the ranks and his nickname had been modified to 'Grizzly', where it had remained ever since. With gray at his temples, he was taking a close look at retirement from the force and politics was a logical next step. Or so Aaron had told me.

I'd liked him when my brother introduced us. His giant hand had nearly swallowed mine. He'd looked tired, but his eyes were kind. Why would a man finishing his career on such a stellar note become involved in murder? Was he? Or was it coincidence? How did he know the victim in my bar? Maybe, hopefully, the car had nothing to do with the murder.

The approaching siren had become several and were nearing at a rapid rate. I put everything back and returned to the bar. Settled on the stool again and waited for the inevitable flood of Blue.

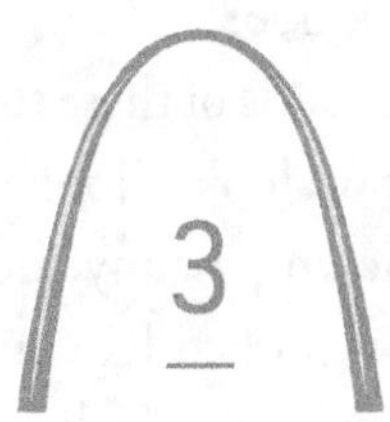

The old saying goes, "There's never a cop around when you need one."

Not true this time. Mostly, I guess, it was because the bar was just down the street from the cop shop, and it was a favorite hangout for the blue crowd. It didn't hurt that my brother brought coworkers there after shifts.

Within minutes, the place was surrounded by blaring cop cars. Some even slid sideways on the pavement, their tires squealing like … well, pigs. Of course, some were geniuses and tried to come in the still-locked front. And when they couldn't, the brightest of the blue breed decided to break the door down.

Good luck. Steel reinforced doors with heavy-duty hinges and locks were among the first purchases I'd made. I hollered, "Around back!" Pretty sure they didn't hear me.

Finally, a detective arrived. He was medium build, Black, and frowning. I knew he was a detective because he came straight in the back door and went directly to the body, stopping short of the blood pool. Following him was a big lumberjack in blue uniform. The name on his badge was Jacobs. He was rubbing his shoulder and motioned toward the front door. "Steel?"

I slowly nodded. He took my name and wrote it in a log book he set up just outside the back door.

Aaron came right on the heels of these two. Though both of us had the 'grown-up kid next door' look, I looked like our father: straight brown hair – mine was down past my shoulders – , freckled nose, and hazel eyes. My brother looked like our mother and was nearly the opposite of me, except for the freckles we both shared. Today, his short sandy hair was a mess, sticking out every which way. His handsome face looked gaunt and his smart blue eyes were sunk into their sockets. The smell of cheap women's perfume wafted from him and lipstick was on his neck.

I said, "If I had to guess, you're working on more than one kind of night shift." My brother was well known for his proclivity with the ladies.

He made a face. Looked past me at the body in the bar and the detective hunched there. "You know who he is?"

There's something about our relationship that made us sometimes act like perverse assholes to each other, even though we were very close. I gave that free rein now. "I don't, actually. But I thought you might, since he probably works out of your shop and all."

He gave a visible start and stared at me. "What? He's a cop?"

I met his gaze with cool, deadpan eyes and waited.

It took a few seconds. No doubt due to his lack of sleep. When he finally got it, he scowled and could have shoved broken glass into me with his glare. "Shit Syl. You nearly gave me a heart attack. That's not funny. I'm talking about the body."

I shook my head. "I don't know who the body is."

Then I smiled. "It actually was funny."

The lab guys arrived just then, carrying in cases and cases of equipment. One of them wore a mask, which was not uncommon in this post-Covid world. He probably had someone at risk at home. Along with the techs came a round giant wearing a white overcoat with the word "Medical Examiner" across the back. He moved in like a train and stepped carefully through the swamp of blood. Settled beside the body and began his examination. The detective said a couple things to him that weren't answered, turned away, and walked back to me.

I shook hands. "I'm Sylvia Wilson, owner of the bar. I found the body."

"Nick Eccheli, Homicide." He stepped back and took an appraising look over me. I got that a lot. He said, "No kidding? You're Boom-Boom's sister? Now I see why he got the short end of the ugly stick."

Boom-Boom was the nickname Aaron's coworkers had bestowed upon him because of the whole late-night-liaison thing with the ladies. We both smirked at the ugly stick line, though it was really an archaic joke.

Aaron scowled at Eccheli. "I suppose you think you're funny, too." He moved off to converse with his brothers in blue, hands deep in his pockets.

The detective and I locked gazes a moment. He wasn't what I'd call super handsome, but he *was* nice. His jaw was square and cleft. His eyes were wide-set and the darkest brown I'd ever seen. No wedding ring either. I don't mind saying a few sparks zinged, but nothing worth writing in my diary about. I'd be interested, if it weren't for the body by the door. Still it was something to keep in mind.

He flipped open a pocket notepad. "May I call you Sylvia, or do you have a nickname, like Sly?"

"No one calls me Sly except my father, and he's dead. Sylvia is fine."

"I'm sorry." He fumbled with his notebook. Cleared his throat. Started again. "So, being a cop's sister, and rumored to be fairly smart, you probably know the drill already. Tell me what you touched."

I'd bought my first bar in Texas when I was 18, having worked in it underaged for a couple years already. Sold it, bought another, which I also sold when Aaron and I moved to St. Louis. This was my third. I had a decent stock portfolio and I was building one for my brother. I was only 22. I thought he could have used a better adjective than 'fairly smart'. He could have just said 'brilliant'.

Yeah, that would have worked.

The murmur of the crime scene guys filtered down the hallway to us, once again reminding me of the happenings of the day. I quashed my ego and took Eccheli on a verbal tour of my activities since I'd entered Smugglers, sans the little trip to the car out back. When I finished, he asked the obvious question. "You know him?"

"Nope. Who is he?"

"No ID. Your video work?" He motioned to the three security cameras.

"Yep. Loads into the Cloud. I'll send you a copy."

"You mind accessing it now? I'd like to see it."

I took out my cell, pulled up the link, entered my password, and selected the most recent upload from 5 AM that morning. The screen divided into three and the video feed from each of the cameras began to play. I paused two, enlarged the third, moved it to the end of the feed, and slowly backed it up until it showed the two intruders.

Standing close, the spark between the detective and I should have grown, but instead it fizzled and died. It confused me; that wasn't the way attraction was supposed to work. As if reading the same thoughts himself, Eccheli shrugged and concentrated on the video.

We watched the skinny guy point toward the front door and the heavy soon-to-be-dead one obediently amble in that direction. Skinny pivoted, turned off the alarm, and followed the big guy to the front. The silver of a knife buried itself in flesh. Jerked back and forth. The killer pushed the victim's body away as it fell to the floor. Went to the register, took out the cash, and left.

Eccheli nodded. "Okay, show me the crowd last night. Let's see if they were casing the place."

We watched the video: the bar crowd filtered in, drank, and wandered out again. Most were cops or retired cops. A few reporters came into the video too, but they usually didn't stay long.

It began to sink in that there had been a murder in my bar. A violent act that had ended a life. Everything and everyone in the video looked sinister. Shadows seemed to take on evil shapes. Every face looked like it had a hidden agenda. I took a deep breath and stilled my mind. Quieted the panic rising in my heart. Forced myself to stop seeing things that weren't there. I focused on the actual images in the video.

Nothing of note happened for a long time. I sped through several hours of tiny people, pausing each time either Eccheli or I spotted someone of the same general build as the victim.

"There." Eccheli pointed at a sixth possible customer. "I think that's him."

I obligingly slowed the video to real time. The man who'd just walked in the back door on the screen had the same dumpy body, the same wrinkled khakis and a designer shirt.

He said, "You know, that could be a security uniform underneath."

I drew in a sharp breath. The victim probably had been a cop at one time, after all. It wasn't really surprising; it was a cop bar, but regular civilians sometimes came in too. And since it looked like he was in the process of robbing me when he'd been killed, I'd leaned toward him being one of the latter. Sadly, I said, "We get a lot of security guys in here."

The man on the screen came in through the back door, walked down the hall, and requested a bottle at the bar from yours truly. Then he turned to face the room. Spying someone he apparently knew, he waved and joined his friend at a booth.

The detective and I leaned in as I made the image bigger. The friend was Martin Degere.

"Shit." Eccheli pulled out his cell and made a call, at the same time handing me his business card. While he explained the situation and the police involvement to Internal Affairs, he pointed from the email address written on the bottom of the card to my phone and back.

I understood from that to email him the videos, which I did. When he finished with his call, I asked, "Are they going to let you keep the case?"

"For now, though they're going to attach someone to the investigation. Do you know the Chief?"

"We met a couple times. He comes in here."

"Do you know who that was with him?"

"No. I said that already."

"Just double-checking." He gave a brief smile. Then, "Anyone hang around with Degere a lot?"

I raced through my memory. Days and weeks. I didn't have a photographic memory, but it was decent. "Not really. They kinda came and went."

"So, no one in particular spent a lot of time with him."

"No one that I remember."

"Do you know whose car that is in your lot?"

I shook my head. No need to confess. Eccheli knew about Degere already.

He said, "I need a list of everyone who has your alarm code."

"Just one person: myself. I don't share it with anyone. Not even Aaron."

"What about employees? Do you give them the code?"

"I have two employees. If I give it to them so they can open for me, then I change it immediately when I get in." I told him about Karyn, my best friend from Texas turned employee, and Tom, a quiet student studying at Washington University.

"When was the last time you changed your password?"

"About two weeks ago."

"I'll need your employees' names and contact info."

I gave him what was requested, adding, "Karyn has a mean ex-boyfriend. Tavon Eaches. Last we heard, he was still in Texas." I told him what I knew.

"What time did you close your bar last night?"

"3 AM."

"Did you see anyone? Hear anything?"

"Nothing."

"You went straight home?"

"I did."

"Can anyone verify that?"

"My neighbors can, if I was too noisy. Other than that, there's the GPS data from my phone and Jeep." No love between myself and the people living around me. I didn't even know their names. My fault, I guess. Hard to make friends when you're always working.

"How often do you clean this place?"

"I do the basics every night. You know: the bathrooms, the floor, the bar, the tables and seats. And I bring in a crew on Tuesdays for a deep clean."

"Do they know the code?"

"No. No one does."

He slowly nodded, and then moved off to speak with the medical examiner and crime scene guys. Having nothing that I could do, I handed my bar keys to Jacobs, then walked down the block to the cop shop, leaving Aaron to answer any further questions from the detective. I gave my official statement and the officer told me it would be several days before I could get back into my bar. That didn't exactly make me happy, but what could I do? I had been dismissed, and they had work to do.

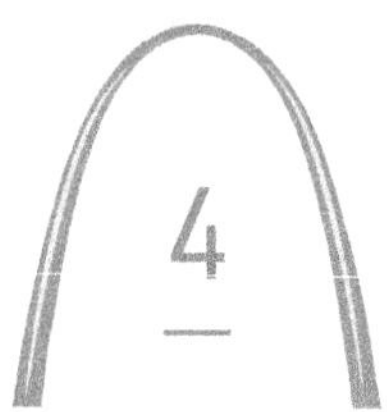

4

By the time I returned to Smugglers, the outside was adorned with yellow police tape. The Corolla had a crime scene guy bagging trash to sort through later. The Medical Examiner vehicle was gone. There was only the one patrol officer – Jacobs – standing guard over the log book. Both front and back doors stood wide open, letting in flies and the burning hot September.

I told Jacobs, "I need to turn off the air conditioning. It's right inside the back door. I can reach it without going in." There was no sense letting out all the cold air when the bar would be closed anyway.

Waiting until he checked with Eccheli via the radio seemed to take forever. Once approved, he logged it in. Then, with him closely watching, I reached into the bar and turned off the air. I stretched a peek toward the front.

The place had cleared out inside, too. The excitement of a body in the favorite cop hangout had worn off, and most cops had gone back to their own work. The lights were on as high as they would go and there was black fingerprint powder everywhere. The body was gone, but footprints of blood tracked in rivers across the room. Waste paper and plastic bags from the science guys littered the floor. With the front door open and the lights up, the room was cast in a glare. I decided the walls were dingy and needed a repaint when this whole thing was over. Everything would get a bath.

Eccheli and my brother were still there.

Aaron's voice was strong and it carried well. The detective was saying, "— doesn't act like a normal millennial."

"She's not. She's been through a hell of a lot."

"Is there anyone else she hasn't mentioned?"

"She has a boyfriend, Bobby Crow. He owns a bar downtown, The Crow."

I turned around and nearly plowed into Jacobs. After apologies, I went around to the front of the bar, fuming. Aaron was telling on me. If I'd wanted Bobby involved, I'd have told the detective myself.

A news van sat two spaces down the street, its occupants unloading gear. I ducked into my Jeep, hoping they didn't see me. Luck favored me, but it wouldn't if I stayed there. I started the Jeep and drove down a couple blocks to a gas station. Pulled in and took out the business card Eccheli had given me. Made the call. "I'm headed home. Lock up when you're done, please. I don't need another robbery."

"Roger that." He disconnected.

I made a face at my phone, Aaron, and the cursed day. Pulling into traffic, I turned left on Jefferson toward I-44, took the freeway west until my exit, turned left on Hampton and then a right. Though technically my address was on Landsdowne, my garage was in the alley behind. It was in St. Louis Hills, which meant my neighbors pretended my Jeep was an Escalade and that I wasn't a bartender who came home in the wee hours. It also meant the mortgage was huge.

My house was a tiny, single-story box with two small bedrooms and a combination living room-kitchen. I'd decorated in calming blues and wood tones. The large beige area rug covered a hardwood floor. The place spoke of comfort. I felt traumatized and wrung out. Comfort was something I needed badly right then.

My dogs greeted me at the door, super-excited to have Mom home so soon after I'd left. Ruffles, the Doberman, earned his name by rumbling deep in his chest with his upper lip caught against his teeth in a pleased smile. That look worried the average person, but when my dog was angry, that top lip curled up over his nose, adding a deep vibration to the sound. He would also lean low and forward as if straining against an invisible leash. Truly terrifying. He'd been Aaron's first, and had some expensive obedience training in him.

Satan, my little, mixed Westie mutt, yapped and bounced back and forth over the top of Ruffles's tall back. Normally a happy dog, when she was angry, full grown men cringed and ran. The moment my small dog felt threatened or fierce, she grabbed the highest point on a person's body she could reach and clung there with jaws that rivaled a bear trap. Usually about crotch height. Hence, the name. She'd been through several homes before coming to live with me.

I loved on my dogs a bit, made some coffee, and then settled under the canopy on the patio behind my house, the two dogs running around me at full speed like idiots. Mom was home in the middle of the day. I had a tall wooden fence around my backyard which, thankfully, kept curious neighbors at bay. Not that many were home at this time. I had plenty of solitude for introspection.

Or I would have, except my cellphone blew up with calls and messages which I didn't answer. All reporters. They'd be waiting forever for a callback. I turned off notifications for all incoming audio messages, calls, or texts.

Someone had been killed in my bar. *My* bar. And all I had to show for my innocence, when I alone knew the alarm code, was a video of a man in a black ski mask. Not very solid evidence.

My parents' broken faces filled my mind. At least their killer had been caught. Small consolation. I barely remembered their voices. Once again, I shook away the memories and took out my phone. I called Bobby.

"Crow," his deep-throated voice greeted me. Though my brother had told Eccheli that Bobby was my boyfriend, he was really just an occasional lover. Lately it had been very occasional. He, like me, rarely took a day off.

"Hey, it's Sylvia. My bar's shut down. Found a body in it."

"Shit! That was you? All the news said was it was a place downtown." I could almost see him, elbows propped on his bar, leaning into the phone. His breath was coming through loudly, as if he were turned into the speaker because he didn't want someone nearby to overhear his conversation.

"Yep. Anyway, thought I'd give you heads up, they'll be by to see you, I'm sure."

"Lucky me. They know who it was?"

"I'm sure they do by now, but I don't."

"You home? Want company?" His voice sounded hopeful.

I paused. It *had* been a long time. The trouble was, I didn't feel much like romancing of any kind. And I didn't feel like having anyone trying to cheer me up. It would be too much bother. "I think I'd rather be alone right now. Watch TV. Try to get my mind off it."

"You sure? I can call Tag." That was his only employee. A skinny kid with more brains than common sense. He was small, but no one messed with him because they knew they'd have to answer to Bobby.

"I'm sure."

"Well, anything you need." Ever the conversationalist, he hung up.

Maybe I should have let him come over. He would have been a good distraction. I could always call him again if I changed my mind. I accessed the cloud and watched the murder again. The two men snuck in. The skinny fellow followed the heavy one to the front door. I witnessed the jerk of the knife through the victim's throat. The throw of the body as it fell. Watched the skinny guy empty the register and leave.

I ran through it all again. And again. I saw the man die a total of four more times.

As a bartender, I had lots of practice watching people. I'd gotten fairly good at reading body language. Plus, when in training, Aaron used to bring home his police psychology books.

Three thoughts struck me now.

First, though money was stolen, I already knew this hadn't been a robbery. Who would rob a bar on a Sunday night? There would be no money. And most thieves took some alcohol when they robbed a place like that. Ergo, the killer wasn't really of the criminal element.

Second, Skinny was way over excited. He'd jerked the blade across the victim's throat in a harsh, ragged move. He'd been jittery afterwards, dropping money, tripping on nothing, and sending his gaze again and again toward the body. It was possible he'd never killed anyone before.

Third, the killer knew ahead of time what a bloody mess he would create. Most people didn't realize how much arterial blood fountained. Why else would he push the body away from him? He either had experience with blood in one form or another, like a slaughter house, or he'd studied it.

Skinny had come into my bar intending to murder his partner. It hadn't been an argument or an afterthought. He'd even brought his own knife.

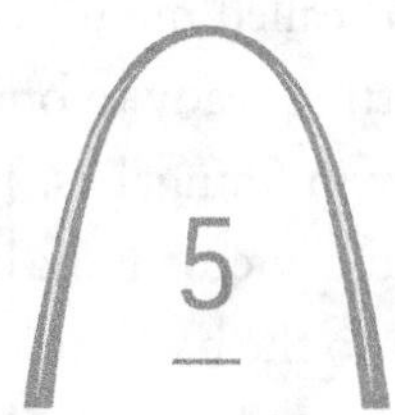

5

Right around 6 PM, the dogs went ballistic. I was lying on my couch, bigscreen TV on, and was trying to distract myself from the murder by reading Peaches's earlier texts about her son's lack of work ethic. She and Uncle Tripp had two children together. Roy was five years my junior. Stetson, the girl, was two years behind him. Roy had just graduated from high school, but wasn't looking for a job. Wasn't signing up for the military. Wasn't considering a school. He just hung around the ranch, only helping his dad when forced. And not very well at that either.

The sudden noise of the dogs nearly made me jump into next week. They growled and lunged against the door as I waded through the melee. I arrived in time for the bell to announce a visitor. As if I didn't know that already. Looking through the peephole, I saw a tall, lean, Black woman: Karyn Washington, who was a long-time friend and bar employee.

We had been next door neighbors in Texas the night her drunk boyfriend, Tavon, had mistakenly assumed my door was hers. It took him a while of lunging against the door, but the hinges finally gave way. I didn't have the dogs then, it was just me in the apartment. I'd stared at him and he'd stared at my Ruger, the one I kept at the bar now. Then the police arrived. After the dust settled, Karyn invited me for apology coffee. We'd been friends ever since. When she'd graduated from art school, she'd called me to see if I had any jobs. As it happened, my bar was getting ready to open, so she'd moved to St. Louis and had taken work in Smugglers. Her name was the artist's signature at the bottom of the photos at the bar. She also waited tables.

I shoved the pooches into the backyard and returned to the front to let in our visitor. September heat rolled into the house as Karyn peered around me for my four-legged guardians, who were pacing the back door. "Is it safe?" She knew my dogs.

"Safe."

"Whew!" She gave an exaggerated sigh, her free hand wiping her brow. She wore a fire-engine red blouse cut deep and huge earrings that nearly touched her shoulders. The sweet scent of jasmine breezed past me as she entered. She held a whip cream container, which she shoved at me. "Chili."

A Texas staple.

"I'll eat it tomorrow. I already ate tonight." Food wasn't something I wanted to deal with at the moment. I opened the fridge only to have Karyn shut it before I could put in the container.

She wagged her finger at me as she spoke. "Nope. Tonight. Now. I know you haven't eaten yet. I know you. But you need food."

She crossed her arms and stared hard at me until I pulled out a pot and started heating the chili. She nodded and settled on the couch, turned sideways so she could talk to me, tapping her toe against the leg of the coffee table. She asked, "How you holdin' up? It's surreal."

Surreal was right. "I'm okay. The cops are going to come talk to you."

"They already did. Handsome fellow, name of Eccheli, came to visit. Wish he woulda stayed longer. Like to do a little investigatin' of my own, if you get my meanin'. Told him all about Tavon. Told him I didn't know where that bastard was, but if he found out, not to tell me. I don't want to know."

We were quiet a moment. I watched the burner beneath the pot turn red. I didn't believe in heating things slowly.

Karyn asked, "So the dead guy was an ex-cop, huh?"

"That's what I understand. Did Eccheli tell you who it was?"

"He said the name was Blaisdale. Teddy, or Robert, or Bob. Or somethin' like that."

"Robert and Bob are the same name."

"They sure are: borin'."

I chose to ignore her comment. "What else did Eccheli say?"

"He asked a lot about you. You know, how long we've been friends. If you were some kind of psycho. That kind of thing. Oh, and he asked me about your friend, Mr. Crow."

"What did he say about Bobby?"

"Say? Nothin'. Just asked what kind of man he was. If he was jealous over you."

"Jealous?"

"Yeah. Apparently jealousy is a big thing with boyfriends these days."

"What did you say?"

"I told him mister borin' ass first name Crow was a good guy."

"Bob may be a boring name, but Bobby isn't. What about Tavon? You think he could have killed a guy like this?"

"Kill a guy? Oh, sure. Kill him like what I got told? I don't think so. Too much blood. You remember how he fussed at those cops gettin' dirt on his shirt when they arrested him."

"Accused the cops of dirtying him on purpose."

"Doubt it's him."

I had to agree.

She asked, "You think you need a lawyer?" She intentionally strung out the word so it sounded 'Laaaahyur', managing to put in that one word her well-known views that lawyers were somehow akin to demons and that ilk, but they acted like they were doing God's work.

"I hadn't thought about getting one. Not until I'm charged."

"Nope. You don't want to be waitin' around until then. Lawyers may be unholy, but you want one ready to jump in and rip some snout the very second there's trouble. Get one now."

"I suppose." Deep sigh. An expense when money would be tight.

"You know I'm right."

I nodded. Decided to change topic. "The bar's going to be a mess when we get back in; it's layered with fingerprint powder and dried blood."

"Hire a bio crew. There's no reason you shouldn't. They'll do a better job anyway. They know how to deal with all that shit."

I shook my head and stirred the pot, sending a cloud of steam and the heavy aroma of spiced beef floating to the ceiling. "With the bar closed, money will be tight. Bio cleaning is no big secret." Just lots of elbow grease and chemicals.

"Seems to me you have only two choices. Either save the money, do it yourself, open the bar at a later date, and hire a new bartender to replace me. Or, hire a crew, get it done fast and well, and open sooner so you can recoup the money quicker. No havin' to replace a bartender who quit because she felt abused. Anyway, the pool tournaments will be startin' next week, so you'll have the money back then."

I turned and eyed her speculatively. I just didn't want to spend the money on a crew. Tom would want the extra money, starving student and all. I could probably talk her into helping, too. Despite her words, she was a rock solid friend. I opened my mouth to tell her how much I appreciated her friendship, but I didn't get a chance to say anything.

She raised her hands. "No. Absolutely not. I'm not cleaning."

I frowned at her. "You're not going to help? What kind of a friend are you?"

"I'm a good friend. Strong shouldered. Chili-totin'. A non-black-powder-shit-cleaning friend. Don't let that burn." She motioned toward my pot.

"I'm standing right here. I'm stirring. Do you see me stirring?"

"I see you flappin' your jaws, talkin' nonsense. That's what I see." Karyn's afro normally looked like a halo floating around her head, but at that moment I thought the halo looked like it belonged to the Angel of Light, Lucifer. Especially with that fiery shirt.

I took out a bowl and spoon and poured the chili. It wasn't super hot, but I'd survive. "You're my employee."

"I quit."

"You can't quit." I settled beside her, cross-legged. "You don't have any money saved."

"Did." She managed to put all the attitude of a rebellious teenager into that one word, wagging her head and squaring her shoulders. "Besides, my lack of job would be your fault. So, I'm gonna move into your spare room and make your life as difficult as I can. Maybe even make your doggies live outside."

I ignored her and took a spoonful of chili, savoring the bite of tobasco. It was a family secret, she'd told me the first time she'd given me some. Most people put the Tobasco in the broth, but her recipe mixed it in the meat. She'd said I was her family too, and so could have the secret.

She'd help clean. She just had to bluster first.

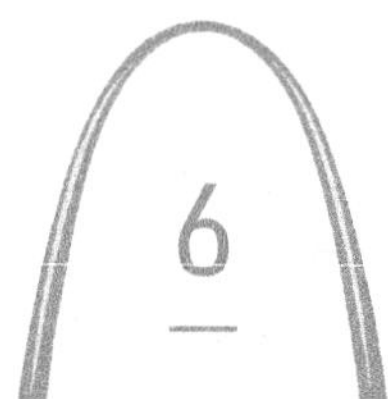

6

Karyn stayed for only an hour longer, but by the time she left, I was feeling much more relaxed about the whole murder thing. Also happier about her helping clean the bar. Though I was sure she was going to protest the whole time.

That evening, I dressed in my blue PJs with the cows on them and watched the game while prone on the couch, the dogs spread across my legs. St. Louis is such a sports town that everyone knows immediately what you mean when you use the phrase, 'the game'. Unless it's in the late fall, when all the professional sports collide for a few short weeks.

I'd never been much of a baseball fan until Aaron and I moved here, but I fell in love with the Cardinals the first time I saw them play. My hope was always the opposing team would powerhouse a long ball and the centerfielder would have to climb the back wall to catch it. Gold glove in the making. History.

Anyway, the Cards were playing their second of a three-game series against Pittsburgh, another team I'd come to respect, and by all rights, I should have been enthralled. My team was attacking the ball as if possessed, but as the night wore on, I lost the bond with my players. The Pirates did, indeed, hit some spectacular balls, staying ahead for the majority of the game, but St. Louis came back from a 7–2 deficit beginning in the top of the eighth, tying it at the bottom of the ninth to go into overtime where the Cards hit a walk-off home run in the 14th inning.

But, I kept flashing to the body on the floor of Smugglers. Seeing my parents. They'd died less than a mile from our small home. The last time I'd seen them, they'd been prone and still, lying in caskets and reeking of embalming fluid moments before we'd closed the coffins for the memorial. Their faces had been patched together and painted as well as the funeral home could, but I'd barely recognized them. At 14, I'd certainly understood death. But I'd never experienced it so close. I had been unprepared for the well of grief that made its home in me. There were days it had threatened to swallow me whole. If not for the knowledge Aaron was just as lost, I certainly would have drowned. We'd clung to each other like seafarers in a storm.

My brother called halfway through the evening, a couple hours before his shift was scheduled to start. The dogs didn't move at the sound of the phone, though they each opened one sleepy eye. Aaron asked, "You okay?"

I was still a little miffed at him for blabbing about Bobby. My voice came out short, terse. "I will be."

He picked up on it right away. "You pissed at me or something?"

"I know you don't like Bobby, but he didn't have anything to do with this."

"Shit, Syl, I know that. But he might know something that he doesn't even realize. Besides, you should have told them yourself."

I had to give Aaron that one. But I didn't have to like it. "What's happening with the investigation?"

"Not much yet. They're still doing initial interviews. But from what I hear about Blaisdale, he was always in trouble when he was a cop. There were citizen complaints about him helping himself to merchandise from convenience stores. There were also allegations of bribery and slush fund money missing. Never any charges pressed, though."

"What about fingerprints, and DNA evidence?"

"The labs are so far behind, it'll take a while to get anything back."

I didn't say anything. By then, Eccheli could have decided I looked good for the murder.

After a long span of dead air, Aaron said, "I guess you know you're a person of interest."

"I figured. You're on that list too."

"Yeah. I think everybody is, now that IAD is involved."

"Any idea when I'll be able to get back into my bar?"

"Eccheli's usually pretty quick with a crime scene. Thorough the first time through. I can't imagine he'll hold it long. I can talk to him."

"Thanks. Is he good?"

"He is."

I didn't know how to ask the next question. Despite the sensationalism by media and novelists, there was a very low percentage of dirty cops out there, compared to the good cops. Still, it was on everyone's mind, especially after recent civil unrest involving the deaths of several black people. No one liked to think that those who were supposed to protect them wouldn't. Or that those same protectors might actually hurt or kill them. And cops didn't like thinking their partners might not have their back when it all went on the line. Nor did they like their ranks sullied by bullies.

Aaron, perhaps entertaining the same thoughts, gave the answer on his own. "He's honest."

"So, I can trust him, is what you're saying?"

"I'm saying *we* can trust him."

At that moment I could have lunged through the phone, wrapped my arms around my brother and planted a giant kiss on him. Instead, I curled my toes in the long fibers of my beige rug.

We again went quiet for a few minutes. Then, he asked, "Want me to swing by? We could grab a bite somewhere before I start shift."

It was tempting, but I still wanted to be alone with this trauma that had reawakened the past within me. "I'm just staying in. Got my PJs on already. Karyn came by earlier with chili."

"Okay. If you need anything, call. Even if it's just to talk. Understand?"

I nodded as if he could see me. "Yeah. Thanks." Hung up. I could never stay mad at him.

Following the game was the late night news, full of stories of mayhem. The lead piece was the murder in Smugglers, of course. Big news that an ex-cop had been killed in a cop hangout. No mention of my bar name. That suited me fine. The victim was named Edward Blaisdale, not Robert as Karyn had said. Apparently, he'd been related to Chief Degere's wife. That explained the connection in the bar. And maybe the car. The news anchor managed a sad and appropriately horrified grimace. My guess was that he wanted the audience to see conspiracies there.

For the next story, about the five week-old robbery at City Capital, the anchor's face morphed into wide-eyed concern. He gave the occasional bob with his head to emphasize certain points. The thieves had made off with over five hundred thousand dollars. Bobbed head. There was no new information, but the FBI – shaken head – was still looking at the bank's employees and were appealing to the public for help. Another bob. The anchor had managed to fill his voice with disgust when talking about the lack of skill in the investigation. And I was beginning to think that most news anchors were failed actors.

A murder had taken place on one of the jogging trails over two weeks ago. The victim was still unidentified. They showed a police sketch and flashed a call-in number if anyone had any information. There were no other updates, but the news anchor assured the audience he would keep them apprised. Such a trustworthy media person.

There were highlights from shootings, car wrecks, thefts, and fires. It was a big city. Each story brought its own facial and vocal expressions.

A story came on about the political race for East St. Louis Mayor. The incumbent was forced to step down when his nephew was recently charged with sedition in the domestic terrorism at the nation's capital. Allegations of misused funds abounded, as well. Politics didn't interest me, and the news anchor just plain annoyed me. I changed the channel and ended up channel surfing.

I still felt unsettled. Still felt as if there was something I could be doing.

I gave up on finding anything to watch and left it on the most recent station. Dumped the pooches off my legs and walked back to my bedroom to fetch my laptop. Set it on the coffee table and slumped behind it on the couch. It didn't want to boot. I stuck my tongue out at it, dug out the power cord, and connected it.

When I typed in Blaisdale's name, hundreds in the St. Louis area appeared. Narrowing the search parameters by adding 'police' to the name brought up news stories about the murder. After the first two, almost all the stories were the same.

Further down the search listings was a single 2013 article about Blaisdale being injured in the line of duty. It said he'd been at an all-night convenience store when it had been robbed. He'd chased after the thief, had cornered him, and summarily had been shot in the hip. He'd been forced to retire early. The man who'd shot him was rotting in prison.

The TV was showing an old black and white western, *Wagon Trail* – which had recently been remastered in color, but this was the pre-colored version. I watched for about an hour before I started surfing again, which is pretty much what I did for the rest of the night. That and watch the guy in my bar be murdered a few more times.

My bar. Had the killing been a personal statement to me? More, the detective was focused on me as a suspect. That wasn't good. I had no adult record. Had only gotten one speeding ticket, and that had been in Texas. Everything else had been when I was a kid. Sealed records. I had to admit, though, the alarm thing was pretty damning.

I decided it was time to pick up my martial arts training again. I'd studied Judo both as a child in Iowa and later in Texas while Aaron had trained in the Academy. I'd quit as a black belt when I started dating the instructor. A pin or hold would soon devolve into kisses and more. Impossible to learn anything that way.

I would start looking for a new instructor first thing in the morning. Perhaps in a different discipline. Something with no holds or pins.

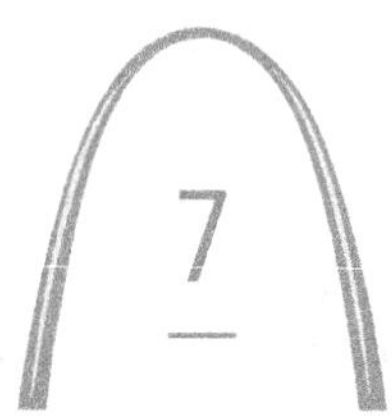

had a bad night, tossing wildly and startling awake, to peer into the
dark corners of my room. Nightmares that had plagued me after
my parents' deaths returned: bodies flying through the air, the feel
of the metal bumper shattering bone, crushed limbs under fanged
tires. Finally, late morning, bleary-eyed and unrefreshed, I rose, wondering if Aaron's nightmares had returned too. Often when we'd first
been orphaned, one of us slept on the floor in the same room as the
other, drawing comfort from just knowing someone else was nearby.

My pups went outside as my breakfast cooked and coffee gurgled.
While eating, I investigated different martial arts on the web. Settled
on Krav Maga. It was a type used by the Israeli Defense Force and
combined bits of several martial arts with some old-fashioned street
brawling. A quick check proved there were a few facilities around
the city that taught it.

I called the closest one.

A gravel-voiced man answered, "Midtown Krav Maga."

"My name is Sylvia Wilson. I'd like to come by tomorrow and
speak to you in person about taking classes."

"What level are you?"

"I'm a black in Judo, but I've never studied Krav Maga before.
What's a good time?"

"I teach all day tomorrow, but I can see you at five. Will that work for you?"

"Perfect."

Appointment made, I started cleaning the house. Normally, I had someone do this for me once a month, but I had time on my hands, so why not save a little cash? Around one in the afternoon, Peaches called. I put down my dusting cloth.

"Sylvia! What is wrong with you?"

"Excuse me?" I pictured her standing with her hands on her hips. Well, one hand anyway.

"Why didn't you call me? Instead, I had to hear it from Aaron." Figures my brother would blab.

"It's no big deal. Some guy was killed in my bar. I'm shut down while they investigate. I'll be able to open soon."

"No big deal? That's not what I hear. I was told you're a suspect. I'm packing my bags and coming right up there."

"No. Really. There's nothing for you to do. I'm fine. Honest." I was going to kill Aaron.

"Are you sure? Coming up is no problem. Just a hop on the plane."

"It's fine. I'm fine. The detective is very good. It's just a matter of time before he clears me."

"You call me if you change your mind. Now you sit right there and tell me all about it."

I looked longingly at my cleaning supplies. Then, I wandered into the kitchen and poured a very big glass of wine, settled on my blue living room couch, and propped my feet on the coffee table. This was going to be a long call. Doubly long because she would surely ask me for a response to the texts she'd sent the day before. Had it only been one day? Impossible.

When the call finished two hours later, I was done for. A nap never called to me so hard. But, I reverted to my original plan and started cleaning again. Hard work always energized me. When I finally quit, the place was spotless. I ate a hearty lunch of leftover Karyn chili and toasted garlic bread. After adding the dishes to the dishwasher and getting it running, I filled the bathtub and went in search of my little white dog, Satan. Found her under one of the endtables by the couch. Pried her out and set her in the tub. She stood panting happily in the bath while I sudsed her. But two minutes into the process, the front doorbell rang. She was up and out like a buzz saw, running to join Ruffles at the door. I was soaked. The bathroom floor was a lake. A river traveled from said lake all the way to the front room and became a secondary lake at the door. She shook and threw dollops of no-tears shampoo that clung to the walls and furniture.

I waded through the growls, barks, snarls, teeth, and soaked dog stench. Peeked through the peephole. Eccheli was standing a couple feet back, staring at the bottom of the door. His brows were furrowed together and he was leaning away as if preparing to run.

I yelled, "Just a minute!" Locked the dogs out back. Satan would come back green with grass stains, but it couldn't be helped.

Back at the front, I opened the door wide. Eccheli frowned, looked my soggy clothes up and down, and peered past me into the sopping house. I said, "Dog wash day. You might have called first. Wait here and I'll mop up so you don't slip."

He nodded. Gave no apology. Of course. He was trying to throw the suspect, me, off guard. Showing up unannounced was a typical tactic that my father, a police detective in our small town, had often employed. I left the door open as I soaked up the water from the hardwood floor in the living room. He came in while I finished the hallway and shut the bathroom door. He smiled and said, "They're pretty good guard dogs."

"Yep." I kept mopping and that was the extent of the conversation until I finished and motioned to the couch. "I'm going to get changed. I'll be right with you."

I waited until he sat, then I went into my bedroom. My pooches would watch him through the glass of the sliding back door. They'd tell me if he did any snooping while I was out of sight. My dad would have investigated while left alone, so I suspected Eccheli would also.

My dogs did their job and went haywire about three minutes after I left the room. Once dressed in dry clothes, I came back to find Eccheli standing near the kitchen. Maybe he had been looking for that famous kitchen drawer that collected everything. Joke was on him. I kept my junk in a filing cabinet in the spare room. I stepped past and suddenly felt bad for my attitude. He was just doing his job. "I'm making coffee. You want some."

"Yes. Thank you." He returned to the couch and waited while I got the coffee maker going. He stared out the sliding glass door at the pooches and asked, "So, the tall one is a Doberman, what's the small one?"

"A West Highland Terrier mix."

"What are their names?"

"Ruffles is the Doberman and Satan is the Westie."

"Satan?"

I told him how she'd earned it. He nodded, but didn't seem to care much. Turned his attention into the room and squinted at the small bookshelf beneath my giant television. Not much there. A few catalogs on bar equipment. A couple signed Harry Bosch books. A glass horse in the Japanese style.

"I have a few questions."

"I'm listening." I stayed in the kitchen, effectively making him either talk over his shoulder or turn sideways and look up at me, much as Karyn had. Maybe I didn't feel too bad about my attitude, after all.

He chose the over-the-shoulder method, twisting as far as he could, but still keeping his feet on the floor. "In your statement, you said the alarm was already off when you entered. Is it possible it was on and you turned it off?"

"It was already off. The back door was unlocked." I pulled coffee mugs out of the cabinet, my favorite Looney Toons one for me and a boring generic white for him. "Do you take cream or sugar?"

"Neither, thank you. You're sure about the alarm?"

"Positive."

"Who has your code?"

"I told you yesterday. No one. Not even Aaron. And I don't write it down either."

"Did you know Edward Blaisdale?"

"Nope." The coffee began the gurgle cycle and effectively silenced Eccheli. Hot bitterness filled the room, comforting my nerves as it always did. I didn't wait until the pot was done, but filled the mugs and brought them to the coffee table, choosing to sit in the recliner instead of beside the detective. The pot continued its monologue alone in the kitchen.

Eccheli hunched forward, elbows on knees, and played with the handle of his mug, turning it back and forth, frowning. Stared at the steam rolling off the hot liquid. Eventually he spoke. "How do you think the killer got your code?"

"I have no idea." I shrugged. This was so not helping my case. "But it was a new code two weeks ago. As I told you yesterday."

He turned and pierced me with his dark, dark eyes. Again, I felt a spark of attraction glow, then sputter and die. It confounded me. Was it really just because I was a suspect? He asked, "Why do you suppose Blaisdale was killed in your bar on a Sunday night?"

I shook my head. "Usually there are minimal funds from a Sunday. Not this last Sunday, though. Strangely busy."

"Busy, how?"

"I guess one of the squads decided to watch a late game there that night. Lots of people. Lots of beer. A good night."

I sipped my coffee, trying to remember everything from Sunday night. I couldn't think of anything that stood out. "The decision to rob my bar, or rather fake a robbery, wasn't from someone who knows me. I only keep the next day's starting money in the register overnight. All the rest comes home with me."

He was silent a moment, and I wondered if my statement had helped or hurt. He asked, "Did you have a grudge against Blaisdale."

"I told you. I didn't know him."

Eccheli nodded. Stood. "May I use your restroom?"

Yet another tactic my dad had employed: 'use the restroom' but 'get lost' and snoop somewhere else. Glad now that Satan had made a huge mess from escaping her bath, I shook my head. "I'm sorry, but it's still waterlogged in there. You'll have to find a gas station or a store. There are some nearby."

He looked about to say something, and then apparently changed his mind. He shrugged and let himself out. No goodbye or anything. Detectives!

I waited until he drove away, then pulled my cell out of my pocket. Googled lawyers. Settled on a Charlie Moore. Called and made an appointment for Thursday afternoon. I took out my mop and opened the bathroom door. The place was one giant ocean. I sighed and mopped.

Then I went out back to fetch my little green and white dog.

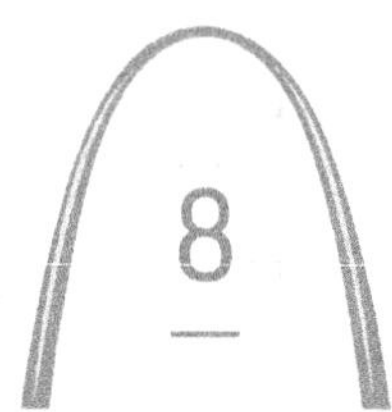

8

I scrubbed Satan's green stripes but they remained, just more pale. After drying her and running fresh water in the tub, it was Ruffles's turn. He stood stock still in the water, with minor trembles running through him. I always wondered if something had happened to him before Aaron got him. Once Ruffles was dried and the bathroom was cleaned, I tweaked my stock portfolio. Aaron's, too. And I watched the murder video a few more times. Supper was a Hawaiian pizza delivered from Pizza Hut. At 7:15 PM, the third and last game of the Pittsburgh series was starting, and I was settled deep on my couch to watch it.

The doorbell rang. The dogs became the Hounds of Baskerville. Sighing, I rose. My front door had gotten more play in the past 28 hours than it had for the last six months combined. Once again, I waded through the teeth, toenails, doggy breath, and cacophony. The peephole revealed a small, round, black woman with orange dyed hair and heavy makeup. Ginger Jefferson. She was a reporter who frequented Smugglers and had become a sort of friend.

I shouted over the din, "I'm not giving any comments."

She shouted back, "I have information about the case."

That got my attention. "Just a minute."

The dogs didn't want to go out back. They'd heard their mom shouting and had to protect her. Ruffles finally went after his obedience training kicked in, but I had to chase my little dog back and forth in front of the door a couple times before she was scooped up. Her growls rumbled against my chest and her little body jerked with intensity. I dumped her outside, turned off the game, and returned to the front door.

Ginger came in, cheap cologne in a cloud around her. "Somebody got murdered in a bar and the owner has been hard to reach for a statement."

I shut the door and nodded, not sure of what to say. "Sorry?"

She landed on the couch, pulled out and turned on the voice recorder on her phone, and laid it on the coffee table. Patting the seat beside her, she said, "Tell me what happened."

"How'd you get my address?" I sat, but put as much space between us on the couch as possible.

She arched a thin, sharp eyebrow. "It's my job to uncover things that don't want to be found."

"I was told not to speak to the press."

"That's their standard procedure. The cops won't tell your side of the story, you know."

My side of the story. Did I even know enough to have a side? "You said you have information about the case?"

"The way this works is you tell me things and I tell you things. We help each other. Understand?"

Ginger was in her mid-thirties and was well known to be the craftiest of the reporter breed. She'd started as a gossip columnist, but had proven her passion in uncovering unsavory details about local celebrities. So, she'd been moved to her own celebrity column, *Scandals*. From there, it was a short jump to being a crime reporter. It was said she had contacts everywhere, and though she was a sort of friend, I never forgot her mission and held to my father's advice: avoid reporters as much as possible, but if not, then it was best to keep answers short and vague. He'd also said that they could be used. Ginger had said she had information. I needed that.

"I don't know anything."

"You know what you saw. What you've heard. How you feel."

"I came to open the bar, found the back door unlocked and the alarm off. The body was lying by the front door."

"As I understand it, you're the primary suspect."

"So far."

"Why is that?"

"They can't find anyone else?" The moment I said it, I knew it wouldn't satisfy.

Her heavy frown scolded me while her thick makeup blushed darker. "We're friends. I'll do you right. Don't worry."

I nodded, understanding only that I was in deep, deep trouble with this woman. Sink or swim, I told myself. "I'm the only one who knew the alarm code."

"That's it? That's not enough to arrest anybody. Nick Eccheli will have to work harder than that."

She hesitated. Then asked, "Did you kill Edward Blaisdale?"

"What? No!" Anger at the accusation forced me to my feet. I thought she knew me better than that.

For her part, Ginger stayed seated. Unperturbed. "Relax. I have to ask these things. That's how an interview works. Sit back down."

"Tell me what you know. I answered your questions."

"The information I have is worth more than what you've said so far." She waited until I reclaimed my place beside her. Began again. "Did you know him?"

"No."

"But he'd been in the bar before. My sources told me that."

"Just because he'd been there, it doesn't mean I knew him. I serve lots of people I don't know. Lots of people I don't even remember serving."

"Fair point." Her eyes glittered like a predator staring at prey. She smiled.

Like a lightning bolt, insight hit me. She'd riled me up on purpose to try to get me to spill something I might not have. Like if I had known Blaisdale. Or even the killer. Clever.

She continued, "I understand there's security footage."

I nodded. Waited, hoping it wouldn't take long; her cologne was giving me a headache.

Ginger narrowed her eyes for a brief second. She patted my arm. "Fair enough. My source tells me there's nothing in the labs so far. Of course, they're way backed up."

I knew about the labs being backed up already, and I was sure she meant that to be comforting, but those two words, 'so far', worried me. It was my bar. My DNA was scattered all over it. Even though I'd cleaned, some of it was bound to be mixed in with the samples taken. "How do you know there's nothing?"

She shook her head, stirring the cologne. "My source is confidential. Anyway, the ME report can cause the most problems. And it's too soon for that."

"Is that all you have?"

"For now." She chucked her chin toward me. "Let's see it."

"You'll tell me what the ME report says when it becomes available?"

"Of course. We're friends." Ginger patted my arm again.

Deal made, I pulled out my phone and played the video of the killing for her.

"Would you send that to me?"

She may have called us friends, but that didn't make it so. I said, "You having that video does nothing to further my innocence."

"It doesn't hurt it either."

"Media sensationalism. No thanks."

She didn't say anything for a few minutes.

I stood again, this time with a cool detachment. "Time for you to go."

"Go? I thought we were friends."

"We are, but you came here on business. That is now concluded: you have nothing more to tell me and I have nothing more to tell you. Ergo, it's time for you to leave." I led the way to the door and opened it wide. As she and the cologne cloud passed, I added, "Don't forget the ME report."

She hesitated and then gave a short business-like nod. "I won't."

Now that Ginger was gone, I let in the dogs and could return to my game, but I just stared at the dark TV, with remote in hand. With a deep sigh, I tossed the remote onto the couch and went into the bedroom. I changed from my shirt into one that was navy blue and clingy. Back out in the living room, I swooped my keys off the counter. The dogs lunged to their feet, yapping and dancing, hoping for an outing with Mom, but settled down just as quickly when I snatched up my motorcycle helmet. Ruffles whined softly.

From the spare bedroom, I wheeled Dad's – well, Aaron's – chromed Harley Fat Boy. The high ape hangers made turning the corners a little difficult, but I managed without scraping off any paint from the wall.

Once outside, I headed onto I-64, but turned in the opposite direction from my bar, into downtown, to a tiny hole-in-the-wall place. The Crow was always packed and I added my bike to the long line in front. While I wound my way to the bar, I shook out my impromptu braid.

The place was filled wall to wall with tattooed men, ragged beards, ponytails, and bare-tummied women. Most were crowded around either pool table, but quite a few lined the bar too. The décor was similar to mine, except it was nothing but photos of bikes. All kinds of Harleys to be precise. There were a few bike parts scattered around the walls and ceiling, too: tires, handlebars, gas tanks. The volume in the place was nearly blinding. And though I knew Bobby had the air going full blast, the place was decidedly thick and hot. And all this on a Tuesday night. I was jealous.

A few interested eyes flashed my way, even though I wasn't sporting any bare skin. But I wasn't there for them. I squeezed into a spot near the end of the bar.

Bobby Crow was, of course, busy dishing up drinks. A mountain of a man, he was the epitome of the stereotypical biker: Long blond ponytail behind a bald dome, full-sleeve tattoos, thick mustache and goatee. He even wore the vest and boots. His face lit up when he saw me and within a few seconds I had a longneck beer. He leaned on the bar, coming eye level with me. No preamble, which was typical of him. He said something, but I couldn't hear it. The guy next to me was on his phone, and by the pitch of his voice, I could tell he'd had a few beers too many. I leaned in and shook my head. Cupped my hand to my ear.

Bobby slapped his hand on the bar and glared at the guy on the phone, who nearly fell off his stool in his effort to escape. There was a brief lull in the volume of the room, but when it became clear no one was in trouble, the volume returned to its normal. Bobby turned his attention to me again. His words came across better this time. "Cops came by."

"And?" I leaned back again, now that we were able to speak at a semi-normal amplitude.

"The usual stuff: my past, your past, us. Lots of questions about you."

"That's because I'm a serial axe murderer."

"I knew that. Explains the attraction. When they gonna open your place back up?"

"I don't know. Not for a few days." I took a sip of the most perfect temperature beer I'd ever had. It slid like melting ice down my throat.

He nodded, straightened, tapped his finger on the bar to say he'd be right back, and went to wait on two equally tattooed guys at the other end. When he returned, he again leaned to eye level with me. "Sucks."

I shrugged. "Nothing to be done about it, I guess. I just wish they'd hurry up. We have a tournament to play."

He nodded again, watched me take another sip of heaven from my bottle. "They know anything?"

"The victim was an ex-cop named Blaisdale."

"Saw that on the TV." He waited on someone and came back. "Your brother get any news?"

I made a face. "They haven't told him anything." Aaron would have called me if he'd found out something. He wasn't good at keeping secrets from me. From anyone, as far as that went.

Bobby gave me a sly wink. "Well then, when we figure out something, we won't tell them, either."

I took another sip of beer and sighed. The amazing thing about the beer at The Crow was that they were all the same perfect temperature. Bobby had ordered in some kind of special fridge with separate compartments designed to keep each type beer at its unique optimum serving temperature. It had paid for itself several times over already; the place was always busy. The fridge cost a mint, nearly five times the price of a standard bar refrigerator, but I had one on my bucket list.

"You have video. What's it show?"

"Not much. Two masked men, one dead and the other leaving. I thought you might take a look." If I was good at reading people, Bobby was a wizard.

He straightened at another customer calling, "Crow!" Before he left me, though, he said, "Too busy now. Stick around."

At my "Of Course," he left. And then I didn't see him for a long while, except for the occasional replacement beer that slid my way down the bar. I watched him work, liked how his body flowed from one task to the next like a well-practiced dancer. He carried that over into his love-making.

Aaron called around eleven. "I swung by your place. Where are you?"

"Crow."

He cursed. "I suppose you have my bike?"

"Someone's got to ride it." It felt good to get in that little dig after all the grief he'd caused me.

He was silent for a long moment, then, "It's my day off Thursday and I have a couple seats to the game. How about steaks at your place before?"

I smiled. As if I'd argue about going to watch my beloved Cardinals. If anything could lift me out of my funk, it would be going to a live game. I knew he probably had bought the steak and tickets for some hot-chick-in-his-bed wannabe but had decided his sister needed to be cheered up instead. He was worried about me. "Sounds good."

We hung up, and for the next several hours, I concentrated on my beer and the conversation that ebbed and flowed around me. As the crowd thinned toward the 3 AM last call, Bobby worked his way down toward me again, towel moving across the equipment below the bar. He looked up at me, eyes glinting. "Got plans?"

I shook my head and grinned.

10

Sometime between closing and dawn, I showed Bobby my videos. We were camped out in my bed, the blanket twisted in a pile on the floor. Bobby had one leg slung off the side, tapping the beige rug with his toes. The A/C was on and the ceiling fan was blowing full on us. Our sweat-slick skin glistened from the light of my phone.

I pointed at the movements on the video. "See, what I can't figure is why the chubby guy goes to the front door."

"There are only three reasons why anyone goes to the front." He stuck his thumb up in the air and added a finger with every point he made. "He's lettin' someone in. He's a lookout. To turn off the alarm."

Bobby had only told me a little about his past, and I'd never pried beyond that. It was the nature of our relationship. But, I was pretty sure he'd run with a rough crowd when he was a biker. His words confirmed it, at least to me. He might have done some time, even. And I thought there was an ex-wife with a kid in his past somewhere, too. I shrugged mentally. He'd tell me if he wanted me to know.

I said, "Well, if it was to let someone in, the skinny guy would have done that after the killing."

Bobby nodded. "And, there was no reason for a lookout. They were quiet, didn't need flashlights due to the amount of security lights you have, and there are damn few pedestrians at that time of morning."

"So, it had to be for the alarm. But it's in back —"

"Which Skinny obviously knew because he didn't have to look for it —"

"But Chubby probably didn't." I stared off into the dark of my bedroom. My stomach dropped. "Shit."

"Skinny's been watchin' you."

I said it again. "Shit."

"Yep." The whir of the fan filled the silence. After a few minutes, he restarted the video. As he manipulated it bigger to focus on Skinny, I told him what I'd figured out about the guy.

"Yeah," he said. "But I think he's naturally a little bit jerky. See how he moves here, by the back door, before the murder?"

Sure enough. Even as we watched, he gave a sudden jerk to his head to face the front of the bar, checking Chubby over his shoulder, while he jabbed the disarm code into my alarm.

"How'd he get my code? Even watching me, he'd have to be awfully damn close to see that."

"Or he tapped into your camera feed."

"If he did that, he could have gone back later, found the videos of the murder in the cloud, and erased them all."

Bobby sighed, his great chest lifting my head so much my shoulder raised off the bed. He said, "I don't know, then. Maybe he went low tech: covered your keypad with a clear film, then removed it with your fingerprints."

"That would mean he's broken in before. Even if just to test the different possible codes. But, it would take a long time to try each number variation. The police would certainly show up before he got it figured out."

I took the phone from him and stopped the image. He kissed the top of my head. Said, "You know I'm not that guy anymore, right? The one who did those kinds of things. He was an absolute idiot.

Dangerous, too. But when I found out I had a kid, I left that guy behind. He's gone for good. Okay?"

I hesitated. Sometimes dealing with Bobby's past was like making an angel food cake: over do it and it could fail. "This guy's pretty great. I like him a lot. But, that guy laid the foundation for this guy. I don't hate that, and I don't hate him, either."

He squeezed me so tight, I thought my ribs would crack.

When he finally let up and I could breathe again, I asked, "Where's your kid?"

"Livin' with his mom. They're up in Brentwood." Deep sigh. "He's six."

"You see him much?" A six year old. I couldn't even imagine what it would be like to have a child, much less one that age. Talk about nonstop energy.

"She won't let me. Took it to court, even."

"That's harsh." Very harsh.

He made a nondescript noise that I took to mean he agreed with my sentiments. From experience, I knew there would be no more conversation on the subject. I returned to my phone and accessed the cloud again, pulling up video after video. Finally, after going back nearly a week, I gave up. Bobby was staring at the ceiling fan. I'd never seen him like that. It really drove home how little we knew about each other. From the beginning, our relationship had been all about chemistry.

I couldn't sleep. So I stared at the fan, too. My mind kept going around and around about the murder and the things we talked about. I wasn't sure when Bobby shook off his funk. I just turned to see if he'd fallen asleep and found him staring at me. He gave his slow smile, like he always did. Pulled me close. And then he made sure the murder was the furthest thing from my mind.

After our romp, we were spent. We drifted off to sleep still tangled around each other. I dreamt of sinister shadows that followed every move I made. It was almost as if they were attached to me, sewn on like Peter Pan's. At times they were in front of me, at times behind. They surrounded me and stared with gnashing teeth.

For a second night, I got very little sleep, waking at nearly seven with an uneasy burr in the pit of my stomach.

Someone was watching me. How far did that extend? Was it just at the bar or here at home, too? I quietly got up and closed all the blinds. When I came back to bed, Bobby was awake. Without a word, he pulled me to lie against him, his thick arms wrapped around me. He leaned his head against mine and closed his eyes again. I felt protected. Safer than I'd felt since my parents' death. I drifted off to a peaceful sleep.

11

When I finally woke again, it was nearly noon. I had quite a few hours before my 5 PM appointment with the Krav Maga instructor. Bobby was gone and the dogs were out in the backyard with massive bowls of water. My phone was propped against the toaster on the kitchen counter, a post it note beside it with 'Syl' underscored by a big arrow pointing at the device.

I turned it on, and a video message from Bobby appeared. His image smiled and said, "My first selfie. Can you call a video that? A selfie?" As he walked, the image jumped around a lot and the background changed from that of the sliding glass backdoor, to the living room wall and TV, to the kitchen ceiling.

He frowned momentarily, his brows all but disappearing beneath the heavy folds in his forehead. Years in the sun did that, I guess. He continued, "You left your phone access to your security site open, so I took a look at videos for the last couple months. Didn't think you'd mind. Nothin' to see. I don't know how Skinny got your alarm number. I'll think on it."

His face softened and he smiled. I knew he was thinking about our lovemaking. I couldn't help but to smile back. As if seeing me, he nodded. "Keep me apprised."

The video ended and I was still smiling.

I dressed in a soft blue sleeveless tee and jeans. Tumbling the dogs into my Jeep, I drove to the nearby Maplewood Doggy Park. I liked the Frenchtown one better – there was just something peaceful about it – but time was at a premium. I had some shopping to do before my lesson.

Maplewood Park was small, and it usually didn't have many visitors, except a few locals here and there. Just right for my dogs. The trees cast a comfortable shade across the bench I chose while my pooches investigated the fenced-in area. The humidity was staggering, painting everything in a haze. I soaked through my shirt within a few minutes.

Despite my dogs' antisocial behavior toward humans, they were downright gregarious when it came to other dogs, and within ten minutes were running around with a collie and two beagles. All belonging to one owner, who thankfully didn't sit near me. The dogs raced after each other and, while Ruffles's long legs easily outpaced the rest, Satan and the beagles were on a par, leg-length wise, so that the three of them trailed the other two, bowling each other over in an effort to catch up.

In between throws of the increasingly soggy tennis ball, while the dogs raced around the park, I opened the St. Louis Post Dispatch website and looked for Ginger Jefferson's article. I didn't have to search far. The short article was the third entry down. The headline read, *Bartender Furious About Murder Investigation*.

A groan escaped me and my stomach clenched. There would be repercussions. Lots of them. The meat of the article was short, due to the murder already being several days old.

The September 5th homicide of ex-police officer Edward Blaisdale has stalled. The labs that have been processing crime scene evidence are backed up and the report from the Medical Examiner's office is delayed.

The security videos from that night definitely show a male perpetrator.

Yet, Homicide detective Nick Eccheli seems to be focused solely on the owner of the bar where Blaisdale's body was found, even though over 17 possible suspects have been identified already.

Sylvia Wilson, the owner of Smugglers, has this to say, "They can't find anyone else."

The investigation seems to rest solely on the fact that Wilson kept her alarm code a secret.

Detective Eccheli refuses to comment.

My jaw was sore from clenching my teeth so hard. I was going to be in trouble with Aaron, Eccheli, and everyone of the blue breed, no doubt about it. I closed the website, tossed the tennis ball, and instead scanned videos older than the couple months Bobby had checked. Someone had been watching me. They'd broken into my bar and killed a person, a vital human being. That didn't sit right with me. I found nothing. I went way, way back, all the way. But there was only one other instance of Blaisdale visiting the bar. It had also been to see Chief Degere. A bulging envelope had been slid across the table. Money?

They chatted a bit, then Blaisdale had moved on to another table, sliding onto the bench seat across from a big square guy with a thick mustache. He bought a few rounds for the both of them. Then they left.

My thoughts drifted to the day my parents died and how grief-stricken I'd been. How completely unable to cope. I thought about the Chief's wife, Patricia. My heart ached for her. I changed my plans. Major shopping would have to wait. I checked the time; we'd been at the dog park 45 minutes. Whistling for the pooches, I walked to the Jeep, thinking about the whole murder thing. I felt violated. By the time I got to my parking space, I was really, really angry.

I scolded myself for speeding out of the parking lot. Driving was no place to take out my fury. Without really realizing, I drove past the turn to my house and was on the way to Smugglers. When I noticed what I'd done, I gave a mental shrug and continued on until I parked in front of my bar.

Staring at the yellow tape across the front door and the unlit open sign, I tried to picture how it had been that night and why Skinny had sent Blaisdale to the front. There had been no pedestrian traffic, so that ruled out having a lookout. Bobby had been right about that.

I noted the security light at the corner of my building. The night had been clear and hot, the face of the bar would have been well lit. No, the thieves hadn't been expecting anyone to join them. No one would have come in that way. That removed the second option, leaving only the excuse of the alarm. Bobby had been right about all of it.

The question remained, though: how did Skinny get the code? I had never written it down and the camera inside was at the wrong angle to see it when I entered it into the alarm.

12

wanted to yell and scream. Lie in bed and hide under the covers. Break a million dishes. Punch someone. Laugh for days and days. Cry for days and days. I wanted to keep driving and never come back. In the end, I slowly drove home from our outing and parked out front.

The dogs launched out of the Jeep as soon as I stopped, chasing each other to the house door to check for intruders. Discovering the coast was clear, they sat like proper pets and waited. As soon as they were in, I relocked the door and turned right around for my Jeep. Stopped at a grocery hot food counter for some lasagna. Made the drive to Chief Degere's house. The yard was small, like mine. Needed a mow, but the brick front had recently been washed. The sidewalk to the walnut door was clean, as was the storm gutter along the street. Cook Avenue. Nice neighborhood. I'd considered it when moving to the city, but ultimately decided the lower crime where I now lived was what I wanted.

There were no cars in the drive, and though the garage was closed, I could see the top of only one vehicle. I gathered the food and walked up the walk. Rang the bell. It took a long time and I was just about to give up when a tiny white woman with brown hair answered the door. Her eyes were red, bloodshot from crying. Water droplets clung to the little wisps of hair that framed her face. She gave me a tremulous smile. Suddenly, I felt like a monster for intruding.

I realized I couldn't remember her name, even though I'd heard it on the news. I said, "I'm sorry about your nephew. I brought you some food." Great opener. I would have rolled my eyes at myself except, well, she'd see that.

She opened the door wide and reached for the bag. "That's very thoughtful. Come in."

"It's lasagna. Store bought; I don't really cook." Liar. I followed her inside, my stomach squelching with guilt.

"I'll just put this in the kitchen." She scuffed away in mint green slippers while I waited in the center of the room. It was decorated in the popular dusty country that had stormed across the nation about 30 years ago. It found residence in the Midwest and was still big in a lot of home decor. Dusty rose couches, brown carpet, and tiny accents of dusty blue everywhere.

Photos were scattered on most every flat piece of furniture in the room, even the TV. And more photos hung on the wall. Some were covered in black cloth. Those probably had Blaisdale in them. I picked up a framed photo that had been flat on the coffee table. A younger Blaisdale and an older version of him who also bore a faint resemblance to Mrs. Degere. A brother perhaps?

The air in the room closed in on me. Everything in this room spoke of a private, haunting grief. I was an intruder and had no business there.

Her voice carried from the kitchen. "How did you know Eddie? Would you like some coffee?"

I lifted my eyebrows. How, indeed? I couldn't very well tell her I owned the bar where he'd been murdered. And I probably shouldn't let her know I was a suspect in the case. I raised my voice a notch to be heard, "I should really go. I didn't know your nephew. My brother works with your husband." Not too big a lie.

"Please stay. I could use some company." She came to the doorway. Motioned to the photo I still held. "That was my brother with Eddie. He died a few years ago."

I carefully set the photo back where I'd found it, saying, "I'm sorry. This must be doubly hard for you."

"It is, yes." That tremulous smile again. "How do you take your coffee?"

"Black, please."

She smiled her thanks at my staying and disappeared into the kitchen again. Within a minute, she came out with two steaming mugs and motioned for me to sit on the rose colored couch. Her smile was brighter. Perhaps my being there wasn't the worst thing. She asked, "What's your name?"

My resolve to keep her in the dark about everything crumbled. I couldn't keep lying to her. She was a cop's wife. On some level, she would probably understand. Hopefully. I remained standing. Maybe she wouldn't recognize my name. "I'm Sylvia Wilson."

She stopped at the far end of the coffee table and set down both mugs, one black and one creamy. She looked me squarely in the eyes, her face set like hardened steel. This woman was not to be taken lightly. She was every bit worthy of being a police chief's wife.

She quietly said, "I know who you are. You own the bar. Did you kill my Eddie?"

I kept her gaze and shook my head. "No ma'am. I didn't. Please believe me. I just came to pay my respects."

Her eyes stayed locked onto me a moment more, and in the silence, the tick of the clock sounded like my death toll. Then she took a deep sigh and looked out the window at the scorching day. "I've always been a good judge of liars. Let's say I believe what you said. The police won't be happy you've been here. Especially my husband."

Mrs. Degere turned her flinty gaze back to me. "And I *will* tell him when he gets home."

She slid the mug of black coffee down the table toward me. Taking the other, she settled on the far end of the couch and returned her attention to the window. She quietly asked, "Was it you who spoke to the reporter?"

I froze. Nodded slowly. "She put a lot of her own thoughts in that article. I'm not unhappy with the investigation. I'm not angry with the police."

She pressed her lips thin, but didn't kick me out. I picked up my coffee and perched on the edge of the one of the recliners, a straight line to the door, in case I had to run for my life. "What was he like?"

The sad smile returned. "He was clumsy. And always making the wrong choices. Always late. Always poorly dressed. Eddie's the only family I have left."

She spoke more to her mug than to me. Steam rolled up her face with every word. "Was the only family left, I mean. Was."

"His car was still at the bar. It was registered in your husband's name?"

She slowly nodded. "It used to be mine. We left it in Martin's name because we didn't think Eddie would make the payments. He did though. But not regularly."

"I looked him up on the internet. It said he was shot in the line of duty."

"Took a bullet in his hip. He worked security after that."

"Where did he work?"

"Hocking Construction."

"Did he make enough there to meet all his expenses?"

She eased upright and stared at me with a deep frown. "Why do you ask? You sound like you're investigating on your own."

"I'm not. I guess I'm just curious. The murder was staged to look like a robbery, but not very well. My theory is your nephew was lured into the bar with the promise of money."

"Nobody's told me anything." She set down her mug. "You know, I remember he once told me he was picking up a few hours somewhere else, too. Didn't mention the name of the place, though."

"So, two jobs might have met his expenses." I nodded and took a gulp of coffee, nearly burning my throat. I set down my mug, too. "Did you get to see him a lot?"

"A couple times a month." She rose. "I think you should leave. I just don't feel comfortable with you here."

I stood and walked to the door. She followed, and when I turned to say goodbye, she stepped right up to my chest. Caught my gaze and her eyes turned hard again. "I'll believe you for now, but if I find out you lied, if you killed my Eddie, you won't be able to run far enough to escape me. I'll make you experience pain like you've *never* felt. Clear?"

Oh yeah. Perfectly clear.

was late for my appointment with the Krav Maga instructor. Not a good note to start on. I pulled up to the Midtown training facility and sat in my Jeep staring at the door, trying desperately to remember the instructor's name. Traffic blitzed past in a frantic, early rush hour. Horns blasted and radios blared. Everyone was angry with each other because of the heat and humidity.

I felt off-kilter and self-conscious about my lack of confidence. Someone had been killed in my bar. It was as good as a personal assault. I was a suspect. And I'd just had my life threatened. I gave up on the name thing. Discipline and sweat would ground me again.

I climbed out of my Jeep and walked to the building. The door shoved open to a cooled front reception, very small with no desk. Just a couple chairs and shelved walls replete with trophies and photos of competitions, stances, and kicks.

The heavy odor of fresh sweat mixed with the acrid bite of cleaning disinfectant. An excited thrill curled in my stomach, and I smiled. I'd really enjoyed my Judo lessons until the unfortunate dating incident.

There was no one in sight, so I wandered toward the wall of grunts and cries that came from a doorless hallway in one corner of the room. I passed two doors on the left side of the hall, one a generic bathroom, the other a janitorial closet, or so the signs said, and into a large room with a rubber coated hard floor. Some upright punching bags, and a low shelf along one wall with a large pile of pads and other items. Filling the room, were six pairs of students practicing kicks of various sorts. The far wall was mirrored, and the reflections of the six pairs practiced as well.

A short grizzled man strolled amongst the pairs, stopping to make corrections or speak to the combatants. He glanced up and saw me. Looked at the clock high on the near wall. Held up two fingers, which I assumed meant two more minutes. I nodded and lounged against the wall to watch.

The pair closest to me took turns on a roundhouse kick in long fluid motions. The next pair over was working on a sweeping kick, aimed at the ankles and shins. I had to admit, I was getting breathless at the thought of trying some of those.

I'd read on the internet that Krav Maga, more than any other martial arts discipline, concentrated on simultaneous defense and disabling of the attacker. Looking at the students before me, who were obviously advanced, but still learning their moves, I liked what I saw. Again, that thrill of excitement curled in my stomach.

By the time the instructor called it quits, I was convinced Krav Maga was the right discipline for me. Sweaty students filed past. Some greeted me, but they all looked dog tired. None of them looked angry; their angst with the weather had been worked out of them. The mirror people left, too.

The instructor approached, hand outstretched. Now that he was close, he looked to be older than the late 40s or early 50s I'd thought when we were on the phone. The grizzled look was from grey stubble and short spikey hair. His eyes pierced into me. We shook hands. He asked, "You're Sylvia Wilson?"

I said, "I am. I'm sorry, I don't remember your name."

"Marshall Teague."

I tapped my temple. "Got it."

"Why do you want to study Krav Maga? Why not continue with Judo?"

I opted not to tell him why I quit Judo. Instead I told him about the murder. "I want something with a bit of teeth. Something I can use right away if I need it."

"Oh, we have teeth. Don't worry. This isn't much like Judo. We do a bit of work with holds and pins, but ultimately, we teach how to keep your attacker from getting that close."

"Lots of kicks." I motioned toward the big room where I'd witnessed the lesson.

"And strikes."

"I haven't done any of that. I guess I'll be starting over. Do you have any classes for beginners?"

"I do, but it's already met for the week. The next class is 9 AM next Tuesday."

"That's a bit early for me. Do you give private lessons?"

"Certainly. Let's go look at the schedule."

"I need something as soon as possible. I'm worried the murder might be a statement to me, since it happened in my bar."

He stopped and looked me up and down. "I have a few minutes. I can give you a first lesson now."

At my nod, he led the way to the center of the floor and motioned to his relaxed frame, looking like anybody on the street. "This is a neutral stance. Basically, it's you just standing, unaware of an impending attack."

"This is a fighting stance." He shifted his feet, his right further back than his left. Bent his knees just a bit and raised his hands: open with the palms faced away from his face. Suddenly, I saw the warrior in him. That was what I wanted for myself: someone who would make people think twice about hurting me.

I imitated him as best I could see. He made a few adjustments to my hands and feet. Nodded. He said, "You want your toes facing toward your attacker. Let's try a basic strike."

He dropped into the fighting stance and shoved the hand over his front foot forward horizontally, level with his shoulder. All in slow motion. The mirror him did the same. "You hit an attacker in the face like this and it will stun him. Maybe even hurt him a bit. It might give you time to get away."

It looked easy enough.

I tried it. He corrected my leg and raised my arm. He said, "Good. Now, raise your shoulder to protect your face when you strike. Also, breathe out at the same time to give your body more room to move."

That shoulder raising thing turned out to be tricky. I kept wanting to tuck my head in my armpit. After several unsuccessful attempts, he said, "Someone's trying to hit you in the side of the head. If he connects, you're out. Use your brain. That's your greatest weapon."

I dropped into fighting stance and gave him a one-two, pretty sure he'd be pleased. I'd been a top-rate Judo student, a quick study. Then again, it was my boyfriend-instructor who told me that.

He said, "That's good. Do it again, but this time keep hitting until I tell you to stop. Don't forget to protect your head with your forward shoulder and breathe out when you hit. One-two. One-two."

Well, that was kind of a compliment there, at the beginning. I struck the air repeatedly and he called out adjustments to my technique. After fifty, or maybe, nine hundred strikes, he put a halt to those.

I asked, "How many times would I strike someone?"

He looked directly in my eyes. And his grizzled stillness brought a stillness right into me. "When someone attacks you, you become an attacker too. You attack right back. And you keep it up until he stops or you can safely get away. Understand?"

"Attack the attacker. Got it." I liked the sound of that.

"Good. Because of your situation, I'm going to teach you things a little out of order. This is how you do a knee strike." Teague moved into a fighting stance and lifted his back knee. Pointed to the raised foot. "See how tight I have this tucked? There are two reasons. First, it puts your strike on the fleshy part right above your knee cap, limiting damage to yourself. Second, it's like a spring load for another, immediate strike. Watch as I move through this."

In slow motion, Teague brought his knee all the way up, striking an invisible attacker in the stomach or groin. In the mirror, his reflection did the same thing. Motioning to the line of his body, he said, "See how I bring my hips forward? This gives power to the strike. Makes it more than a jab. I quickly return my leg to be able to strike again. Now you try it. Try and drive your knee right through your attacker."

He picked up a large pad he called a tombstone and nodded he was ready.

I tried it. Even though Teague had leaned into the hit, he took a bracing step back with the impact. The guy in the mirror did too. He said, "Good. Yes. Now one more thing. The minute you hit the bag, snap right back to the fighting stance to prepare for whatever you have to do next. Right away."

I nodded my understanding, and when I struck next, I thought I did what he'd told me. But instead, I heard, "Don't let your leg dangle. Snap it back right away."

Four more strikes and he was still saying the same thing. Each time, I thought I'd done it right. On the fifth, Teague grabbed my leg and flipped me onto my back on the mat. My breath whooshed out and I lay there, blinking up at him. Though short, he towered over me, flat on my back as I was. He raised his eyebrows and said, "That's why you don't let your leg dangle."

Teague helped me to my feet with a strong pull. We resumed our positions: me at the attack, and him behind the tombstone. He said, "Don't worry so much if you're doing it right. There is no right or wrong in Krav Maga. Just the best ways for power and effectiveness. Think street fighter. Just try to keep me from grabbing your leg. I want you to strike repeatedly."

That sounded like a challenge to me.

I struck three times in a row. The best he could do was a quick slap on the side of my knee as it left. After the third attempt, he straightened and said, "Good. Now, what was the difference?"

"I wasn't focused on the strike, just about you not catching me."

He pointed his finger in the air like an exclamation point. Like his hair. "Exactly."

He set up again and we practiced a few more times. Happily, I didn't end up on the floor even once. Teague called a halt. "Okay, that's good. Practice it until I see you again. How about Friday at one?"

I assured him I'd be there. As I walked away, I felt a new sense of confidence building. Become the attacker. Don't let anyone catch me. Think street fighter. Hurt the attacker before he hurts me. I could do this. I'd bet Mrs. Degere could too.

I went home and ate a mystery frozen something from a plastic container while watching the first game of the Highway 70 series between the Cardinals and the Kansas City Royals. Always a fierce rivalry. Fell asleep on the couch in the second inning. I woke again in the sixth, saw there was still no score and went to bed early.

14

had another night of startling awake every hour or two. When it was finally Thursday morning, I rose and checked my phone MLB app for the score to the previous night's game. The Cards had lost to the Royals 3–0. Second game in the series was 7:15 tonight. And I'd get to see that game in person, courtesy of my brother.

I putzed around the house all morning, taking a broom to my ceiling corners for cobwebs, deep-cleaning my beige living room rug, and wiping the fronts of all my kitchen cabinets. While a hot pastrami sandwich was cooking in the press for lunch, I tried to figure if I had enough time to do some serious grocery shopping. Aaron would be over around 4:30 so we could grill the steaks and still get to the game around 6. Parking being what it was. My appointment with the lawyer was at 2. Maybe I could zip through the store really fast on my way home.

After eating my sandwich, I climbed into the Jeep, leaving two pouting dogs in the house. I was halfway to the lawyer, when it occurred to me that I hadn't asked Eccheli when he would release my bar. I'd have to ask Aaron. Or maybe Mr. Charlie Moore could help with that. Isn't that what lawyers were for?

It didn't take long for me to drive to the attorney's downtown address; traffic was light for a Thursday. The Arch was shining in the windshield at me and a feeling of okayness settled on me for the first time since the murder. I wondered if the feeling would last. I hoped it would.

Moore, Mancini, and Schmidt wasn't hard to find and within a few minutes I was seated in the waiting room of the firm. Everything I'd researched about Charlie Moore hadn't prepared me for the frail man who came to escort me to his office. His smile was genuine when he firmly shook my hand. He wore a grey suit jacket that hung on him like it was two sizes too big and his skin was sallow. His head was bald, except for a few wisps of hair behind his ears. He looked sickly, and I wondered why he wasn't wearing a mask.

He must have caught some expression on my face, or maybe it was just standard when meeting someone new, because he said, "Cancer. My wife died of Covid. The kids are long grown. All I want to do is practice law until the day I join my wife."

As if that explained everything – and I certainly wasn't going to ask about his apparent death wish – Mr. Moore led the way to his desk, a large walnut affair that was nearly covered with open books and stacks of paper and dark brown folders. He motioned to the matching plush chairs in front while he removed his jacket and claimed his own seat behind the desk. I sat in the chair nearest the door, not fully committed to needing a lawyer yet.

While he thumbed through a file which I assumed was mine, I looked around the office. Everything was either walnut wood or burgundy cloth. Little dots of gold highlights popped out here and there on picture frames and matching pen-pencil sets strategically placed within the walnut bookcases that lined the walls. More gold was peppered in the tie-backs for the long burgundy drapes that hung on either side of the fourth story windows. A gold central chandelier, instead of crystal, rained light down on us. There was a small section of wall that displayed more gold framed photos of a younger and healthier Charlie posing with St. Louis celebrities: Bob Gibson, Nelly, John Goodman, and a few others I didn't know.

My lawyer eventually cleared his throat, looking up from the file. "You shouldn't have spoken to the reporter, Ms. Wilson."

I shook my head at my gullibility. "I realize that now. But at the time, she said she had info about the case. Anyway, most of what she wrote she got elsewhere."

"It still makes you look bad. And we need you to be a friend of the police and the court." He hesitated, and when I didn't say more, he softly added, "Tell me what kind of trouble you've gotten yourself into. I want to hear the whole true story in your words. Don't leave anything out."

He leaned back in his chair and laced his fingers across his chest. As I began speaking, he closed his eyes. I told him everything, even Eccheli's rude attempt at snooping in my house. That brought a smile from Moore. At least he wasn't sleeping.

When I finished, he opened his eyes and leaned forward again. "Have the police charged you with anything?"

I shook my head. "I think it's just a matter of time before they do. I'm the only one with the alarm code."

He waved it off. "Your detective knows that can be thrown out of court. It's circumstantial. Why do you think you need a lawyer?"

He didn't ask me if I committed the murder. Was he giving me the benefit of the doubt? Or did it just not matter to him? I searched everything I knew, but found no valid answer to his question. "I just want to be prepared in case they *do* charge me."

"I understand that. But, honestly, there's nothing I can do until you are arrested."

"Actually, there is. My bar is my sole means of income. The longer it's closed, the more suspicious I look to my customers, even if I'm never arrested. I need to reopen soon."

"All right, I'll get started on that right away. Meanwhile, no more talking to reporters. It's my job to find information for you, should the need arise."

We stood and he escorted me to the door where we again shook hands. As I rode the elevator down, I had mixed feelings about my new attorney. Though I guess most people did when it came to lawyers. Maybe, like Karyn asserted, it was intentional. I just hoped Mr. Charlie Moore would do whatever he could to get Smugglers reopened soon.

15

When I returned home, I pulled into the back parking space and came through the gate, loaded with bags from my speed grocery shopping. Aaron – the only other person to have a house key and know my house alarm code – was sprawled in a chair under the green striped awning on my patio, drinking from a beer can that was dripping with condensation. My dogs lounged on either side of him, bare bellies on the cement. They hadn't even moved at my arrival. Some protectors. The pooches loved Bobby, but they worshipped Aaron. Ruffles never forgot he'd been my brother's when he was a pup.

Aaron rose and took several bags. I frowned at him. "I didn't see your truck when I drove by out front. How'd you get here?"

"Uber. I figured you were right about the bike. Thought I'd take it home."

"You keep it here because you're worried about it getting stolen."

He shrugged. Which, in Aaron speak, meant he was done talking about it. He opened the sliding door and I led the way inside, noting the creased pillow on my couch. Apparently my brother had been here a while. Maybe even the whole time I'd been out.

We unloaded the groceries. When we finished, he went out to start the grill, and I reached into the fridge and pulled out two giant potatoes. Stabbed them a few times, and popped them in the micro-wave, setting the timer for 15 minutes. I had mixed feelings about him taking Dad's bike. It belonged to my brother, but I'd gotten used to riding it. And, I felt closer to Dad with it here. Guess I'd have to get used to it being gone.

I joined my brother on the patio with my own beer. The humidity was crushing, and half the time we rubbed our beers across our foreheads to cool us down. We were both silent, watching the heat waves rise from the grill as it warmed.

Finally, when Aaron put on the meat, he brought up the newspaper article. "How could you talk to a reporter like that? I thought you knew better." He shook his head, his back to me, and adjusted the placement of the already sizzling steaks with tongs. A flame belched from burners below.

His shoulders slumped. "Eccheli's furious. He froze me out of his investigation."

"Because you're my brother."

"Because of that damned article."

"Am I still a suspect?"

He nodded. "What do you think? Eccheli's not going to let a reporter sway him."

"Shit."

"Yep." He went into the kitchen and brought back two more beers, even though I was only half finished with mine.

"Any idea when Eccheli's going to let me back into my bar?"

He shook his head. "Sorry."

"So, an ex-cop was killed in my bar and we don't know anything. No one's talking because I'm on the suspect list. The detective in charge of the investigation is mad at me. And I can't get back into my bar."

"About sums it up."

"What am I going to do?"

"What are *we* going to do, you mean. I don't know, but we'll figure something out."

I smiled and tipped my beer bottle toward him. He raised his in answer and, when he took a swig, I swiped my eyes with my thumb. He'd hold it over me forever if he saw how much his words had touched me. Twice now, he'd brought me almost to tears by reminding me I wasn't in this alone. Bobby had too.

Aaron rose and turned the steaks. "I overheard the ME telling Eccheli at the bar that it looked like it was personal because of how deep the cut was. I'll try to find out more from someone I know at the ME office once the report comes out, but don't hold your breath."

When he returned to his seat, I showed him the videos and told him what Bobby and I had deduced. His question was immediate. "How'd he get your code?"

"I don't know. But I'm sure that's why I'm a suspect. I only keep it in my head. I've never told it to anyone."

"Not even your brother," he said drily, eyebrows knit together, and disgust plain on his face.

"Aren't you glad now? You'd be a suspect, too."

"I think I might already be, by association. At least, a secondary one."

"How could they suspect you?"

He parried with another question, leaning forward, his elbows on his knees and looking directly at me, beer dripping on the cement. "You think it's a frame?"

To hear him put it that way made chills play xylophone on my spine. My stomach rolled and my jaw clenched. I shook my head. My voice was nearly a whisper. "I don't know."

"Hear anything about Branden?"

I'd dated Branden Moore about a year ago, but he'd become possessive, jealous, and I'd had to break off our relationship. That hadn't stopped his obsessing over me. So in the end, I'd banned him from Smugglers and even swore to him I'd get a restraining order if he persisted.

I slowly shook my head again, watching Aaron's forced nonchalance. I said, "He hasn't been around since the night you threw him out of the bar. I can't believe he would have done this. Despite Branden's stalking tendencies, he isn't violent."

"He might have progressed." Aaron rose and opened the grill. Heat waves, suffused with the smell of charring meat, folded to the top of the awning. My stomach kicked with a violent growl. The dogs perked up, cocking their heads and looking around for what caused the noise. We laughed. Aaron fussed with the steaks, and came back. Then he asked, "You know where he is? Think I'll go visit him. See what he's up to."

"As far as I know, he still lives in the same place."

He smiled. "I've heard rumors that Eccheli's IAD partner, Johnson, is interviewing the cops that hang around your bar. Specifically the chief."

"Well, I'm pretty sure the chief didn't do it, either."

He shrugged yet again. "IAD is involved. They have to investigate."

I snorted. "And while they're doing that, the killer is getting away."

"Not if I can help it." He grinned and the freckles crinkled on his nose. Suddenly he wasn't a cop, just the all-American boy I'd grown up with. Nodding toward the grill, he said, "These are probably done."

I went into the kitchen and brought out the silverware and glasses. I went back and plated the potatoes, got some salad I'd made for supper the night before and a half finished bottle of Merlot. The chill Aaron's words had evoked only intensified and the steak, my normal go-to comfort food, didn't assuage it.

I said, "I've started martial arts again. Krav Maga this time."

"Don't date the instructor." He grinned at his bit of wisdom.

I stuck my tongue out at him.

My brother did his best to divert my attention, chatting about family and how often Peaches had been calling and texting. Moved into the different investigations he knew. Ended with, "They tapped me to work the City Capital task force, now that Piggot is in the hospital. He's got a broken pelvis. Lucky to be alive, if you ask me."

No kidding. Piggot had been one of the patrolmen assigned to work the robbery. In his spare time, he was an avid bicyclist, and could often be seen riding his bike in the early dawn hours. A car had caught the back wheel of his new Colnago with its bumper as it passed, sending Piggot flying. His $3800 road bike was a crumpled ball of metal.

"Wow! That's great!" My congrats sounded forced to me, but Aaron's grin was big and he seemed not to have noticed. So much for my inside line to the case. Updates would be harder to get.

He said, "The job isn't much of anything. Mostly scut work. The agent in charge, Dawes, actually says commands to me like I'm a dog: sit, stay, fetch. But the other guys are cool. Right now, Dawes is reinterviewing everyone, which is good for me. Maybe I'll pick up a few things on the way. He's already warned me there will be long hours. Maybe a few short trips."

I pointed my beer at Aaron. "You won't have as much time to date."

His face clouded. I could see that thought hadn't occurred to him. Then he shrugged. "Worth it. And I'm still talkin' to Branden."

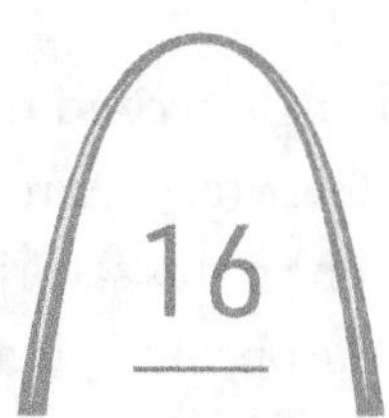

16

The baseball game that night was a sellout, as were most in St. Louis. Doubly so because of the nature of the Highway 70 series. Both Missouri teams, the Cards and Royals only played each other once a year and were fierce rivals. It didn't help that the current manager of the Royals had been booted from the Cardinals. Sadly, it was only a two game series. Parking was chaotic, even though Aaron and I were over an hour early and had ridden the bike so as to come and go easily.

The line at the gate trailed through the lot filled with tailgaters who offered beer, burgers, and brats to everyone who passed. Cardinal emblazoned red scarves, the gate giveaway, were worn by everyone. Even though it was way too hot for them, no one seemed to care. People stepped on my toes and barked my heels. The closer we came to start time, the more people pressed against me. But, at last, we were through the gate wearing our Cardinals jerseys, with our own scarves wrapped securely around our necks, sweating buckets. The important thing was, we were wearing our scarves.

Inside, lines snaked to the different concessions and the museum. We fell into the line that went through the entry tunnel to the tier for our seats. Aaron, of course, took the seat closest to the petite brunette in a tank top, landing me next to the fat lush with beer dribbling from his beard. Lovely.

The seats were good, though: second tier, outfield. Near the left field foul line, but in fair territory. Aaron was always hopeful of catching a homerun from one of his favorites.

The game started with the opening pitch thrown by a hometown hockey player who'd been drafted into the St. Louis NHL team, the Blues, and had subsequently won the Stanley Cup with them. He did an okay toss, though obviously baseball wasn't his sport. The fans gave him a standing ovation that lasted a full five minutes. St. Louis has always been known as a huge sports town, no matter which of its teams played. Players who came here never wanted to leave and, often, those who had been traded away came back to the city to retire.

Then the game was off and running with the crack of a bat and a belch from my neighbor into my ear, bathing my face in beer and digestive fumes.

I only paid attention with half my mind. The question turned round and round in my head: what if it wasn't just circumstantial that I looked guilty? What if someone was trying to frame me? I still didn't think it was Branden in the murder video. He didn't move the same, even though he was about the right size. But, it wouldn't hurt if Aaron checked him out.

In the middle of the fourth inning, the Royals were ahead 2–1. Aaron nudged me hard and pointed at the JumboTron. It showed two burly fans, red-faced and probably inebriated, fighting in the stands behind the home bullpen. Security was involved and actually received several blows too. Surrounding fans no longer paid attention to what was happening on the field, but stood nearby watching and sipping their beverages.

The two combatants clutched and flipped over the seats behind them, knocking a drink out of a spectator's hand to send it spraying down on the warming relief pitchers.

Emilio Juarez, a red-hot pitcher whose career had taken a hard dive the moment he set foot in the Cardinals dugout, took exception. He flung his glove on the ground and monkeyed up the side of the bullpen. Launching himself at the two miscreants, he used his fists to good excess and ended the fight. Security escorted all three out of the stands. The two fans were banned from the stadium, according to the JumboTron. Juarez was ousted from the game. He'd probably be fined heavily and suspended for a few days.

The view on the big screen shifted to the fans. It made me acutely aware of being watched. Was he here? The killer? I crossed my arms and huddled in my seat, trying to make myself small. I didn't feel safe, and I couldn't get over someone being killed in *my* bar. I'd always thought of Smugglers as a safe place where the toughest of the blue breed could relax. But it hadn't been safe enough. Not for Blaisdale. Maybe not for me. I shivered, cold in the blinding hot September evening.

My emotions seemed to be running in waves like those in the ocean. One minute, everything was fine, and the next, I was terrified for my life. My parents' deaths kept racing through my mind. I took a deep breath and slowly blew it out. Did that several times until I calmed.

I hoped Eccheli found the killer soon.

A group of exuberant fans started a wave going around the stadium somewhere in the top of the seventh inning. The score was 2–3, in favor of the Cardinals. When the wave came around to us, Aaron and his neighbor, Hot Chick, both joined in. Next to me, Fat Guy did too, spilling beer and nachos down his stomach. I sat in my seat and waited for the moment of calm to return.

The next time the wave came around, Aaron gripped my bicep and hauled me to my feet with him. "You're going to have fun in spite of yourself."

Hot Chick shot me a glare. I guess she didn't appreciate my brother's attention being diverted. I smiled back at her, winked, and blew her a kiss. She snapped her gaze back to the game so fast I was surprised she didn't get whiplash.

I tracked the wave around the stadium, as did the JumboTron. I didn't want my picture up there for everyone to see. When the wave got four sections away from us, I stood and excused myself for the bathroom, making sure to step on Fat Guy's toes in the narrow confines between rows. He'd be a bit more careful about crowding me in the future.

If I thought I was escaping mayhem by fleeing my seat, I was sadly mistaken. The concession area was chaos. I realized I'd made a grave error: 7th inning stretch was looming, and many ardent fans had decided to get the jump on the between-innings concessions. The bathrooms were a joke, both women and men dancing and fidgeting in gargantuan lines that didn't seem to move at all.

That feeling of being watched only followed me as I strolled the walkway, trying to stay in the middle of the traffic, dodging mostly overweight men and running, screaming children. My mother had loved crowds like this. The more the merrier. But I was like my dad. The only crowd he'd liked was that of a restaurant or a bar. Solitude in a group.

I constantly checked over my shoulder to see if anyone was following. There was no solitary corner, quiet table, or bench where I could scan the crowd for someone watching me, so after one lap, I returned to my seat, noting the wave had disintegrated and no one was staring at me. Aaron handed me a famous Nathan's Dog and beer. There was a question in his smart blue eyes.

I took the offered snack and said, "Bathroom."

Satisfied, he turned back to Hot Chick, the game, and the final remains of his own hotdog. Nathan's Dogs were legend at Busch Stadium. Mine was bacon-wrapped, slathered with baked beans, pico de gallo, spicy aioli, and crispy fried onion. Heart attack in the making. And oh-so-good. Normally, I would have downed it faster than a speedball. As it was, I ate a few bites and gave the rest to Fat Guy, as an apology for trodding on his toes. Gloom settled on me again, swirling my thoughts into a dark cloud of what-ifs and maybes.

Aaron should have saved his tickets for a girlfriend, the game was lost on me. The ninth inning came and went without me noticing. I wished we hadn't come. The Cards won though, spanking the Royals, 2–7. We were now just half a game behind the leaders, Cincinnati. The Pirates were a game-and-a-half behind us. And Milwaukee was two games behind them. The Cubs were half a game below that. It was a close race; who'd end up in the post season, which was just a few weeks away, was still anybody's guess.

It took us nearly forever to get out of that stadium, then twice as long to get out of the parking lot. Aaron stayed right behind his new girlfriend, the one from the seat next to him. I was almost afraid he'd make me take a taxi home, but he somehow thought being cool to his sister would score more points with his next conquest. After a lengthy goodbye with Hot Chick and exchange of phone numbers, we were finally on the way.

The good thing about Busch Stadium was that it was smack downtown. Exits everywhere. I'm sure from space, the cars leaving the game must have looked like roaches scattering from a kicked sandwich. The bad thing about it being downtown was the number of events in that area each evening. It took us a long time to exit the lot, but once out, we made excellent time home.

Aaron "Boom-Boom" Wilson didn't stick around. I assumed he was heading off to, once again, earn his nickname. Last big hurrah before being slaved to the FBI. As for me, I went out and sat on the unlit patio, watching my babies tumble over each other in mock ferociousness. After a couple hours, I went to bed. For the fourth night in a row, I slept poorly. I tossed and turned for a couple hours, until my dogs, who must have decided to take matters into their own paws, camped on either side of me, effectively pinning me beneath the blankets. Then I fell into a deep sleep, interrupted every few hours when I woke from a mayhem of dreams about murdering cows.

Somewhere near dawn, I woke in a cold sweat. I wasn't just any suspect in the murder; I was the primary suspect. They had no real proof I hadn't hired the guy on the video. I'd been far too passive in accepting Eccheli's judgment in the case. But it was looking like if I didn't do something, I was going to jail for a very long time. I needed to stop feeling sorry for myself. Time to get to work. Time to be a detective like my dad.

I remembered he'd kept notebooks. Tons and tons of them in boxes in the garage. A new notebook for each case. They'd been filled with schematics, notes, and charts. It helped him clarify his thoughts and plans, he'd said.

I reached for my phone, and opened my note app. I labeled the document Groceries so if someone happened to snoop, they probably wouldn't be interested in opening anything with that title. First, I wrote everything I could remember about finding the body. Beneath that I added thoughts and two questions. Why staged to look like a robbery on a Sunday night? How did the killer get my code?

I wrote what Bobby and I decided about the killer watching me. No real questions there yet except the ones already asked. Next, I added what had transpired with Ginger Jefferson. Left a space for questions and moved on to my visit with Patty Degere. Made note that there was a second job besides Hocking Construction. Put down the question, How did Blaisdale have so much money? Then I wrote down what Aaron had told me. Finally, I added Charlie Moore's name. I put under his name, "Alarm = circumstantial."

It made me feel better.

17

I stayed awake to welcome in Friday morning. Even though it was the unofficial beginning of the weekend, the street was absolutely silent. My neighbors had all gone to their various places of employment. By 10 AM the weather was just as thick and humid as the day before. A grey spread of clouds covered the sky from horizon to horizon, holding the heat close to the city. But that wouldn't stop me; I had work to do. I'd decided to start with what Patricia Degere had told me about Blaisdale working two jobs. One was at Hocking Construction. I would start there. But I wouldn't speak to the manager, they rarely knew what was going on. I would see if there was a receptionist I could bond with. Lunchtime would be best. What I found out there might show me where to go next in my investigation.

Step One of my plan made, I had nothing to do until noon. I wandered my house aimlessly. Sat on my blue couch. Checked out the evening's event listings in the paper. The Fox had a Broadway production of The Lion King. It was a 900th tour, or something like that. Saw it the first time. Nothing good at the movie theaters. Nothing at Powell. Didn't feel like going to a comedy club.

I got up. Straightened the beige rug. Went to the fridge. Took out food, but didn't want it, so put it back. I went out to the back patio. Sat. Got up and wandered along the shrubs lining the wooden fence, intending to check them for dog pee damage, but stopped when I realized I'd walked half the fence without looking at a single plant.

I went back inside. Peaches called, filling my ear with her high-pitched southern drawl. "Honey, how *are* you holding up?"

"I'm bored. There's nothing for me to do."

"Clean the house. There's always that," Peaches said. I could almost see her nodding.

"Cleaned everything four times in three days. There's nothing left to clean." I frowned at the shine on the range hood.

"Honey, there's *always* something to clean. You just have to find it. In *my* opinion, people just don't put enough elbow grease into their problems. America – hell, the *world* – would be a better place if only people would *just* apply their excess energy."

Peaches was getting ready to launch into one of her famous diatribes. Probably on her eldest child, Roy, again. I had to nip this in the bud or I'd be stuck on the phone with her for another hour, if not more. "You know, Peaches, I think you're right. I need hard work. I'm going to go do that right now. Bye! Love you!" I hung up.

I needed back in my bar. I'd had enough of sitting around and waiting on other people. I needed to live my life.

I pulled out my phone and called Eccheli. Got a recording. It was my guess he screened all his calls, keeping his actual time on the phone to a minimum. I'd learned a few things as a business owner. One of them was how to deal with people who probably wouldn't call you back.

When it came time for me to leave my message, I said, "Detective Eccheli, it's been four days since the murder in my bar. According to the security videos, you haven't been back in there. I assume you're finished. I'll be heading to Smugglers in the next few minutes to begin cleanup unless I hear directly from you. Thank you."

I'd barely disconnected when the call back came.

"It's Eccheli. I need a couple more days before you get back in. You know how it works." I heard lots of voices in the background. Sudden raucous laughter. It didn't sound much like he was investigating anything.

I nodded to myself, I did indeed know how investigations worked. I also knew bureaucracy dragged its feet whenever possible. "Look, you can have it as long as you want. But the pool tournaments are starting Monday, and I'm not going to be the one to tell your two dozen coworkers, including those higher up, that they aren't going to compete. You'll have to do that."

The tournament players who were higher-ups were probably pushing him already. There was a pause on the other end. Not quite what I wanted. A little more push was needed. "Also, I have an event scheduled in there tomorrow night with someone coming in from out of town. I had to pay big bucks to fly him in. It's too late to cancel. But I can see about an outdoor venue permit somewhere. Who would I call about that?"

"I don't —"

"I'm sure someone in one of the offices probably knows more about that. I'll just call around and see what I can find out. If I tell enough people the story, sooner or later, I'm bound to get answers."

I could almost see the hamster wheel spinning in his mind: the more people I called, the more trouble I was bound to raise. His voice was tight when he spoke. Bordering on angry. "No, it's okay. I'll tell you what. I might be able to squeeze in a couple hours tonight and first thing in the morning. Would midday work?"

"It certainly would, Detective. I'll meet you there with lunch and a cleaning crew." I disconnected before he could object. Midday tomorrow. Perfect. And lunch to apologize for my being such a bully.

Now I had to line up someone for my newly invented event. I began a search of entertainment. I didn't have a stage, per se, but I could shift a few seatings, put the jukebox in a different corner. I settled on a comedy act that, true to what I'd told Eccheli, cost me a fair bit of change to bring in on such short notice. Then I contacted the advertising firm that I'd used when I opened Smugglers. More money going out.

And there would be no time to repaint.

My regular cleaning service also had a crew that did biomedical cleaning, so I scheduled them for the next day. I called the showroom where I'd bought the pool table. When I asked them to recover and deep clean my table, they couldn't get someone there for a couple weeks. However, I could trade it in on a new one and have it installed Monday morning. I ordered it, gulping over my dropping bank balance. It was going to take me forever to recoup what this murder was costing.

I called my two part-time employees. Karyn was thrilled to not have to clean. Tom, a student at WashU, wasn't; he'd been counting on the extra money. I told them both I'd have extra hours for them at the event and during the tournaments.

I also called Almera Security. They were a giant in their field and boasted twenty-four/seven in-office help.

A man named Elijah answered. "How may I assist you today?"

"I own one of your security systems. Do you keep my alarm code?"

"We do not. That's your code."

"What happens if the alarm goes off and I'm not available to reset it?"

"We can reset it from here."

"Without my code?"

"We have our own reset code."

"So, to be clear, you can turn off my alarm from there."

"In extreme circumstance, yes."

"What about my data in the cloud? Do you keep record of my password there?"

"No, Ma'am. Again, we have our own Admin password."

"I need to speak with your supervisor."

"I'm sorry. He's in a meeting. I can leave him a message to get back to you."

"Please do that. Tell him, this is Sylvia Wilson. As he undoubtedly knows, someone breached my alarm and killed a man on my property. Tell him, I gave no one my code. Tell him, I want to know how this could have happened."

"I believe Mr. Tate will call you back immediately."

"Thank you, Elijah. I'm sure he will."

"Please stand by your phone."

A moment later, the phone rang and a heavy voice said, "Hello, Ms. Wilson. This is Gordon Tate."

"I assume Elijah informed you what has happened at my bar."

"I can assure you, Ms. Wilson, that the incident in no way had anything to do with us."

"I'm not trying to affix blame. I'm simply trying to figure out how this could have happened."

Deep sigh. "I'm sorry. It's the same thing I told the detectives. No one could have breached our system. The firewalls are too rigid."

"Would you be able to check if my own personal alarm code was used?"

"The detectives also asked that. I told them they needed a warrant."

"I appreciate that. I'm the client, however."

"Indeed. It shows here that you did use your code three times early Monday morning: 3:21 to set, and 4:07 to unset. An hour later to reset."

"I see. Thank you. You've been most helpful."

"You're welcome. Anything else, just call."

"Actually, there is one more question."

"Yes, Ms. Wilson?"

"I'd like to know the times I've accessed my cloud and set or unset my alarm over the last three months." A big stretch of time, but I didn't want to miss anything.

"That could be quite extensive, I'm sure. Would you like me to email it to you?"

"No, just print it off please. With the changes made to the cloud at those times. I'll pick it up."

"Certainly. It'll be waiting at the front desk tomorrow."

"I'll be by. Thank you again." I hung up and looked at my watch. Nearly noon. After smooching on the dogs, I locked up the house and hopped in the Jeep. During the drive to Hocking Construction, I turned on the radio just in time for the ad I'd placed for tomorrow night's venue.

The announcer came on first. "Tonight! One night only! Comedian Zach Zimmer at Smugglers!"

Then it segued to a sound bite from one of Zimmer's shows. "So, Zachary Xavier Zimmer. Yes, it's my real name. You think I chose this? My parents did. What kind of parents name their kid Zachary Xavier Zimmer? Did they say 'Let's see how much fun we can have'?" The radio filled with canned audience laughter.

Finally, the announcer came on again. "Zach Zimmer, 9 PM Saturday at Smugglers! 2212 Olive. $35 at the door."

Not bad. At the top of each hour, after the news, the ad was supposed to be longer. But this was good in between. I expected a packed house. A political smear ad followed for the East St. Louis Mayoral race. I turned off the radio.

18

Hocking Construction was just shutting down for lunch when I arrived. A couple pickup trucks loaded with locked boxes kicked up dust as they sped off the lot. Workers, both male and female in the construction uniform of heavy boots and webbed toolbelts, collected in small groups and plunked down on front steps of partially constructed homes. I opened a trailer door that read the construction company's name with Terry Milfin as foreman.

The receptionist was a tiny girl dressed in big hoop earrings that gently bumped her shoulders. She wore a pink polka-dotted tee and was wedged between the wall and a very close desk. The nameplate said Vonda Karrik. She looked up from a sandwich that looked suspiciously like cream cheese, sprouts, and cucumber on whole wheat. "Oh, Mr. Milfin isn't here. We're on lunch break."

"It's okay. I'm not here about business. I'm Eddie Blaisdale's friend. I just want to talk. My name's Sylvia." I entered. The office looked to be just a regular house trailer, with the bedrooms converted to private offices and storage.

She raised her eyebrows and wiped her mouth with a napkin. Her nose was pointed enough to be used for a thumbtack. She pointed to the bronze nameplate on her desk. "I'm Vonda. Are you a cop?

'Cause they've already been here once. Made Mr. Milfin mad because they had him wait for a sketch artist. Wasted his whole afternoon."

I smiled and shook my head. "My brother worked with Eddie. That's how we met." Sorta. The trailer floor swayed drunkenly when I walked to a folding chair and settled it across from her at the desk.

"It's real sad what happened to him." The receptionist's voice was subdued.

"Yeah. I can't get over it." Hung my head appropriately. "I always wanted to visit him here, when he was working, but he wouldn't let me. He said friends weren't allowed."

"They're not." She leaned forward and whispered, "But he had one or two of his friends visit."

"Really? I feel insulted. Which ones? What were their names?"

"He told me, but I don't remember. Sorry. But I know for sure one was from his other job. A dark-haired guy with a mustache. I don't really remember the other one much, except he was kinda geeky." She looked around and leaned toward me. Whispered again, "Eddie was going to take me on a trip."

I raised my eyebrows. "Really? He must have been making good money."

She laughed and leaned back. "Not here. Probably from the other place."

She hesitated, then said, "He was always talking to me and got us both in trouble plenty of times. The boss threatened to fire him for it. He wanted benefits, you know?"

I nodded that I did indeed know and assumed Vonda was speaking of Eddie wanting benefits, not the boss.

The receptionist continued, "He wasn't *that* kind of friend. As if. Ew!"

Her hand flew up to cover her mouth, and her eyes opened wide. "Oh God! I shouldn't have said that. I mean, he's dead!"

"It's all right. He can't hear it."

She looked at me, uncertainty clouding her eyes. Dropped her hand and settled into the rest of the story. "When he told me about the trip, I asked him if the money was from his aunt, and he said it was something like that. I said I'd think about it. I didn't really want to date him, but I mean, I've never been anywhere else. You know?"

"A trip is a very big deal."

"It really is." She chased a crumb of bread around her plate with her finger. "You probably think I'm a bad person. But maybe I could have loved him, once I got to know him better."

"Anything's possible." I shrugged and considered where to go next. Blaisdale wasn't earning enough money to make regular payments on a car, but he was going to take Vonda on a trip. It smelled more and more like he'd broken into my place hoping to score some serious cash. That meant it wasn't a spur of the moment thing. He and his killer friend had planned it ahead of time. So, it wasn't just my bar that had been hit. Yet, the Sunday night thing still bothered me.

Deciding I'd gotten everything I could there, I stood. "Do me a favor?"

She nodded.

"The detective who's in charge of the investigation is also a friend of mine. You need to tell him all this."

"I guess…"

"Please. So he can catch the guy who killed Eddie. Do it today."

I stayed until she agreed. Then I left. As I walked to my Jeep, I passed a lean bowlegged man in construction boots. He was walking in the opposite direction, toward the office, and had his ear to his cellphone. "I don't care what you promised him. You promised me delivery two days ago. Now get them to me!" He stabbed his phone shut and glared at me. I smiled pleasantly and continued to my Jeep.

Almost immediately, Peaches called. I put her on speaker while I headed to my Krav Maga lesson.

She began, "Honey, how have you been?"

"Good. I'm good. I'm driving right now. Can I call you back this evening?"

"Things settlin' down for you?" Either she hadn't heard what I'd said, or most likely just decided to ignore it.

"Heading that way. I'll call you back this evening." I hung up, knowing I wouldn't. I'd just talked to her that morning. Honestly, she was going to drive me crazy.

19

learned elbow strikes in my Krav Maga lesson, and I was sore all over. But I drove to the Degere house again. Like last time, the Chief wasn't home. Unlike last time, Mrs. Degere met me at the door. Her lips were pressed into a thin line and her eyes held that same guarded steel in them.

"What now?" she asked. No 'hello'. No 'how have you been'. I couldn't really blame her. But, at least she was talking to me, which meant she might still believe I hadn't killed her nephew.

"I'd like to see your nephew's home. Where in Metropolitan Village was it?"

"Why?"

I shook my head. "There has to be something somewhere that will help solve the murder. Something that will prove I didn't do it. I just want to make sure the police have everything."

She hesitated. Looked far off at something unseen. Snapped her gaze back to me. "I have a key. We'll take your car."

I blinked. This was a turn I hadn't expected. She left the door. Returned half a minute later, holding up said key. "My husband doesn't know I have this. And I don't want him to. Understand?"

I nodded. She stepped out and locked her front door. Obediently, I led the way to my Jeep. We drove in silence. Thankfully, it only took ten minutes to navigate to Metropolitan Village. Finding a parking space, on the other hand was a bit dicier. After another ten minutes of driving around the block again and again, someone pulled out near the apartment doors and I slipped in.

Number 31 was one of the lower rent units. But still, I couldn't figure out how Eddie Blaisdale could afford an apartment there. Living by himself. And a car. Even with two jobs. Security didn't pay that well. And the other job was only occasional. He had to be supplementing with robbery.

Mrs. Degere – Patty, she told me to call her – peeled back the police tape and pushed open the door. A noxious wave of rotten food and body odor hit us. Clothes were strewn around the room and over the back of a broken mustard yellow recliner that faced an old TV. Plates littered the floor on either side of the chair. The kitchen area was part of the same room. Beer bottles covered the counter, except in front of a crusted microwave. TV dinner boxes and trays overflowed from the trash.

Patty wrinkled her nose and rushed to open a window. I wandered, idly lifting porn magazines, bills, and junk mail with my toe. I didn't see any pay stubs, which might have meant the second job probably paid cash. There was no desk. No table. Just the recliner and the TV. Across the room, a door opened into a bedroom with a stained and stripped bed, covered in a mound of blankets. No pillow. A closet was mostly empty, except for a couple suits and his police uniform. As near as I could tell, most of his clothes were on the floor in the living room. No dresser. The bathroom opened off of the bedroom. It smelled like stale urine and I didn't go in.

Back in the living room, I gravitated to the stained recliner and pulled off the cushion. Plumbed my hand way down into the cracks at the sides, but found nothing. The police had been thorough. I could almost see Eccheli there, his shiny shoes pushing filthy shirts out of the way. Tucking his hands into the same change collectors I was.

"What are you looking for?" Patty stood near the window she'd opened, taking deep breaths of the fresh air.

I shook my head. "I don't know. But there's got to be something."

"The detectives have probably found everything of value already."

"Does this look right to you? Is anything missing or where it shouldn't be? Is there something here that's new?"

She gazed around the room, hands on her hips. "It looks the same to me as it did. Not that I came here often. Only one other time. About a year ago, Eddie had the flu and I went shopping for him."

I followed her gaze. If all of Blaisdale's clothes were out in the living room, it stood to reason that was where he dressed. Where did he dump his pockets when he changed? Two feet from the other window was a large swath of pants. I crossed to them and stood in the center of the pile. Looked out the window. Saw the parking spaces and my Jeep.

Glanced down at the window sill. Nothing. But, just as I was turning away, I saw a tiny scrap of paper, trapped between the glass and the screen. There was something scrawled on it in black ink. I eased open the window – which was quite a feat, considering its age and how many coats of paint it had – and plucked up the paper with my fingernails. The writing was cramped, as if it had always been a small scrap, though somewhat bigger because the rest of it was missing. All that remained was *–gne* and below it a *5*. Miniscule stress folds suggested the paper had been pulled through or out from under something. I bent close to the window and looked at the underside, but nothing was there. The rest of the paper was gone.

Patty joined me. Her voice was breathless, excited. "It looks like part of a name and phone number."

"Can you get an envelope or something to put it in?" She left. I carefully placed the scrap on the windowsill again. Pulled out my phone and snapped a photo as Patty tore something paper in the background. She returned with a magazine bill in one hand and its envelope, torn open on the end, in the other. I took the offered envelope, dropped in the paper, shook it to the bottom, folded over the torn end, and held it out for her.

I said, "I'm a suspect. I can't take it to the police. But you can. Besides, I have no justifiable reason to be here. You do."

She took the offered clue, eyes wide. Nodded. We left. Neither of us said a word the whole trip back. I dropped her at her house and went home to flip through the TV channels until the first of a four game series against Houston came on.

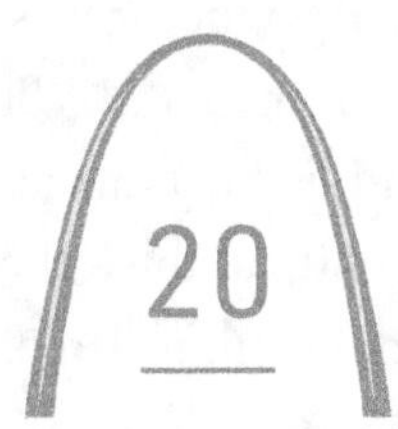

20

Saturday morning, I decided to get up around nine-thirty. It was five days since the murder, but it felt like it had been a month since I'd been in my bar. While the pot of extra-strong coffee was perking, I let the dogs out and peeked at the sky. Same grey cloud-cover. Great. I hoped it meant something. It was already hot and thick and a rain would relieve that. I hadn't seen the kid who mowed my lawn in weeks. My poor shrubs in the back needed rain. Much longer, and I'd have to start watering them. If we weren't under a water restriction by then.

The dogs finished their business and came back inside to settle on the cool kitchen linoleum. I stepped over them and checked my fridge for ingredients for Eccheli's lunch. I had a cantaloupe, some prosciutto, cherry tomatoes, and a head of lettuce. That was a beginning. I also had a baguette of crusty French bread and some aged cheddar. Now I just needed something to drink, but since we were having lunch at the bar, the problem was solved. No need to go shopping today.

My cellphone pinged with an incoming message. I looked at the notifications bar really quick. Peaches. I was probably in trouble for not calling back the night before. Typical Peaches. I loved her, but I decided to leave it until later.

It pinged again. She was definitely going on a rant.

Then a thought occurred to me. It was so obvious I actually hit my forehead with the heel of my hand. "Stupid!"

Satan lifted her head and stared at me from where she was cooling her belly. Ruffles let out a soft rumble. The cellphone pinged again.

I was being investigated. I couldn't supply lunch for the detective. And if he was as honest as Aaron had said, he definitely wouldn't take it. The stress level amped up, pinching my stomach. Then, the vindictive streak inside me surfaced. If Eccheli wanted to consider me the primary suspect, that was his tough luck. I would take my lunch and eat it in front of him.

Another message announced itself. And another.

I poured myself a giant mug of black coffee, smiling in anticipation as the bitter steam rolled into the air. Then I pulled out the melon, cut it into long spears. Skinned the slices. Wrapped prosciutto around them. Threw them on the grill. The dogs investigated the backyard like they hadn't been out just a few minutes before, suspicion in their high backs and stiff legs. While the grill fire hissed and popped, I tore up the head of lettuce and halved the cherry tomatoes. When the melon was done, I set the spears on my cutting board to cool while I changed. I left my phone in the living room so it could notify my furniture of incoming messages.

I decided to wear something a little flashy because of the event, but it had to definitely be as expendable as all my bar clothes. Beer had a way of ruining good shirts. I chose a soft grey brushed cotton blouse with ivory colored buttons. My favorite jeans and my black sneakers. Added a string of raindrop pearls with matching earrings. Brushed my hair until it looked like living mahogany.

When I returned to the main part of the house, my phone was quiet. Apparently, Peaches had finished her one-sided thoughts and was waiting for a response from me so she could begin again. She'd be waiting a few more hours. I had work to do. Though, I checked the notifications to be sure there were no texts from other people. All 21 were hers.

My thoughts kept returning to what Vonda had said. Blaisdale was coming into some money. Patty Degere had pretty much confirmed it, but it hadn't been from her like he'd told Vonda. And it couldn't all be from the second job. I called Aaron and was put immediately to messages. My guess was he had an overnight visitor and had turned off his phone. I left a message asking him to check into other local robberies.

When I returned, I sliced the wrapped melon into tiny bite sized pieces, dumped half of them on the lettuce and tomatoes, and added basil and a raspberry balsamic vinaigrette. I put a lid on the bowl, packaged the remaining cantaloupe separately for some other time, and slid them both back into the fridge. I started humming a tune I'd heard on the radio somewhere.

Finished with the salad, I cut a thick slab off the baguette and some slices of cheddar. They each got their own bag and joined the bowl of salad in the fridge.

Lunch was done and it was only a little after eleven. I felt much better. Far less stressed. A quick phone call to the cleaning service I'd booked yesterday confirmed they would be at the bar on time. I still had nearly an hour to kill. Plenty of time for me to pick up the security list at Almera. Then head to my bar to square things away with Detective Eccheli.

The cleaning crew would take some time, but then I would open.

I was back in my bar.

21

I packed up everything and drove to Almera. The front office of the security company featured a tall reception desk that curved into the room, making the waiting area small. Pale peach walls complimented the peach rug. Somewhere, a dehumidifier hummed. An aged secretary smiled. She handed me the requested cloud access list and asked if there was anything else I needed. I thought about how Aaron's crime profile books said criminals often returned to the scene of the crime. I asked to speak with Elijah.

Within minutes, an exceedingly tall Black man appeared. He could have been a basketball player. Maybe was in younger years. He flashed a smile and shook my hand. "Pleased to meet you Ms. Wilson. What can I help you with?"

His smile was infectious and I found myself smiling in return. The heat of interest sparked deep in my belly. Elijah must have felt it too, because his eyes glittered. Bathing in the warmth of natural attraction, I wondered what had caused the spark between Eccheli and I to fizzle so fast that very first day he'd interviewed me at Smugglers. Romance was supposed to happen just like what was happening with Elijah; the fire building upon itself.

The secretary cleared her throat and the tall security agent jerked his gaze toward her, letting go of my hand, the spell broken.

I explained what I needed. "The camera has to be small enough it won't be noticed. And it has to be something that can't be picked up by any electronic scanners."

"So, no wireless. I think I have something for you." Again, that smile. "If you'll follow me, we'll go take a look."

He walked beside me in the narrow canyons between cubicles. Each time we bumped against each other, my skin burned pleasantly where we'd touched, feeding the growing fire between us. We passed into a hallway where signs on doors read, "Cables", "Transmitters", and "Mobile". We entered the door that said, "Cameras".

It was a large room with full metal shelves lining the walls and a large empty table in the middle. Cameras of all types covered every square inch of shelving. Labels dictated which type we were viewing.

Elijah picked a spot midway across the back wall and lifted something that looked like a tiny Phillips screw with a wire running off it. "I think this will do the trick."

I took it from him. The camera was the size of my pinky nail. The other end of the wire had a USB. "This attaches to a computer? I don't have a place I can put one."

"It'll store the images until you're ready to download."

"How much time do I have on it?"

He made a face. "These mini cams only have a few hours. This one has two. It's best if it's attached to something it can constantly download onto."

"If I find an adapter, I can attach it to a cell phone. I'll take it."

"Good, I'll add it to your account."

"Um, about that. I'd like a second account set up. Under a different name."

He hesitated, frowning. "Surely you don't think we had something to do with your break in?"

"I don't. But I want to be able to prove it. More importantly, I want my name cleared. And I want the real murderer caught." I had to admit, this last gave me pause. Was my motivation just what I'd said? Or was it also because of the ghosts of my parents?

He nodded. "I understand. We'll need Mr. Tate's approval."

"Certainly." I have to admit I was a little bit sorry to have someone else intrude on my solo time with Elijah, but business was business. He made the call and Mr. Tate was more than willing to help prove his company's innocence. "We have provisions in place to set up a dummy account under any name you choose. The address will be here. We won't send you a bill, but you'll have to pay by week in advance."

"Let's start with a couple weeks then. Use the name Carl Tyler." That was the man who'd given Satan to me. It was a common enough name that nobody would look at it twice. Elijah finished setting up the account. I paid the receptionist and then left. Romance would have to wait until a more opportune time, though I did invite Elijah to visit my bar.

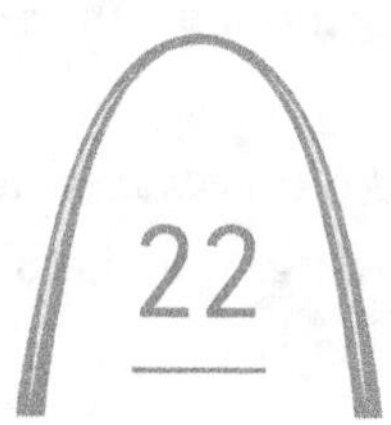

22

I stopped at a local WalMart and picked up a small burner cell and an adapter for the camera. The ad for my event played two times on my way to Smugglers. The news said the mayoral candidates were all to be featured that night on TV. Because of the incumbent's nephew there was a quick recap of the rampage at the US Capital. Also, the Cards were winning their afternoon game against Houston, 6–5.

Pulling into the lot behind my bar, I noted the back door to the building was wide open again. Not seeing a vehicle, I wondered if the door had been left that way by the last people who'd gone in. As thick as the humidity was getting to be, it would take forever to get it out of there. Not to mention theft possibilities. My temper was growing as I walked in, but dissipated the moment I heard the murmur of voices.

My gaze immediately dove all the way down the hall to the front door where the body had been. I could almost still see it there. The place looked the same as the last time I'd seen it: black fingerprint powder and trash everywhere. After a deep breath, I closed the door and switched on the air. I placed my lunch on the bar. Eccheli and an Black woman I could only assume was his IAD partner were seated in the same booth the security video had shown Blaisdale and Chief Degere seated on the night of the murder. They hadn't noticed my entrance, but seemed to be role playing, working out the murder. The voices were all wrong though. There was something intimate flowing in the tones they used.

My parents often spoke that way when they thought no one was around. Only loud enough for the other person to hear. That explained the dying spark between me and the detective. It appeared he already had a lover.

I picked my food bag up about six inches and dropped it on the bar. Eccheli nearly jumped through the ceiling, but his partner coolly turned her head to stare at me with hard, proprietary eyes. Even with that, she was lovely. She wore her hair in a long afro that she had tied behind her, the ponytail flaring wide over her shoulders, accentuating her heart-shaped face. Perfect pouting lips were glossed in red that came off wine-colored against her dark skin. I could see why Eccheli toed the line in the romance department.

Walking toward her, I held out my hand. "I'm Sylvia Wilson."

She shook, not with a woman's half-finger grasp, but a solid grip that meant no nonsense. "I know who you are. I'm Detective Johnson. You should know that we can't take your food. You're part of the investigation."

We? There had been no mention of inviting her. I turned to face Eccheli directly. "I realized that right after I hung up. I apologize."

It caught him off guard and his gaze involuntarily slid toward the woman. She was definitely more than a roll in the hay. Live-in? Wife? Neither wore a ring, but that meant nothing. Most cops didn't, so as to protect their loved ones. He returned his gaze to me, and he nodded his forgiveness. "We have some questions."

"Of course. Do you mind if I eat while we talk? I haven't had anything today." A small lie. I'd had a slice of toast four hours ago. Without waiting, I pivoted, returned to the bar, and laid out my lunch. With the small torch I used for flammable drinks, I toasted the cheddar onto the baguette.

The two detectives joined me and I suddenly felt guilty for my vindictive streak. They were only doing their jobs. Setting down the torch, I said, "Look. I know you can't take anything from me. But, you can buy a non-alcoholic drink, right? It comes with appetizers." I gestured grandly toward my display of melon salad and melted cheddar toast.

Detective Eccheli looked doubtful and Mrs. Detective, as I was starting to suspect, based on the constant threatening vibes, pressed her lips tight and glared even harder at me.

"No? Okay, then. I didn't want to be rude. Maybe some other time." Or definitely not. Especially with the daggers spiking from her eyes in my direction. No, I didn't like her at all. I came around the bar and fetched the corner stool, bringing it back behind to sit directly opposite the Mr. Detective.

That vindictive streak once again rose up within me. I made sure the two detectives saw how good my meal was. The still melty cheddar strung from my bite of the baguette. The melon was juicy and it dribbled down my chin. The beer was in a heavy, iced mug and little ice crystals floated across the surface.

All in all, perfect. I stabbed a forkful of salad and shoved it in my mouth.

Eccheli placed his phone on the bar, voice recorder on. He announced this was an interview with me and gave the date. Then he began with the questions. "You told me the alarm was already off when you entered. Is that right?"

I nodded, mouth full of smoky, prosciutto-wrapped melon. Belatedly, I realized I had to speak my answers. "Yesh."

He nodded. "Who has your code?"

I swallowed so I could be understood. "As I told you. No one."

Johnson's gaze sharpened. She asked, "So, how do you think the killer got it?"

I paused, trying to decide whether to tell them Bobby's part in trying to figure out what happened. Then decided not to. I continued,

"I honestly don't know. He could have mounted a camera somewhere or put a thin plastic cover over the alarm keypad at some point and removed it later, after I'd had a chance to use it."

Johnson said, "But he still would have needed time to work out the code based on a number of combinations. The alarm would have gone off by then. According to the video, he had it all figured out already. And we found no evidence of a camera."

I really didn't like the woman. And she technically hadn't asked a question, so I looked at Eccheli and waited. My melty cheddar suddenly tasted much better.

Johnson leaned against the back of her stool, and it squeaked a protest. Mr. Detective gave a grim smile and asked, "How well did you know Chief Degere?"

"He was a customer. Met him at a couple parties, but only briefly. So, not well."

"What was he like when he was here?"

I shrugged again. "Pretty much just a guy's guy. Liked beer and football. Never loud. Never annoying. A decent tipper."

"Did you interact with him?"

"Only to get him beers, or when he asked me to change the channel on the televisions."

"Did you see him with anyone, regularly?"

An ambiguous question. "Did I regularly see him with anyone, or was he with anyone regularly that I saw?"

Johnson leaned forward again. She frowned and narrowed her eyes. "The second."

"Not anyone regular, no."

"Now, the first."

"He was popular. Lots of people stopped by to talk to him. People bought him beer. Well liked."

"You said earlier, you interacted only when he bought beer from you."

I retraced my part of the conversation. "No. If you check your recording, I believe you'll find I said I got him beers and changed the television channels. He didn't necessarily pay for those beers. They were often bought for him by various other people. All this will be on the security videos. I'm sure you've already seen them."

Eccheli jumped back in. "What about the victim, Edward Blaisdale? Had you seen him before?" He slid a photo of the man, still living at that time, in front of me.

I shrugged yet again. It seemed to be my safety net for the moment. "I couldn't tell you. From what I saw, he seemed pretty nondescript. But, looking back through the security videos, you probably saw that he'd been in here before the crime, so, I probably served him. I sure don't remember him, though. We get quite a few ex-cops."

"Do you remember him sitting with Degere?" Johnson again. It was plenty obvious she was IAD.

"I remember lots of people sitting with the chief, on and off throughout most nights. I don't specifically remember him at all, but it's on the video."

Eccheli briefly touched his wife's arm, which confirmed their relationship to me. My father had done that all the time. Mr. Detective asked, "Does anyone from that night stand out in your mind?"

I stared at the center button of his shirt while I replayed my memory of that night. "No. Not a soul. But as I told you, it was strangely busy."

"Nobody who didn't belong?"

"I don't know everybody, I'm sorry. I wouldn't know if someone belonged or not."

"How about new faces? Any of those?"

"There's always one or two on a busy night, so probably. But I don't remember them."

"Why would they stage it to look like a robbery on a Sunday night?"

"I have no idea. I don't keep extra money overnight."

"Even though it was a busy night."

"That's right. I always take it home."

Mrs. Detective's turn. "Anyone with a grudge against you or your brother?"

"Not that we know of. But I told Detective Eccheli that on the first day."

"So, you have no idea why Edward Blaisdale was killed in *your* bar on a *Sunday* night?"

I slowly shook my head. That was the ninety-four dollar question that had been plaguing me. "He was here. He saw it was busy." I shrugged.

A noise came from the back hall and I peeked around the corner. Identifying the rose-colored uniforms, I said to the detectives. "Cleaning crew."

I was sure they already figured that. I slid off my bar stool, motioning toward the waiting workers. "If there's nothing else, I need to get these people started."

"One more thing. Patty Degere dropped off a piece of paper she'd found. She was pretty vague on how she came across it. Though she did admit she'd spoken to you on more than one occasion. Vonda Karrik claimed you made her promise to bring in some information she had. Then there's the matter of the newspaper article. Unless you want to be arrested for impeding an investigation, you need to back off."

"Helping isn't impeding." I shrugged yet again. I would do what I would do. He would do what he needed to do. No two ways around it.

Eccheli shook his head. Johnson deigned to comment. I didn't watch them walk out, devoting my attention to the cleaners, though I did glance up just in time to see Eccheli take one last look around as he headed out the back door.

23

The crew cleaned like they were possessed. While they did that, I turned off my cameras. I didn't want any record of my new spy cam's existence. Deciding to install it front and center on the bar, I unscrewed a bolt in the mounting of the tap and drilled a bigger hole so the wire would fit through. The phone was behind the bar and a convenient beer sign hid the wire connecting the two.

Amidst the sounds of vacuuming and the astringent odors of cleaning solution, I adjusted the angles of my other cameras. Anyone could see their location, but at the initial installation, I'd bought special casings that hid the direction they viewed. The mystery guy had known their focus. Either he'd accessed the feed at Almera or on my phone. He was very tech savvy. Or, he'd been very good at guessing.

Now all I had to do was to wait for the guy to come back and get him to move close enough to the tap to get a good look at him on the spy camera. It had been five days since he'd killed Blaisdale. Five days for his nerves to work on him. He should be making an appearance; the crowd tonight would be perfect cover.

I went down the hall, looking on the walls, ceiling, and framework for drill marks, putty repair, sticky residue, or anything that would be evidence that the killer had placed some kind of mini cam there. There was nothing to be found. I even checked the bathrooms.

I turned the security cameras back on in time to open the bar for the day.

Karyn wandered in about an hour after the cleaning crew left, though she wasn't scheduled until 7:30. "Now that I don't have to help clean, I thought I'd give you a hand setting up."

I made a face at her, complete with stuck-out tongue. She brushed off her shoulder in reply. There had been no customers yet, so I'd been filling the bar coolers as full as I could get them. She went to the storeroom and carted out boxes of mugs that she stacked against the wall while I finished. Then we wheeled out extra kegs for the tap.

We paused for a couple icy brews. I'd had the game on, but it was over now. Houston won 7–5. We so didn't need to give up any points. Luckily, the Pirates had lost their game too, so they were still a game and a half behind. Peaches had texted a few times. I made a mistake and answered the first. Ignored the second. It was all the same thing again. She was worried about me.

Karyn asked, "How's the investigation going? Do you know?"

"I don't know much from the police side, except the labs are way backed up and the ME report is delayed. But Aaron said he overheard the ME say to Eccheli it looked personal. And according to Blaisdale's aunt, apparently he was working two jobs. I went to the one and got a description of someone, but no one seems to know where the second job is."

"Wow! You're like Nancy Drew, right?"

"Who?"

"You know, that chick that solved mysteries for her dad. It was on TV when we were kids."

"I never saw it."

"I did. All the time. What else have you found out?"

"Not much else, honestly."

We were quiet a bit more, nursing our beers. I was thinking dark thoughts about what would happen if another suspect wasn't found. I assumed Karyn was thinking the same, best friends and all, but then she said, "I saw your Jeep downtown yesterday."

"I'm learning Krav Maga. There's a training studio down there." I was a bit disappointed in my friend's apparent lack of concern for me. I took a drink. The cold ice crystals slid easily down my throat and I forgave her.

"What the hell is that?"

"What? Krav Maga?" I told her.

"Ah. I thought about joining an aerobics class somewhere." She drank heavily from her mug and smacked her lips afterward.

"You could join me. I promise you'll get a workout. You'll learn some self-defense too."

Her brows nearly crossed in a frown. "I don't know."

"Well, you can come watch my next lesson. See what it's about."

"Maybe." She shrugged. Then after a minute, "Any thoughts about where to put the pool table?"

I nodded. "Many, and none of them happy at the moment." The usual Saturday afternoon crowd had landed while we were working, and now I saw the booths I'd have to relocate to accommodate the pool table were occupied.

Karyn put her hands on her hips. "Why move it at all? We can leave it where it is. Use it as the stage."

I stared at her. Why not? When I'd bought it, I'd had a custom wooden cover made for it. Nothing fancy because the vinyl cover would fit over that too. But it was heavy enough to support a person. The crowd could build around him. Even if something leaked through the cover, I was getting a new table Monday, anyway. "Karyn, you're a genius."

"True. Don't tell anyone, though; it'll ruin my reputation."

We finished our beers, waited on a few customers, and took down the lighting fixture over the pool table. Then we dragged the wood cover out of the store room and took off the vinyl cover. The cleaners had done a great job getting rid of the blood, but the felt was blotchy from the chemicals. It sobered us. But we had no time to dwell on our thoughts. We had work to do.

It took a bit to get the table set up as a stage, but we finally managed with the help of a couple guys who wanted our phone numbers.

Karyn gave them the bar number. I gave them Eccheli's.

Zachary Xavier Zimmer was decent as an entertainer. I gave him a B–. The crowd Saturday night liked him well enough and drank plenty of beer. I had Tom, a big guy that wouldn't hurt anyone, on the door, collecting money and keeping peace. Karyn and I were kept hopping all night tending bar. And, though the cleaning crew had done wonders, I caught glimpses of smudged fingerprint powder that had rubbed off onto people's clothes.

The Blues were in town and, as the reigning Stanley Cup champs, were playing a preseason game against the Chicago Blackhawks. Powell had finally opened its doors on its most recent concert. There were a couple semi-stars singing in town, too. Thankfully, the Cards had played their game in the afternoon.

Plus, rain was imminent.

Still, the place was packed.

As I waited on customers, I tried to make them stand in front of my hidden camera. I kept wondering if one of them was the killer. I studied every face, but the room was too busy to keep track of them all. Which was a good thing, I guess. It meant more money in the till. And I'd view the video later. All in all, it was a good night. We were all beat by the time I set the alarm and locked the door.

Driving home, I wondered if the murderer had been there. Laughing at Zimmer's jokes. Drinking beer I'd served him. Had he been watching me, as he had when figuring out the code?

Had he watched Blaisdale, too?

The thought sent fire into my blood. I was sure Eccheli had already checked and was miles ahead of me in the investigation. But the moment I parked the Jeep in front of my house, I had my phone in my hand, watching Sunday night's video. Blaisdale came in the door, straight to the bar. I handed him a couple beers and he made a beeline to Degere's table.

I waited and watched three more people come in. Always glancing around the room, hollering to someone, then to the bar for a longneck, and then always to join a table. Someone came in the back door and came directly to the bar. He kept his head bowed and none of the cameras caught his face. He took his tap beer to an empty table and sat. Though he wasn't facing Blaisdale and Degere, he cautiously glanced their direction many times, still with his head down. I wondered if anyone would have seen his face, looking at him directly. Point in fact, I didn't even remember waiting on him.

This guy left a few minutes before the victim. Maybe he wasn't the killer. But, like me, he was probably on Eccheli's radar as a person of interest.

Tonight's video – the one with Zimmer – wouldn't post until morning. I took a look at the video on the burner phone I'd had my micro camera loading into, but with all the faces who'd come in for the event, and without a frame of reference for the killer, I was still in the dark.

Frustrated, I turned off my phone and went into the house. The dogs jumped all over me, coating me in slobber. No doubt they'd been worried that they'd heard my Jeep, but I hadn't opened the door in a prompt manner.

I let the dogs out to do their business, let them back in, and then stumbled to the bedroom.

The sleeping issues of the past few nights gave way and I fell into a dark, dreamless sleep until late the next morning, when Ruffles, tired of waiting for me to wake, bounded onto the bed and licked my eyes open.

My first thought was about the killer. There was only one way he could have gotten my code. He had to have placed a camera of his own somewhere in my bar. No two ways around it. And he must have fixed my videos to hide its mounting and removal. He was tech savvy enough to manipulate my videos in the cloud without Almera being any the wiser.

I let the dogs out, noting the still grey sky and the suspicious lack of rain. It was decidedly cooler, though, so the rain was coming today. The event video would have posted by then, so I settled on the couch and pulled up my account in the cloud. Watched the video closely. If anyone was dodging cameras, I couldn't tell.

I called Bobby.

"Crow." His voice was soft as if he had been asleep just a few seconds before.

"Shit. Did I wake you?"

"No. I was just watching some TV. What's up? How goes the thing?"

"I saw a guy in the video who watched Blaisdale, but he left first. They must have met up afterward somewhere. The outside monitors didn't show anything. Any ideas?"

"Absolutely none. They could have met anywhere. You sure it's the guy?"

"I'm not sure of anything. I just know Blaisdale didn't look guilty, or uncomfortable. And I didn't see he'd been casing the place. I don't think he knew about the robbery at that time."

"What's the guy look like?"

"He never shows his face. That's part of why I think it's him. If he accessed my videos, then he knows where the cameras are facing."

"You're SOL, then. Hey, you still taking part in the pool tourney? Or are you just gonna lie low until this whole murder thing blows over?"

"What? Yes, Smugglers will still be in the competition."

"Good. 'Cause The Crow team's gonna kick your ass."

"We'll see. I have some videos I need to compare. Want to help?"

"You cookin'?"

"Yep." Though I had no idea what. "Let's use the big screen at the bar, but I have something else to do first. I also have my regular cleaning crew coming, so we'll have to keep it short. Around 12:30?" I'd have to turn off the cameras again to keep the killer from seeing what we were doing. That made me smile.

Bobby gave a grunt as he shifted positions. I pictured him on his bed facing the TV. He lived in a one-room unit that was way too small for a man his size. He said, "I'll call Tag and meet you there."

We disconnected and I packed the rest of the prosciutto, some swiss cheese, a loaf of dark rye, and a jar of sliced dill pickles. That would make a great sandwich on the grill I kept at the bar for personal use. Assuming it wasn't raining by then.

I minced some melon and packed that too. I also grabbed a leftover baked potato, peeled and smashed it, added mustard, coarse black pepper and salt, and packed it. Checking the time, I dashed to the bedroom, got changed into heels and a smart blue dress, and packed a set of work clothes.

The dogs watched every move I made and sat eagerly when I grabbed my keys. I motioned toward the front door. "Okay. Let's go."

They launched like missile rockets for the exit, albeit one a bit closer to the ground.

25

I drove to the west end of Forest Park, the top of the Arch in my windshield, and pulled into the parking lot behind Aaron's apartment building. 'Lot' was a generous term, in this case. It was a narrow stretch of pavement with diagonal spaces that left barely enough room for vehicles to pass. Aaron's pickup, too long for the conventional spaces, occupied one of the two parallels at the far end of the building. Sometimes I could slip into a space reserved for an absent tenant. No such luck this time. I parked on the street in front.

I carefully climbed out of the Jeep; skirts weren't really made for those kinds of vehicles. Walked around to the passenger's side and told the pooches to 'stay' through the door. I'd learned from experience this was a necessity. Once leashed, they were allowed out. They were excited to be someplace new, though it really wasn't. It had just been long enough since they'd been there that it seemed new to them. I threaded Ruffles's leash through the hand loop of Satan's to space them apart, snagged the backpack with my change of clothes, and into the apartment building we went.

Aaron's building was located near the University. Student housing. Very quiet this time of morning on a Sunday. Today was September 11th. Mom and Dad had been gone eight years now, killed on an anniversary of the infamous terrorist attacks. The silence of the neighborhood seemed fitting. While the whole world held a memorial for those killed in New York and Washington DC, my brother and I would hold our own little vigil for two people who'd died on a quiet country road in the middle of nowhere. My dogs came along because, well, they were family too.

My heart grew heavier as I climbed the steps, and when my brother opened the door, I saw on his face the same consuming grief I felt inside. We hugged tightly. He smelled of aftershave and shampoo, his hair still spiky and damp. He wore a black suit with a crisp purple tie.

The dogs scooted past us into the apartment and I dropped the leashes to let them explore. Aaron's place was a typical single man's home: black sofa and matching chair, nice stereo for his preferred LPs, and an even nicer TV and gaming system. Normally a neat and tidy place, today boxes were stacked haphazardly all along one wall.

He followed my gaze. "I cleaned out my storage for the bike. Dawes has kept me so busy I haven't had time to deal with the junk."

I nodded. That explained why I hadn't seen the bike in the lot. "Best place for it, though I miss riding it."

"I'll bring it over for visitation." He smiled briefly, but somberness dropped over him again. Some years, we laughed and talked about our favorite memories. But most years were like drinking from a jagged can of sorrow. This year was like the latter. The dogs settled quickly, then dove into naps. We sat quietly, sharing our mutual pain, drinking a bottle of Mom's favorite Pinot Grigio, even though it was early in the day, yet. Aaron had also put out the ritual cheddar and crackers that had been Dad's nightly snack, but I could barely choke them down.

We did this rite every year, though it turned us inside out, because in the shadow of the 9/11 terrorist attacks, no one else seemed to remember our parents. And someone should.

My thoughts kept flashing from my happy memories of when my parents were alive to their crushed faces, to Blaisdale lying on the floor of my bar. I dragged my mind back to my father, to my mother, to their savaged faces, only to leap to Blaisdale again. Around and around and around. Would they forever be linked in my mind? Would I ever be able to think of my parents without thinking of the man killed in my bar? The thought made me sick to my stomach.

The soft pit-pat of rain hit the window. Finally. I concentrated on the sound, trying hard to still my thoughts about bodies on country roads. A body on my bar floor.

After an hour, I rose and went to the bathroom to change into my bar clothes. I came out to find Aaron pouring the remains of the wine down the kitchen drain, tears brimming his eyes. We held each other tight for a long moment. Then I kissed him on the cheek, gathered the pooches, and left.

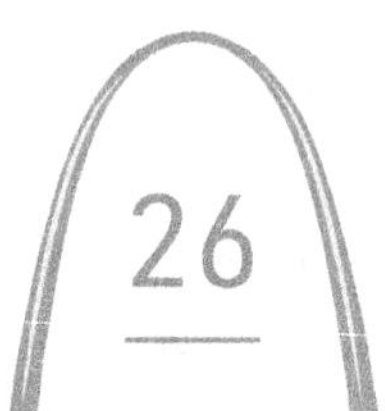

26

The rain was steady as we pulled into the back lot of Smugglers. Bobby, dressed in neon yellow rain gear, had just arrived and was parking his bike. He dismounted, but his wide smile gave way to a frown when he saw who I'd brought. Apparently taking to heart my earlier warnings about Satan's attack tendencies, he cupped his hands over his crotch and turned his hip toward her fast approaching teeth. Ruffles made his own deep-throated bid right alongside her.

I called the dogs back to me. Ruffles responded to his obedience training and turned, still growling. Satan, however, was always my disobedient child. I knew from experience that she wouldn't listen to my call, and that any physical interference on my part would only make things worse for Bobby.

Instead, I turned right around, jangled my keys, whistled, and opened the Jeep door again. Wet dogs in the vehicle. I'd be days airing it out.

What started as a direct bullet for the intruder ended up a long curving arc that brought my little dog right back into the Jeep. One thing she loved above all else was going for a ride.

I turned on the Jeep's air conditioning, shut the door, and joined Bobby at the back entrance.

He wore a pained look. "What gives? She knows me."

"She knows Bobby-at-the-house. Bobby-at-the-bar might be a completely different person. It remains to be seen."

"I guess."

I unlocked the door, turned off the alarm, and said, "You can set up the grill in the storeroom, and I'll put the sandwiches together."

He gestured toward the Jeep. "What about the dogs?"

"When they calm. It won't be long." Bobby took off his rain gear, a puddle forming at his feet. He mopped it and we busied ourselves about our tasks while the air conditioning kept the pooches cool.

True to my prediction, when I let the dogs out they made a bee-line inside, only to wait while I dried them. They took no notice of Bobby. Sometimes the dogs came there with me, but not often, so they entered stiff-legged and big-chested, and ran, noses to the floor everywhere, covering the same ground again and again.

When the sandwiches were finished cooking on the grill, and were all melty and stringy, I shut the storeroom door, turned off the cameras, dug out some chips, and we all settled in front of the big screen, with the video from the night of the murder playing.

I pointed out the guy when he entered the bar behind Blaisdale. "See, he's hiding his face."

"Doesn't mean anything." He reached for a second sandwich. After a few minutes, he added, "But he sure seems suspicious."

Satan cuddled up to Bobby on the bench, mesmerized by the food. Pretty soon his thumb was rubbing behind her ear while he slipped her little tidbits. Ruffles sat at attention, staring unblinkingly as my sandwich moved from the plate to my mouth. When I was full, he got the rest.

When the guy left on the video, I reversed it again to the point where he'd entered. Then I pulled up the Zimmer event videos from my normal cameras and played them beside the first one.

I checked my watch. The cleaning crew was due to arrive any minute now. Rising, I checked the grill to make sure it was cool enough, then called my loyal pooches to the storeroom. It would smell like wet dog for a few days, and Karyn would complain, but I could live with that. Satan actually sighed when she had to leave Bobby's side. I think she was completely besotted with him.

I threw down a blanket I kept for just such a reason and filled their water bowl. I turned on a radio to confuse noises, and then I shut them in. Returning to the bar, I took out the melon I'd brought, blended it with some ice cream, divided it into small dishes, and poured brandy over it.

Bobby didn't look up when I handed him a dish until he took a bite. "Damn, woman! Where do you come up with these things?"

I shrugged. Most everyone liked my cooking.

The cleaners arrived while we ate. They were my regular crew that came every Tuesday to give the place a once over. I had to pay extra to get them in on Sunday, but the place was disgusting from the event and still had the remnants of fingerprint powder missed from yesterday's crew. Those had been from a different branch of the same service, though one person was the same. Falling into their usual rhythm, my four regulars began work. The gleam in their eyes and quick smiles told me they were anticipating a heavy tip. Plus now they could skip Tuesday cleaning as well.

After about twenty minutes, Bobby paused the video and leaned into me. "I think that could be our guy, standing next to the jukebox. See how he runs his thumb along the rim of his glass?" He enlarged the appropriate video to show me. Then he ran the pre-murder video. Pointed.

Thumb running the rim of the glass.

I watched his angle of sight. He was frowning hard at where Blaisdale had fallen. "He seems to be paying more attention to the front door than Zimmer. And see, he doesn't laugh at the jokes."

"Well, truthfully, I wouldn't either," Bobby confided. "Your comedian wasn't that funny."

I made a face at him and took the remote, running the event videos in reverse at triple speed. We watched the guy's thumb circle the other way and his head bob as he looked down from the front door to his drink. Then we saw him stand up and walk backwards to the bar. When he turned around to face the bartender, Karyn, I paused it and pulled up the video from my mini spy cam.

Moving forward at high speed, I finally stopped at the same time stamp. We both leaned forward. I said, "So, this is our guy."

"Yep."

The man shown was lean and fairly handsome: dark wavy hair, bright blue eyes, square chiseled chin.

I pressed play at normal speed and we watched him walk away. Bobby leaned back against the bench. "Yep. See that hitch in his right leg?"

I frowned. Hitch? I watched closely. Sure enough, when the guy put his weight on his right leg, his stride was a bit shorter. "Knee injury?"

"His knee and hip seem to move fine. Most probably something internal. Kidney stones or somethin'." He picked up his empty ice cream dish, pointedly looking into it.

"No more melon ice cream, just vanilla left now. Want some of that?"

"Nah. I should probably go. Tag doesn't know how to do inventory. Your brother can probably get a face ID on the guy." He motioned to the screen.

Disappointed Bobby wasn't staying, I obediently scooched off the bench to let him up.

He rose, circled his arm around my waist, and pulled me into a heavy kiss that burned my lips and made my insides quiver. He reared his head back and looked into my eyes. He didn't say anything for a minute, and then he cocked his head to the side. "Call me."

As he walked away, I pursed my mouth and puffed out a big gust of air. How did a 240 pound muscle-bound biker unsettle me so? I whispered, "Damn!"

I pulled out my phone and called Aaron. He answered on the first ring. "Wilson."

"Can you identify someone for me?" I told him what Bobby and I suspected. "I think this guy we found is the killer."

"Send it to my phone. I checked on Branden. He's been in the nut ward at WashU for a couple weeks now."

"What?" Shock ripped a hole in my stomach and I nearly dropped my phone.

"Yeah, it seems he got over you pretty quick. Fell in love all over again and started his stalking game. Her daddy is a judge and got him put away."

I nodded, glad Branden had help. Also glad he'd been locked away when the murder was committed. For all the things he was and wasn't, he didn't need the kind of in-depth inspection a murder investigation drew.

Aaron continued. "Eccheli can't find Blaisdale's second job. He's got a warrant to the IRS, but that could take forever. He's also got a BOLO for Blaisdale's friend that visited him at Hocking, but St. Louis is a big city. That could take a while, too. All the labs are backed up, so there's nothing there either." He hung up.

For a moment, I pictured the teenaged boy who'd come directly home from school to our uncle's farm every day to work so we always had a place to stay. Our uncle had never demanded it, but he'd appreciated every bit of sweat Aaron had given him. Hard working. Dedicated. That was my brother. Small wonder he'd been tapped for the bank robbery task force.

I smiled and sent the image. Shut off the big screen and turned all the cameras back on.

27

The fourth Cardinals-Astros game, due to start at 3:10, was called for rain. To be rescheduled at a later date. I spent the next couple hours on inventory. Though, I kept the bar decently stocked, the impromptu event the night before had seriously depleted my reserves. My puppies were happy I spent time with them in the storeroom. When I came out again, the cleaning crew was packing up.

After they left, I put on my jacket and took the dogs outside to do their business before opening. When they were done, I dried them again and shut them back in the storeroom.

On Sunday evenings, there was no suppertime crowd to speak of. Like so many times in the past, I thought of adding a small menu to my bar. Nothing fancy: burgers and pizza. Every person who went to a restaurant had the potential to skip coming to Smugglers. Even worse, they could go to a competitor bar after eating. Adding food might be a smart move, but it might not. There would be more rules and regulations, and I wasn't sure I wanted that. There was plenty of time to think, though. Because of the expenses incurred from the murder, I didn't have any free capital right then and it would be a while before I did.

The solitude in the bar balmed the edges of my psyche that had gotten roughed up by the craziness of the past few days. I'd been going non-stop for a week and I just needed some time to rest. Still,

I couldn't quite just sit and relax. I finally decided to go through the Almera printouts. Over the last three months the cloud had been accessed only once before the investigation. But it hadn't been me.

I pulled out my phone and watched the video at the time it had been accessed, nearly fourteen days ago. Two Fridays before the murder. Right after I'd changed my alarm code. And after the bar was shut for the night. There was nothing out of the ordinary. I circled the date on the printouts. I went back to my phone, peering intently at all three videos. Finally saw something. When I'd first bought the building, there was a small hole above the baseboard where someone had apparently attached a wall door stopper. It had subsequently been torn off, removing part of the plasterboard with it. It had been repaired right away, but there was the hole again in the video, nearly a year after it had been fixed.

I wandered down the hall to make sure. Because ... well, because. The wall was completely intact. It was something that might help prove my innocence. Though, I wasn't sure how.

I opened my notes on my phone and entered my findings of the day. Rereading my notes from after the Zimmer event reminded me of something Bobby had said in the very beginning: 'He's been watching you.' It was something I'd disregarded later when I decided the killer had used a camera to get the alarm code. But I hadn't found any mounting holes or sticky residue. I opened my security videos again and started looking. There was nothing in the two weeks since changing the alarm code. Nothing the week prior to that, either. That made me feel a little better. Maybe a lot better. But still, how had he gotten the code? And what was my next move?

My phone chirped, announcing a call from Peaches, which effectively stopped any more investigation.

"How are you doing?" she asked, her voice quiet. She was referring to the memorial service Aaron and I had for our parents. When we lived in Texas, she sat with us every year. My uncle too.

"Today's always a hard day." Even admitting it brought the sharp sting of tears. I swiped at them with the heel of my hand.

"Tell me how it went."

I pictured her sitting on her couch, patting the seat beside her like she always did when she wanted me to sit with her. So I hunched lower on my bar stool and told her about the wrenching silence. The bitter taste of the loss of our parents. Aaron pouring out the wine with tears in his eyes.

"My memories kept flashing from my parents to the guy who died here, in Smugglers." My gaze flicked to the front door.

"Honey, maybe that's why it was so hard. Because of that death."

"Maybe."

"How's that going?"

I filled her in on what little I knew about the investigation, including what was on the videos.

"You're going to take that to the police. No cowboying like you always do. No back talk."

I laughed out loud. It was so Peaches.

The front door to the bar opened and Ginger Jefferson came in, shaking out a hot pink umbrella. I hoped it was news about the ME report that brought her to Smugglers. I watched her glance around the empty room as Peaches's voice on the phone turned hard. My aunt said, "I mean it. You hear me?"

I knew from experience that tone meant no nonsense. "Yes, Ma'am. Promise. Got a customer. Love you." Disconnected.

Ginger met me at the tap. I asked, "You're working on a Sunday?"

She shrugged. "I have to work when there's work to be done."

"What will it be tonight?"

She looked around the empty room. "Oh, I don't know. Surprise me."

I nodded. We'd played this game before. She wanted nothing expensive, but with plenty of fruit and plenty of alcohol. And nothing as mundane as a screwdriver or mai tai. "Go take a table. I'll bring it to you."

A check in my bar fridge produced a peach, which was ironic given who'd just been on the phone. I peeled, pitted, and tossed it in my blender with a little sugar syrup. Whirred it until the peach was pulverized and poured about a jigger into the bottom of a champagne flute rimmed with sugar. I added a half shot of golden tequila. Filled the rest with champagne. Added a fat paper straw and wedged a slice of lime on the rim. Took it to her booth on a tray.

"This is a Smugglers' Bellini." I set the glass in front of her and gave the drink a little twirl with the straw. The peach in the bottom rose up like a cloud at sunset.

"Oh, it's good enough to bear the Smugglers name?"

I shrugged and slid onto the bench opposite her. "If you like it yes. But if it sucks, then no."

She gave a full-throated laugh and lifted the glass to look into the cloud. "If it's bad, is it free?"

I grinned. "Why not?"

With a wicked glint in her eyes, she took a sip. Licked the sugar off her lips and set down her glass. With a deadpan face, she said, "It's terrible. I'll take two more."

"As luck would have it, I have just enough left."

She slid the glass across the table for me to try. The tequila and champagne blended into a smooth effervescence and I wondered how triple sec would taste thrown into the mix. But the lime was all wrong, even though there was tequila. I should have used lemon. It was still good though. "I see what you mean. It's vile. Just vile."

Our laughter was loud in the empty bar. It made me keenly aware that things might never go back to the way they were. It was possible the murder would be the end of my bar; some places never recovered from something that devastating. I asked Ginger, "You heard anything?"

"Will you give me another interview? A better one this time?"

"You got me into a lot of trouble. The detective won't even talk to my brother. And I'm worried how it'll affect business and the upcoming tournaments."

"I'm just trying to make sure he's doing his job. Looking at all the possibilities. Eccheli knows that."

I slowly nodded. "If you give me something more worthwhile than what you've given me so far. Then, when it's over. Yes. I'll give you everything."

She leaned in. Tapped her lacquered fingernails on the base of the champagne flute.

28

had to turn my ear toward Ginger to hear her whisper above the sound of the rain on the bar windows. The empty room seemed to amplify the noise. It seemed odd the reporter would whisper when there was no one else there, but maybe she thought someone might come in at an inopportune moment. She softly said, "My source didn't tell me much. Just that it looked like it was personal. And since you didn't know Blaisdale, you're in the clear."

I opened my mouth to tell her that not only did I already know this information from my brother, but that Eccheli probably didn't believe I didn't know the victim. But was interrupted by my name being called out. I turned and saw a couple of men coming down the back hall toward the bar. They were members of my tournament team. No doubt there to practice. I noted Ginger's sharp gaze their direction and excused myself. There would be no more information from her tonight. But that was okay. She wasn't getting diddly from me. Ever again.

I fetched beer for my two guys and another player who came in the back, tracking mud. Brought Ginger the two promised drinks. She dropped thirty dollars on the table. "For all three."

She winked and waved away the change.

From then on, the place started jumping. It made me happy and was a good sign of things returning to normal. Customers settled at the booths or tables. The jukebox was kept busy, as was the now chemical-stained pool table, which I assured the players would be replaced before the tournament. Pool balls clacked and players laughed. Glad to see my team practicing. Though we weren't playing them first, we would eventually face the team from The Crow. They were formidable.

An hour later, I was mopping up tracked-in rain and mud by the doors and under the tables when Ginger left, popping open her pink umbrella. She opened the front door, letting in a spate of rain drops, blew a kiss my way, and shut the door behind her.

Around 1AM, Elijah from Almera showed up. Tall and lean, he was good looking in all the right ways. If there was one word to describe him, it was 'smooth'. He wore a crisp black suit and an overcoat as if just coming from the opera, but there were no operas in town. His shoes were trim and shiny. He ordered a scotch and soda and carefully pulled up a stool at the bar.

I set the drink in front of him. "Nice suit."

"Midnight mass."

I frowned. "I thought that was Saturday night into Sunday."

He took a sip of the scotch. Nodded. Said, "Normally, yes. But this was in memoriam of a deceased parishioner. Special request in his will."

"Ah." I didn't know what to say to that. Good for him? We stared at each other a few minutes. Not really one of those comfortable silences.

Finally, he looked around the bar. "Busy."

My turn to nod. "For a Sunday, it's very busy. I halfway worry there will be a body here in the morning again, though." I laughed.

He laughed too, but it sounded forced. "How's the investigation going?"

"I don't know. They let me back in here, that's all I care about." I shrugged. Not true, but it was my business, not his. I went to the other end of the bar to fetch a round of tap beers for the current players at the table. Elijah's gaze followed every move I made.

When I returned, I asked, "Miss me?"

"I missed the view." He smiled. Pretty damn sexy mouth. And the smile went all the way into his eyes. Like a cat. I grinned back, but couldn't think of anything clever to say.

"What do you do when you're not here?" Was that small talk, or was he fishing for an invite somewhere?

"Nothing. I'm never not here. When this place is closed, I go home, sleep, eat, shop, play with my dogs. Then I come back. Not much else."

"So this place is your passion, then." He nodded. Looked around again. Didn't seem too impressed by what he saw.

"Pretty much, yeah." I frowned. We were both working hard at rekindling the spark that had been between us at Almera, but it just refused to flare. I knew why: my lips still tingled from the memory of Bobby's kiss. "But I have competent employees. I can take a day off here or there."

Again that smile. "Maybe we could have dinner sometime this week, then."

I shook my head. "Not the next few weeks. I have pool tournaments. It will take all three of us to keep up."

"Ah." He slowly nodded, regret clear in his eyes. "Maybe I'll call you after that?"

"Sure." I shrugged and gave him a card. "You can call me here. That's easiest."

He pocketed the card, tossed back his drink and stood. Looked on the verge of saying something, but chose to leave instead.

I blew out a frustrated breath. I was pretty sure he wouldn't call. And that was my fault, because of Bobby. But maybe I'd go hunt him down after the tournaments were over. Give it another shot.

The bar stayed busy right up until closing time. I announced Last Call early, figuring on a line. I was not disappointed. The full length of the bar was crowded with loud, happy people. I saw no one leaving yet. I really should have called in either Tom or Karyn. Most ordered tap beer, so it wasn't too bad.

While I waited for the crowd to disperse, I cleaned behind the bar. Nobody made a move to the door. I cleaned the two empty tables. Flicked the lights off and on. Got nothing. Watched the two pool players until the moment the shooter was ready, then flicked off the lights for a count of three. Brought them back on.

There were more than a few evil glares facing me.

I shrugged. "Sorry. The bar's closing. Pack it up."

"When the game is over." The taller of the players stared at me defiantly.

"Doesn't work. You knew the bar was closing when you started the game. Out. Now." I waited. Nothing except the clack of cue ball against pool ball. I nodded to myself. Desperate times called for desperate measures. I went into the storeroom and snapped the leash on Ruffles's collar. Brought him to the center of the room.

Cleared my throat. "You all are fine police officers, but surely you know that rules aren't made to be broken. I said, the bar is closing. I can either call on-duty patrols, or you can take your chances with Ruffles." I nodded toward my dog. Gave a little hiss.

Ruffles responded like the obedience trained dog he was. He wrapped his upper lip around his nose and sent out a deep throaty growl. He leaned against the leash. From the storeroom came Satan's vicious series of high-pitched barks.

As one, nearly everyone in the bar straightened and headed toward the door. The two who didn't were the current pool players. They refused to look at me. Ruffles swiveled his hips against me more, so he was able to face them.

I said, "Gentlemen. I'll tell you what. I'll let you two have the table free next time you play so you can finish this game. Take a photo to show the placement of the balls."

The tall one pulled out his phone and snapped the pic. Nodded.

Then they were on their way. I followed them to the front door and locked them out. Locked the back door too. Let Ruffles loose and opened the storeroom door so Satan could join him while I cleaned. It didn't take long. When I was ready to go, I emptied the register, set the alarm, opened and relocked the back door, and pottied the dogs. We all climbed into the Jeep.

I sat a minute and slowly sucked in a long breath of air. Let it out again. It had been a long, busy day. But I felt good about it.

I made a call.

Bobby answered his phone with, "I'm on my way."

We both arrived at my house simultaneously. The dogs, who knew Bobby-at-the-house, didn't even bat an eyelash at him. The rain looked good on him, tasted good on his skin. We were halfway undressed by the time I got the door shut behind us.

29

When I finally woke, it was nearing nine Monday morning. Less than six hours of sleep, but I had a full day planned. The pool-table guy would be at the bar at one-thirty. I needed to detour by the cop shop to see Eccheli on the way. My pooches needed some mommy time. And there was a Krav Maga lesson scheduled for this morning. Bobby snored loudly beside me and the dogs were seated close to the bed, staring at me. I grabbed a robe and let them out. It was still raining and I wasn't complaining.

On my way to the kitchen, I picked up clothes that were scattered everywhere, fishing my phone out of my jeans pocket before I threw them in the laundry area. The green light was flashing. I had a message.

I put Bobby's clothes on the bed beside him. He was still snoring.

Back in the kitchen, I made coffee and checked my message. Aaron's voice said, "Sorry, there's no match for your customer. I need clearance to access the other databases and, since I can't justify it with the task force, you should probably go to Eccheli."

I made a face at the phone and plugged it into the charger. Let in the dogs one at a time and rubbed them semi-dry with a towel. Mopped up their footprints.

I settled at the kitchen table. Somewhere during my second cup of coffee, I heard stirring in the bedroom. A few minutes later, Bobby came out, dressed in yesterday's clothes, mustache and goatee still damp from the bathroom sink. He smiled and kissed me on the cheek. Poured himself a cup of coffee. Laughed. "Twice in one month. These are dangerous times."

"Huh. Twice in one week. The world just may end."

During our history together, he'd learned I really didn't make breakfast, so he set about making scrambled eggs and bacon. While he cooked, I told him what Aaron's message had said.

"Good luck with that." He slid a plate in front of me and settled with his own across the table. We ate in silence and when we finished, he stood, put on his rain gear, pulled me against him and kissed me with tenderness. "See you when I see you."

It was our standard goodbye, and it made me grin. He walked out the door. Within seconds, his bike's full-throated roar sped away from the house. Back to normal. Though, the house felt a little empty without him.

I dressed and, as soon as the phone was charged, called in my liquor order with my supplier. Then, I spent some time rough-housing with the dogs. By the time we finished, both were panting and I was exhausted. I called Eccheli and made an appointment to stop by on my way to Krav Maga.

When I eventually arrived at the police station, shaking rain from my umbrella, Eccheli was waiting at the front and led me to his desk. He looked tired, with big bags hanging under his eyes. Johnson was seated in the next cubicle, though if she was IAD, it probably wasn't her real desk. Not a bit of bags under her eyes. Probably used hemorrhoid cream for that. It made me smile. Butt cream on her face.

I really didn't like her.

I had printed off some photos of the guy Bobby and I decided might be the killer, and I dropped them on the desk in front of Mr. Detective, telling him what Bobby and I suspected. I then showed him what I discovered in the printouts and the videos. "I was going through my account. Found this."

Johnson made a rude noise and said, "You're a bartender. Let us do the police work. You just go back to enabling drunks." She stood and moved off with a file folder.

Eccheli watched her leave, a deep frown dividing his forehead.

A memory of my parents fighting the day they were killed struggled forward. Dad had the same look on his face when Mom stormed away. I firmly clamped down on the memory and muttered to Eccheli, "I can't imagine why you married that."

He whipped his head to stare at me, eyes open wide. "What do you know about us?"

I pointed my thumb at my chest. "Bartender? Hello? I watch people for a living."

Leaning toward him, I said, "I understand your reasons for keeping your marriage a secret. Other cops wouldn't want to work with you. Or protect you, for that matter. I won't tell anyone. Bartenders are discrete."

I reached for the photos and printouts, but Eccheli slapped his palm on them and glared at me. He motioned down the hall. "Go talk to your brother or something. Leave me alone. And leave this case alone."

I heard a long low whistle and turned toward it. Spied Aaron, who dog-trotted to catch up to a tall black man in an overcoat. I assumed it was the infamous Agent Dawes, since he was slapping his thigh for Aaron as if calling a pet. They were headed for the exit. I hadn't even known my brother was there, hadn't even looked for him; the task force office was in another location, I'd been told. No chance of catching him before he left, either.

I turned back to Eccheli. "You're welcome for the work I did."

After one last look at Johnson's back, I left. If he wasn't going to arrest me for interference, then I had a lot of work to get to. I could have danced away from his desk; I was no longer the only primary suspect.

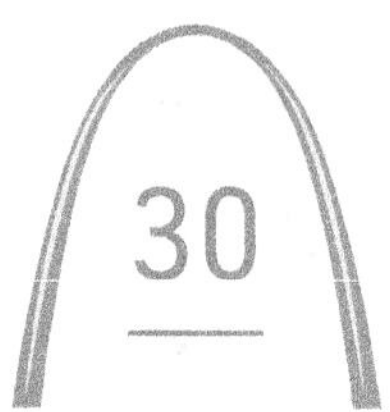

30

Karyn's place was pretty much halfway between the bar and the training facility, so I picked her up for my third Krav Maga lesson. As we rushed under an umbrella through the rain from my Jeep into the building, she grumbled, "How did you even talk me into this?"

"Because you love me."

"Hah!"

We walked into the training room and Marshall Teague met us with a raised eyebrow, Spock-style. Karyn stared at the wall of mirrors.

"She wants to learn how to hold the pad and things for me. Maybe she'll even take lessons," I offered.

Teague pointed some six feet away. "Stand over there."

Karyn obediently took her position, watching us in the mirrors, and I moved to the center of the mat with my instructor. He asked me, "How'd practice go?"

"Uh, okay I guess." I shrugged.

"We'll see."

I showed him my elbow strikes. He seemed pleased. The very first knee strike I did, however, he caught my leg and dumped me on the mat. I let out a string of expletives and Teague raised both his eyebrows this time.

Karyn burst out laughing and finally turned her attention into the room. She said, "Oh god! Yes! I've got to learn this, just so I can dump her ass on the ground. Sign me up."

Teague actually cracked a smile and helped me to my feet again. He asked Karyn, "Do you work at the bar, too?"

I turned and looked at her. Up until then, I'd assumed the killing was either a random thing that happened, or at the worst might have been a message to me. There was her ex-boyfriend from Texas, Tavon, the one who'd tried to break into my apartment. He had quite the violent streak. But, Aaron had said that Eccheli had discovered Tavon was in jail during the time of the murder.

At Karyn's pensive nod, Teague asked, "Do you have time for a quick lesson after Sylvia's?"

She looked doubtfully at me; the pool-table guys were scheduled to be at the bar at 1:30 and I had to pick up supplies. There was also lunch to be had. I held up my hand and went to my bag. Dug out my phone. Called Tom. When he answered, his dorm room was loud in the background with people laughing and shouting. "Will you open the bar for the pool-table guys?"

"Whew! I'm glad you called. I'm down to my last nickel. And my roommate is here with his friends. I'll head right over." Doubtless, studying while waiting. He always carried one or two books with him, in case the bar was slow.

Both employees had their own keys, but I gave him the new alarm code and disconnected. I nodded at Karyn and she brightened.

She said to Teague, "Of course, but it'll have to be really short. We drove together, and she needs to get to the bar."

"We can do that. Just to get you started." He beckoned to me. "Let's get going again."

He took his stance with the tombstone and motioned for me to strike with my knee again. As he worked, he coached Karyn. "See how I hold this? I don't want to put my hands behind, or I'll get sore wrists." He demonstrated, then invited her to take his place.

She did well, checking her stance in the mirror, but she wasn't quick enough at the leg-grab thing. She seemed disappointed. "I'm going to get faster."

Teague then took my lesson into knife attacks.

"There are many ways to disarm someone with a knife, but this is the easiest. When someone comes up behind you," he moved behind Karyn and reached around her, putting a fake knife against her throat. "The very first priority is securing the blade."

He traded places with her, talking to me. "Grip the arm holding the knife and pull it down. Even a little bit is good. You just need to get the blade far enough from your throat so you can move."

He showed me in slo-mo, pulling Karyn's knife down, turning, and punching. Then he did it again. Looked pretty easy.

I came in and took his place. No problems. "Karyn is docile, though. She's just letting me do it. A real killer won't be so easy."

"Remember what I told you last time: think street fighter. Stomp on his foot. Crash the back of your head into his face. Whatever you have to do so you can get that knife off your throat."

We practiced a few more times. Karyn even fought after making me promise to not break her foot or her nose.

Next he showed me a simple disarm-strike-kick combo if the knife came from the front. We spent the rest of my lesson time practicing that.

Then it was Karyn's turn. He started her back at the basics.

When her brief lesson was finished, we paid, and I bought some practice pads and a tombstone. We raced to the Jeep, rain popping against my umbrella. Once situated, I asked her, "What's with your mirror obsession?"

"A new idea for a series of photos for the bar."

I looked at her doubtfully and she shook her finger at me. "They won't be x-rated. Get your mind out of the gutter."

"I wasn't the one staring at the mirrors."

31

The yearly pool tournament was big, boasting 23 sponsor bars with 5 two-man teams apiece and as many single players as signed up. There had been talk about splitting into two tourneys, but as yet it hadn't happened. We ran every weeknight, all a bar's games against a competitor in one night. The three-quarters with lower percentage total wins were eliminated. The ones left standing would continue on into elimination rounds. At that point, we had enough space to start the singles tournaments. Same rules applied.

My new table had been installed in plenty of time for me, Karyn, and Tom to play its first couple christening games. The pool-table guys had done great work leveling it. It was identical to my last mid-priced table, except I'd splurged a little and gotten one with a bit of marbleized veneer on the sides and legs. I had to keep reminding myself it was an investment. But I was oh-so-broke. Karyn won with a huge grin on her face and a demand for a pay raise, which I denied.

Anyway, tonight we were hosting a little sports bar near the Pier, HomePlate. I didn't foresee a problem beating them soundly, but sometimes things happened out of our control. People got distracted. Blaisdale's murder had to be first and foremost on everyone's mind. I decided to sell tap beer for half price to help everyone get over it. It would also get a few tongues loosened. Gossip would abound.

Some of my regular cops were bound to know something about the investigation.

The opposing team came early, dragging muddy footprints across the floor. Lakes and rivers formed under the tables and in front of the register. Tom took the first turn mopping. Half of my guys weren't even there yet. I set the players up with a round, answered their questions about the murder with, "I don't know anything," and left them to their own devices. By the time the rest of my guys arrived and the first tourney game began, they were stewed and more than a little curious about Eccheli's investigation.

My team easily won the first game. In the middle of the second, I was leaning hard against my side of the bar, eavesdropping on the night desk sergeant from the cop shop, who was deep in conversation with an armchair jock of the opposing team. Karyn was running the tables. It was Tom's turn to mop again. I had the A/C up full to alleviate some of the stuffiness the wet weather brought, though reports had it that the rain was letting up.

The precinct's representative was speaking. "They keep saying it wasn't a break in. That the killer had the alarm code."

"So…. who are they looking at? Gotta be an inside job, right?"

"What do you think?"

A voice from down the bar drowned out the response, "I'd like a Budweiser, please."

I held up my hand to indicate I'd be with the speaker in a minute, and focused all my attention on the conversation at the pool table.

It was back to the cop again. " — only seems to prove even more that it was an inside job."

"Had to be, right?"

The voice from the end of the bar interrupted again and a shadow fell across me. "Bartender?"

With a sigh, I shifted my attention from the murder discussion to the person standing in front of me. He was a handsome man: dark wavy hair, a voice as smooth as his complexion, lopsided smile, and startling blue eyes that I'd seen in a photo taken by my spy cam.

I was staring into the eyes of the probable killer.

In a split second, a million possibilities flashed through my mind: speed dial Eccheli, shout for help, speed dial Aaron, grab the guy, tazer the guy, speed dial Bobby, hit the guy over the head with a bottle, run away, speed dial 911, and on and on. I finally decided to befriend the guy, hoping to learn some information from him. After all, any of the options I ran through could fail easily. And he couldn't hurt me with all the other cops here. I would dial Eccheli as soon as I could without raising suspicion, though.

I asked, trying to keep my voice level, "Tap or bottle?"

"Bottle, please."

"Glass?"

He shook his head.

I leaned into the fridge, fetched his bottle, and set it in front of him. Gestured to the pool table. "You here for the tourney?"

"Excuse me?" His bright blue gaze went from his bottle up to my eyes. The irises were a bit big. Probably contacts. Still, the underneath color had to be blue or the contacts would show a green tint.

"The pool tournament. Which bar do you follow?" I didn't take him for a shooter, but if he named a bar, it might give away his location.

"Uh, this one, I guess." He smiled self-consciously. Handed me a ten.

"So you're from around here then? I think I saw you in here Saturday night for that comedian."

"Just visiting relatives. But, yeah, I came Saturday. It was a good time." His studied gaze was guarded now.

"Your relatives are cops?" I handed him the change, noting the scar dead center on the heel of his right hand.

"Office workers at City Hall. I heard the advertisement on the radio Saturday and came back tonight to see what the place is really like. These are all cops?" He partially turned to face the room, making an encompassing gesture, but his gaze moved directly to the spot where Blaisdale had dropped.

"Mostly. Not the competing team, though."

"I see. Thanks for the beer." He raised his bottle to me and wandered to a table in the corner, by the jukebox. He sat so he had a view of the front door with only a small turn of his head. I watched as, again and again, his gaze sought out the kill spot.

I went into the back room and called Eccheli. "He's here."

"Who's there?"

"The guy in the video. The photo I brought you." I heard the grunt of his chair as he shifted, or maybe, hopefully, stood. My hands were shaking from an adrenalin rush, which was novel for me. I'm usually cool under fire.

"Don't do anything. I'll be right there."

I nodded as if he could see me and hung up. It didn't take him long to arrive. But during that time I was on pins and needles, working hard to keep from staring at the guy. Didn't want to spook him.

When Eccheli arrived through the front door, he had the missus with him, of course. The volume in the room ceased immediately. Even the opposing team quieted, picking up on the vibe. Not a soul said a word. The only sounds were the jukebox and a couple already hit pool balls knocking together. All eyes were pinned on the detectives at the door. I had no doubt that quite a few of the customers thought I was going to be arrested.

Neither detective looked at me. They scanned the room and made a beeline toward the corner table where the possible – probable – killer sat. Eccheli slid into the seat opposite the guy, while Johnson stood at the end of the table and effectively blocked all escape.

The guy startled and slid an accusatory glance my way.

I, of course, leaned on the bar and watched the show. Someone shot a ball into a pocket at the table, and the spell was broken. Volume returned to near normal. Still, more than a few necks stayed craned toward the table in the corner.

Karyn slid her tray across the bar and came around back with me. She whispered, "What's going on?"

"They're interviewing a suspect."

She nodded and watched a moment. Got bored and went to refill her orders.

I, on the other hand, was mesmerized. It seemed as if Eccheli chatted with the guy forever, but when I checked the clock, it had only been seven minutes when the suspect stood and edged past Johnson. Had to give her credit, she didn't budge an inch in the intimidation factor. Stood her ground and made him go around. Nice.

The room quieted again, as if everyone was holding their breath.

As the guy passed the bar on his way out the back door, he locked his gaze on me. His eyes were like the coldest depths of a glacier. And harder than iced diamonds. A chill ran down my spine.

I stood my ground like Johnson had. Met his gaze with one of my own, which I hoped was just as tough as his.

His lips curled into a snarl. And then he disappeared into the back hall, out of sight. The guy hadn't expressed any anger at any of the cops in the room. Not even at the two detectives. Just me.

Eccheli followed, escorting the suspect out.

Karyn stared at me open-mouthed from the booths in front of the big TV. Johnson stayed at the guy's table. She pulled out an evidence bag, wrote on it, flipped it inside out, and grabbed the suspect's bottle. While sealing the red zip top of the bag, she walked over to the bar. "Mind if I take this?"

What was I going to do? Tell her she couldn't remove it from my bar? Ask her to pay for it? I shook my head. Motioned for Karyn to take over dishing drinks for me.

"Who is he?" I asked Mrs. Detective because I wanted to keep tabs on the creepy guy who'd threatened me with his glare.

Instead of answering my question, she parried with one of her own. "Why did you turn off your cameras?"

"What?" I glanced at Eccheli, who'd just returned.

He met my gaze, eyebrows raised. "You turned off your cameras yesterday and the day before. Why?"

Wow. These two were really on top of what I was doing. "I'm operating under the assumption that whoever broke in that night has access to my video feed somehow. I turned off the cameras Saturday to hide the fact that I was installing a secret camera, and yesterday to view the video from said camera on my big screen."

I showed them the spy cam and the burner phone. "It only loads directly onto this phone."

Mr. Detective nodded. "That's where you got the photos you brought me."

I nodded. "I can send you these videos regularly, if you'd like."

Mrs. Detective said, "I'd like." She gave me her phone number.

I manipulated the little phone and looked up at Eccheli. "Done. Who was the guy?"

Truthfully, it didn't matter if they told me or not. I had the video feed. I could find out for myself. But, I was hoping they'd let me into the investigation, at least in part. After all, I'd brought them a viable suspect, which let me off the hook a bit. That had to count for something.

He hesitated, and then, as if reaching a decision, pulled out his notebook and slid onto a bar stool. "He says his name is Lee Garret. He has a Canadian passport and says he's from Alberta. He's just here visiting relatives who live in Creve Coeur."

"Long way to come for a beer. You two want coffee?" I snuck a look at the notebook upside down and memorized the address of Mr. Garret's relatives. Being able to read upside down had come in handy over the years.

He nodded. "Love some. Garret said he'd come here the first time on Saturday night to see your comedian. Then came back today because he liked the place."

I poured the piping hot coffee into two deep mugs and slid them across the bar with cream and sugar. "He told me his relatives work in City Hall. And he wore colored contacts. Those irises were just too big."

"I saw that." He lifted the coffee, started to take a sip, and grimaced. Obviously thinking better of it, he set the mug back down. Probably a good idea – as thick as the steam was coming off of it.

Johnson held her mug near, letting the steam roll up her face. A habit I indulged in. Creepy.

"He had a scar on his right palm."

Eccheli shook his head. "Left."

Johnson set down her coffee and said, "You're both right. The scars are on both hands, and they transect the heels of the palms. That's Carpal Tunnel surgery. Our boy's a techy. Or at least an office worker. Lots of data entry."

I could have dropped my jaw. Bobby and I were ahead of the detectives on that point. I wondered if it had been sound advice to 'not tell them anything', as Bobby had put it. But I wondered if they would have listened, given my reception when I dropped off the photo.

Eccheli checked his notes. "He said he works as a dental assistant."

She shook her head. "Not a chance."

"Does this mean I'm not the primary person of interest any longer?" I looked directly at Johnson this time.

"Let's just say you've been bumped down the list." She gave a half-smile at that, then quickly hid it by picking up her mug and sucking down some coffee.

I noted that the edge of dislike I had for her was beginning to soften, and I regarded her with suspicion.

Loud voices came from the pool table, and we all three looked that direction. Game 2 had just finished, HomePlate triumphant, and the players for Game 3 swarmed in, thumping backs and spilling beer on the exiting players.

Eccheli looked at me. "Is it ever quiet here?"

I shook my head. "Only when the place is closed due to murder."

Johnson snorted into her mug. Could I construe that as a laugh? With a sigh, she lowered her coffee. "Why didn't he get rid of the murder video? I mean, he's techy, he easily could have. Especially considering how he'd replaced the video of his first break in."

I shrugged. "No point. He was too small to get rid of the body by himself, and he'd just killed his only help."

Johnson watched me with calculating eyes. She slowly nodded, and then slid off the stool.

Eccheli raised his eyebrows and glanced at her empty mug, then back to his still full one. "We leaving?"

She shrugged. "Things to do. Bad guys to check out."

He heaved himself off the stool, slugged back a giant gulp of coffee, grimaced at the heat of the liquid, nodded to me, and followed his wife out the back door.

I went back to cleaning tables, serving half-priced beer, and watching the games. My mind, however, kept replaying the guy's cold blue stare as he walked past me out the door.

32

Smugglers was hopping busy all night after the detectives left. The distraction of the murder pulled harder on the HomePlate team than my guys, who played it cool. Still, the third game took forever. Lots of stupid mistakes that cost my guys enough to lose. But they settled nicely and took the fourth and fifth, finishing the match for the night. The visiting players stayed and they all spent the rest of the night shooting bull and making trick shots at the table.

I still felt the malice of Garret's stare bear down on me. I was jittery and my stomach was locked into a painful knot. More than one glass shattered on the floor at my feet. Finally Karyn pushed the mop into my hands and took over the bar work. Though the rain had stopped and the air was on, the humidity was still high, making the walls close. I kept trying to gulp in fresh air. If ever there was a case of becoming suddenly claustrophobic, it was then. Karyn said it was just a panic attack. Still, I was glad I had a late crowd to keep both my employees there with me until I left.

The volume in the bar spilled into the street as I locked up. I drove home and parked in front of the house, too tired to go around back. Even before I opened my door, I knew something was wrong. There were no happy whines or yips coming from the other side. Energy zinged through me and all thoughts of sleep left.

I stepped back from the door and crept along the edge of my house until I reached the A/C unit on the side. Behind it was a loose siding board I slid out of the way and retrieved my .357 Colt Python. Like my brother, I admired a fine firearm. The Colt was the same one used by one of the bad cops in the Clint Eastwood Dirty Harry movie, *Magnum Force*. I had providence on it. I hadn't had enough money to buy Dirty Harry's gun. Had to take what I could get. In retrospect, I wished I still had the money spent on it.

Including the Colt, I had a total of four guns at home, all registered. One of which, Bobby knew about. Two different ones Aaron knew. And certainly, no one at all knew about the fourth. I'd had the one I now gripped in my hand less than a month.

I moved to the front again, checking shadows before dodging into them. Reaching the door, I leaned into it, listening. Silent as a ball of cotton. The key slid smoothly into the lock and turned. I eased open the door. Watched and listened for any movement or noise. Nothing. I slipped my arm in and turned on my lights. The alarm was already off.

Mayhem erupted from my backyard as my dogs snarled and threw themselves at the sliding glass door with angsted fervor. I hadn't let them out there. Maybe Aaron had stopped by. But the dogs were clearly upset, and they wouldn't be if it had been my brother who'd visited.

Even if there was a noise, I wouldn't hear it over the violent ruckus. I sidled into the room. Nothing but my blue furniture and beige carpet. Through the glass door, I saw Ruffles was foaming and standing stock still. When he moved, it was with the stiff-legged, high-toed, movements of a mechanical being. His upper lip was curled completely over his nose and the resulting sound came through the glass like an outboard motor. I'd never seen him so livid, and I honestly wondered how he could breathe like that.

Satan was throwing herself at the door again and again, as if she were a small missile that would weaken and eventually punch through the glass. I could picture the trauma her body experienced every time she made contact. If I didn't do something fast, she would be covered in bruises, maybe even broken bones.

Something had upset them so much that even my presence didn't calm them. Moving quickly through my home, I cleared all the rooms; no one was hidden anywhere. Then, I put the safety back on the gun, set it down, and went to focus on my poor dogs. I pulled out the rod I kept in the track. That's when I noticed the dark brown handprint on the sliding door.

Unless I missed my guess, that was dried blood.

I pulled my cellphone and dialed Eccheli. It took him a long time to answer, and he didn't sound too happy, but his sleep-cracked voice got animated the moment I explained what had happened.

He said, "Don't touch anything. We'll be right there."

"My dogs might be injured. I need to go out there and check them." Satan had calmed a little, but she still paced the window in agitation. Ruffles was standing stock still, growling.

He hesitated. "Do you have kitchen gloves?"

"I have painter's gloves." Actually, I didn't. But I did have some of the gloves the police left behind at the bar. Close enough.

"Perfect. Go out to them, don't let them in. We'll get there right away." He disconnected.

I probably was working my way back up Johnson's 'person of interest' list with this middle of the night phone call. Nothing to be done about it.

When he'd said they'd get there right away, he wasn't kidding. I'd managed to find my gloves, put them on, and had only been outside a few minutes. I was sitting in the soaked grass, trying to calm a frantic Satan so I could inspect her for injuries when my cellphone vibrated against my thigh.

Eccheli asked, "We good to come in?"

"Yeah, we're out back."

The minute the front door opened, Satan became all claws and teeth and twisted out of my arms. She threw herself at the glass door, ballistic missile at work again. As for Ruffles, I was used to his snarls, but the intensity of the one he gave at that moment scared me.

I watched Eccheli and Johnson as they entered my house. Saw how he noticed my Colt Python on the counter, pointed it out to Johnson, and how she nodded and pocketed it. I certainly hoped she was going to give that back; it had cost me a pretty penny.

As the two detectives cleared the house, again, flashing lights of an arriving squad car ricocheted off the back fence of the yard. I would probably be as popular in my neighborhood as a scorpion. At least there was no siren.

Mr. and Mrs. Detective returned to the front room. Eccheli leaned close to the glass, studying the handprint. Johnson stared out the glass at me and pointed at the door handle. When I shook my head, she pulled out her phone and called me. "How are the dogs?"

I shouted over the violence of growls and barks. "Ruffles has no injuries, but I can't get Satan to hold still to check her!"

"Want me to call animal control to tranq her?"

I hesitated. I didn't want to do that to my dogs, but I didn't foresee Satan letting me check her any time soon and that bloody handprint scared me. I nodded to the woman staring out at me, feeling somehow like a traitor.

She disconnected and made the call.

Cops and crime scene people began to fill my home as car after car arrived. A tech busied himself scraping some of the dried handprint into a paper collection packet, while another dusted for fingerprints on the front door, the counter, the sink, everywhere. The lights in the neighboring houses came on.

I heard the familiar throaty rumble of my dad's Harley out front, followed shortly after by Aaron's frame filling the doorway. He made a beeline to the back door, and would have opened it if it hadn't been for Johnson's quick grab. The conversation that followed between them was quite animated, and he finally called me.

"Johnson thinks the dogs are too angry for me to come out."

"She's right. We're waiting for animal control to come sedate them." They'd calmed some, but every time someone made a big move in the house, they went crazy again. Really, my neighbors were going to hate me.

He ran his free hand through his hair. "What the hell happened?"

As I told him the sequence of events, his mouth pressed into a tight line and his brow furrowed into a dark chasm.

"I'm staying with you for awhile," he said. "No arguments."

Eccheli leaned over Aaron's shoulder, speaking into the phone. "Animal control is here. They're set up around the side fence of the yard with their tranq rifle. They don't think you should try giving the dogs the shot yourself; they might turn on you, as scared as they are. Once they're down, I need you to come inside so you can tell me what happened."

I agreed with the assessment that my dogs might be too emotional to get the shot from their beloved mom. Pain was pain. At that point, they'd attack anyone who hurt them. Ergo, Animal Control and their tranq rifle. However, the emotion my dogs felt wasn't fear. They were furious and ready to tear someone apart.

I nodded, stood, and walked to the far end of the yard; my soaked jeans weighed heavy on my hips. My heart broke both times the gun was fired. Ruffles went down without a sound, but my little white dog yelped and nearly turned a summersault before she fell.

Aaron came out immediately, wrapped me in a bone-breaking hug for what seemed a long time. Someone had broken into my house and maybe hurt my dogs. My heart burned with fear for them. When he pulled back, he smiled and ran his fingers under my eyes. "Tears for your babies."

I shrugged. Of course I had tears for them.

Together we straightened out and checked their sleeping bodies for injuries. We found none. Then, I phoned the on-call number for my vet and left a message. I needed to make sure they were completely okay. No drugs, or slow poisons, or anything.

We went inside.

Somewhere during my explanation of the events to Eccheli, my cell buzzed: the vet calling me back. I gave her a brief overview of the happenings, and she agreed to meet me immediately at the clinic.

Johnson shook her head. "Your Jeep is hemmed in. I'll drive you."

The surprise must have shown on my face, because she actually laughed at me before she went to start her car. Why was she being nice?

Aaron lifted the sagging Ruffles and I took Satan. When I opened my front door, I was blown away by the number of spectators, most in their pajamas. Though it was well after four by then, neighbors filled the sidewalk behind the crime scene tape, and gawked from open windows and from across the street. I had no idea there were so many people who lived near me. I certainly never saw most of them. News vans lined the road and reporters shouted at me while their cameras swiveled my direction.

The scent of hot wet asphalt from the recent rain filled the night. The bushes on either side of the house glistened in the false lights with raindrops poised to fall. My sidewalk was filled with earthworm trails.

Aaron bumped me from behind, pushing me down the steps with Ruffles's rump. "Just keep going," he urged. "You don't want to talk to anyone."

"You're right about that." I ducked my head and made straight for the detective's car.

Johnson started her vehicle and pulled away from the house. As she wound past the news vans, crime scene vehicles, and staring neighbors standing in clusters in the road, I ran my hand through Satan's coat. It gave me comfort and, though I knew she was sleeping, I pretended it gave her comfort too.

Once onto clear road, Johnson glanced down at my hand smoothing Satan's fur. "I have a dog, too. Well, a giant rat, really. She's a teacup Chihuahua. Dogs are amazingly resilient and very forgiving."

I smiled at her. I'm sure if I'd thought about it first, I wouldn't have. But I was rattled and would take compassion from anywhere.

She glanced in the rearview mirror at my cop brother. She spoke carefully, making it obvious to me because I knew the truth that she was trying to hide her relationship to Eccheli. "My husband makes fun of my dog, says he doesn't like her. But I sometimes find them cuddled on the couch together, watching a movie."

I smiled again, wondered if I was sick because I found her so likeable, and suddenly thought of how my dogs loved Bobby. I made a mental note to call him after finishing with the vet. Well, as soon as he would be awake.

I also made a mental note to find out Mrs. Detective's first name, now pretty sure I was coming down with something. Probably from the stress.

The parking lot for the vet, Dr. Nelson, was empty, except for her vehicle. We carried the dogs through the spotted puddles, into the building, and directly to the exam room. Gateway City Vet Clinic was situated right downtown, not far from the bar. Four vets worked out of it, including a specialist in exotics. The building was situated on a big lot with a heavily-soundproofed boarding kennel attached. The front office was divided into two waiting rooms: cats or dogs. Six exam rooms graced the walls, and we went into the center one on the dog side, where Dr. Nelson waited. Thankfully, she was my regular vet. I didn't want to deal with explaining my dogs to someone new.

She palpated the dogs' abdomens, checked their gums and eyes. Ran her hands over every part of their sleeping bodies. She drew blood. "I find no injuries, nor do I see any signs of poisoning. But the blood will better tell that."

She studied me, doubt in her eyes. "I can keep them here …"

I shook my head. She knew my dogs. Everyone knew my dogs. They had special labels on the kennel doors that read 'Bad Dog'. No need to put the world through their separation anxiety. "I'll take them home. You can call me with the results or if they need more tests."

She nodded, relief clear on her face. "Give them lots of TLC. And give them some vitamin K, just in case of poison."

Aaron and I scooped up the pooches and the vet helped us out the door to Johnson's car. She stuffed a vial of the required vitamin into my pocket. "The test will be done first thing in the morning."

On the way home, Johnson asked, "Do you want to tell me why you have a gun?"

"No offense, but have you lived in any city before?" Then I told her about the history of the pistol. "It's a collector's piece."

Aaron, in the backseat, chose not to say anything, but I could almost read his thoughts. He now knew of three of the weapons in my house.

Johnson asked, "Is there anything we're going to find in your house that we should know about?"

"Are you searching it?"

"A crime has been committed. I assume you want us to catch the asshole who did it. So, yes, we're doing a thorough investigation."

"I have three more guns hidden around the house. And the one in your pocket."

From the backseat came, "Jesus, Syl!"

Johnson raised her eyebrows. The dash lit her face and I could almost see my name inching even further back up her 'person of interest' list. "I need you to show us where they're located."

I nodded. I could find new hiding places when the police were done. There was something more important on my mind right now. "Why didn't he just kill them? I mean, if he's Blaisdale's murderer, and he's trying to send me a message to shut up, wouldn't he have killed them?"

Even in the dim light of the car, I could see Johnson's frown. "We don't always know why killers do what they do."

"I don't know him. He doesn't know me. Why did he kill someone in my bar? Why did he terrorize my dogs? Why did he wait so long after the murder to do that?"

"The link between tonight and your identification of him is unmistakable. Are you sure you've never met him?"

I shook my head. "I don't know him. I don't remember seeing him in my bar before the murder. But that's what security videos are for. Here's a question, how'd he get into my house? That's a different alarm code than the bar. Aaron and Bobby are the only other people who know it."

For some reason, Johnson decided to keep her own council on her thoughts. By the time we returned home, most of my neighbors had dispersed and the crime scene crew was packing up. Pre-dawn light was tinting the horizon. The stars winked down from above, happy to be able to see Earth again. The humidity was gone and the gentle breeze was cool, sweet, and clean. It was going to be a beautiful day. As if the cruelty of the night hadn't happened.

Aaron fetched the dog crates from the spare bedroom and put my babies in them for safety when they staggered awake. I dutifully showed Johnson and Eccheli all my weapons in their hiding places. Mrs. Detective returned the collectable pistol she'd pocketed and they left. It was just Aaron and me with the dogs. He held out a cup of fresh coffee.

I shook my head. "I need to sleep."

"You won't. You'll fuss over the dogs, and you'll rethink the day's events. I know you."

"That may be, but I've got to try." As if he knew everything about me. Hah! Sometimes my brother just irked me.

He settled at the table. "Don't worry about your pups. I'll take care of them."

I raised my hand in farewell and marched to my bed. It turns out, Aaron was right about not being able to sleep, but it was out of anger, not fussing and worry. And certainly not fear. I was sure Lee Garret was responsible for the break in. I remembered that glare; it had been full of promised malice. I wanted him caught and caged.

After a while, I heard the dogs struggle through their wake up, Ruffles's low and confused growl, Satan's high-pitched whimper, and

Aaron's quiet voice reassuring them both. Then the back door slid open and shut, followed by Aaron's deep sigh and the sound of coffee pouring. All went silent.

Except me.

I tossed and turned, fluffed and punched my pillow, threw blankets off and pulled them back on again, and stared at the clock, the ceiling, and the dawn light peeking through the blinds at the window. Finally, after an hour and a half, I got up. Tugged on a black tee and jeans.

Aaron met me at the kitchen with a coffee and raised eyebrows.

"Shut up." I took the mug and joined him on the couch.

For a long time, we didn't say anything. Then he rose to his feet. "Gotta go to work."

"I'll make some breakfast." I automatically rose.

"Already ate." He lifted his eyebrows, again. It seemed he was doing that a lot lately, and it was another thing that annoyed me. He quietly asked, "Four guns? Really? That's a bit of overkill."

"It's none of your business. But, the last one was a bargain, considering the history. It's a collector's piece. I like them all. Each one is different. If I ever get time, I'm going to join a gun club again."

"Whatever you have to tell yourself."

"It's all true." I seriously wanted him to leave now.

"We'll talk more about it later. I'll be back after work to sit with the pooches." He leaned over, pecked my cheek, waved at the dogs outside for some odd reason, and left.

I sat alone in my front room, listening to his bike drive away. Then I rose and did a half-assed job of cleaning up the fingerprint powder and trash left behind. I opened the back door for my snoozing dogs. They staggered to their feet and jogged unsteadily into the house. I shut the door after them, dropped the rod in the track, and set the alarm. Then I curled up again on my blue couch. One at a time, my pooches climbed up with me: Satan curled in the crook of my knees and Ruffles flopped on my legs beside her. Finally, I fell asleep.

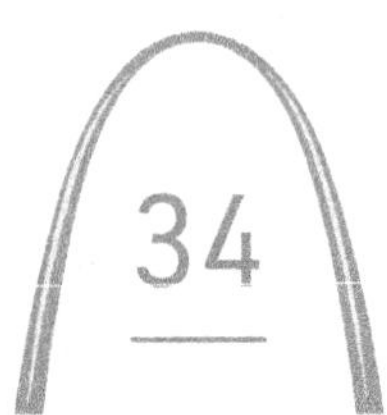

34

I woke a little after 8 AM when a motorcycle of a different engine pitch than that of my dad's rumbled up the front sidewalk to the door. The dogs lifted their heads and cocked them to one side. Neither made any effort to move.

Bobby.

I extricated myself from my blanket of dogs, unlocked the front door, turned off the alarm, and crawled back under the dogs.

Bobby knocked, and when I shouted it was open, he let himself in. Shut the door, came over and stared down at us, worry creasing his forehead. Ruffles's stump tail thumped against the cushion and Satan wriggled in excitement bumping my legs off the couch. She really was in love with the man, as long as it was here at home.

I said, "Sorry I didn't call. I meant to. It was crazy, and then …" I sighed and shook my head.

He shoved the coffee table out of the way and squatted beside me, his knees popping in protest. And I was pretty sure his jeans were going to split from the strain of his bulging thighs. Reaching over, he ran his hand down my cheek. "No worries. But I have to say it surprised the shit out of me to see it on the news."

"I'm okay. He was gone when I got home. But, the vet's going to call me any time now with the results of the blood work she had done on these two." I jutted my chin toward the warm lumps on the couch, the small one still wriggling.

He nodded, not taking his gaze off me. "You hungry?"

My stomach was still all in knots, and I shook my head. It seemed not to have mattered. He rose, knees popping again, and headed to the kitchen. It was true I was a gourmet cook, but Bobby made the best down home food. Soon, a pan was snapping and popping with sausage, eggs, and fried biscuits.

Despite myself, my stomach gave a loud rumble, and the dogs' noses were busy twitching.

My cellphone rang and I lunged for where I'd left it: the corner of the coffee table, now several feet away thanks to Bobby. The dogs spilled onto the floor and trotted over to investigate the aromas coming from the kitchen. It was the vet's number on the phone.

"Dr. Nelson?"

"Syl, I'm sorry I'm late calling. I had to wait for Animal Control to get back to me."

I glanced at the clock. 8:25. "I don't understand. Why would you need to speak to them?"

"I found traces of Telazol in both dogs. That's a common brand of tranquilizer used with dart guns. It turns out Animal Control doesn't use Telazol; it's too expensive for them and sometimes lasts too long. I'd say that's what your intruder used."

"Will they be all right?" My heart was in my throat. Bobby turned toward me, listening from the kitchen.

"I don't see any problems with them recovering, even when dosed with the two different drugs so close in time together. But keep an eye on them. Are they up?"

"They got up, but they're sleeping a lot."

"That's common and will probably last through the day. As I said, keep an eye on them. And remember to give them the vitamins."

I said my thanks and hung up. Frankly, I could have worshipped her as a goddess at that point. Unexpected tears of relief flooded my eyes. The harder I tried to stop them, the worse it got until I was blubbering like a baby.

I'm not exactly sure when Bobby slid onto the couch behind me, wrapping me in his thick arms, but he stayed until I calmed down again.

I'm not a crier, and I felt the need to explain my irrational action. I whispered, "I was so worried about the dogs."

"I know. Me, too." He wiped some stray hair out of my face, gave me a squeeze, and slipped off the couch again. Back in the kitchen, he took the now cold eggs, chopped them up and put them in the dogs' dishes. Started some fresh.

Anger rose up inside me again. I was angry at the guy who'd killed a man in my bar, invaded my home, and drugged my dogs. It made me furious. I wanted to rip apart Lee Garret – I was positive it had been him – with my bare hands. And, watching Bobby dish up the eggs and reheated sausage, it made me angry that my life, and the lives of those around me, would be changed in ways I couldn't yet predict. Also, I was getting really, really tired of my emotional roller-coaster ride.

We ate in silence while I contemplated that last one. My dogs would have to go with me to work. Just a minor inconvenience. But I wouldn't be able to come home alone for a while. My nice, safe neighborhood suddenly seemed just as menacing as the rest of the city. I reached for my phone again and called Eccheli.

"Did anyone call in a noise complaint about my dogs last night?"

"In fact, they did. The call came in at 2:13 AM and a patrol went by not even fifteen minutes later, but they reported no noise."

"Why the hell wasn't I notified at the bar?"

"That's what I've been trying to find out."

"Let me know, would you?" I hung up before he could give me some excuse not to call back.

I told Bobby what Eccheli had said. "They should have called."

"Isn't it protocol, given what's happened to you?"

"I don't know. But I'll make sure it will be now."

He smiled for the first time since he'd arrived. "Of that, I have no doubt. So, do we have a plan yet?"

It warmed my heart that he'd automatically included himself in my plans as Aaron had. I reached over and plunked a kiss on his freshly overburdened, biscuit-filled cheek.

"Well, I'll obviously have to take the beasts with me to work."

"And then they'll come over to my place to meet Bilbo." The named critter was a fish. A black Moor, to be exact. It had been with Bobby for almost three months now.

He pointed his finger at me, just as I opened my mouth to refuse. "I know you can take care of yourself. But, you need help, and you know it."

The thought of moving in with him, even temporarily, filled me with trepidation. I didn't want to jeopardize the great no-strings-attached thing we had going. Glad to have another option, I said, "Aaron's already made plans to stay here."

Bobby slowly nodded, but I thought I saw a trace of relief cross his features. He'd been worried about it changing our relationship, too. "What do you need me to do? We'll have to do it on the down low so your detectives don't put a stop to it."

I chewed on my lower lip. Something my mom used to do when frustrated. It was a habit I was quickly forming. "Here's a question: why would our killer need a camera, or anything, to get my alarm code, when he's shown himself as a tech genius? He could have gotten the admin code from the security company. He'd already hacked them to tamper with the video. And he bypassed the house alarm."

"Maybe he was hopin' no one would notice the tamper? Tryin' to throw the investigation off track?"

"Maybe." I still wasn't convinced. "But why? What's he really hiding?"

"Don't know." Bobby spread his hands wide. "Something else in his life? Something else techy? His job?"

That made sense. I said, "We already know he works with computers. But maybe he's not just techy. He could actually be working in the computer industry. Software or something."

"That would be something to protect."

I told him what little I'd learned from Eccheli and Johnson. "We need to know more. I'll see what else my brother can find out. Blaisdale worked two jobs, but Patty Degere had no idea what the second job was. It could be a tech firm. But there are, like, millions of those around here."

"Leave the leg work to the cops. I'll go to this asshole's address and see if I can tail him."

"I'll go with you." I jotted down what I'd memorized from Eccheli's notepad and handed it to him. I petted the pooches, locked the door, and joined Bobby on his bike.

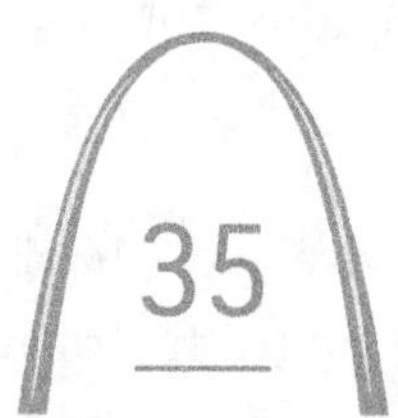

35

The address Garret had given for his relatives was only twelve minutes away. We parked in front of the tiny, two-story house. It was unremarkable: no porch, no awning over the door, no shutters. Nothing but a plain white box with a black roof. The yard was equally miniscule and equally unremarkable.

I rang the white doorbell beside the plain white door. I stood directly in front, Bobby to the side, so as not to spook anyone with his biker looks. When no one answered, I rang again. And again. Finally, after the fourth ring, an elderly lady answered and we both stepped back to give distance.

The smell of over-burned oil and something else rolled out of the house. My eyes teared and I peered past the woman's frail frame. Cats were everywhere. I could put a name to the unknown stench: kitty spray. I was allergic to cats. My throat tightened, and I swallowed hard, suddenly regretting the breakfast.

Bobby wrinkled his nose, and his mouth pressed into a thin line. He glanced at me, then tightly said, "We'd like to speak with Mr. Garret, please."

The woman shook her head, putting her hand on the doorjamb as the sudden movement seemed to unbalance her. "Garret? Who's that?

Is that a first name or last? Two detectives were asking about him. Woke me up before the sun this morning. Scared me half to death."

"What's your name, ma'am?"

"Mrs. Gwen Boyle."

"How long have you lived here, Mrs. Boyle?"

"Well, let's see." She squinted her rheumy blue eyes. "It's going on twelve years now, I guess. I moved here just after my Leroy died."

I took a deep breath and gave Bobby a smile, thankful that he'd stepped in. I collected myself and showed her the picture of the killer. "Do you know a Mr. Lee Garret?"

The woman stared at the photo and slowly shook her head, hand gripping the jamb. "No, I can't say I do. The police asked that too. Who are you?"

I opened my phone and googled 'Blaisdale'. Enlarged a photo of him in uniform and showed that to her. "What about him? Do you recognize him?"

"A police officer? I can't really see him well." She gripped my phone and pulled me close to her. Lost the picture. I found it again, enlarged the face, and showed it to her, cupping all the buttons and pads to keep her from pressing them. She wrapped her gnarled hand around mine. Tiny tremors passed under her skin. Again, she shook her head. "No. I can't say that I know him either. Who are you people?"

"Thank you, Ma'am. If you remember anything or hear of anyone who uses the name Lee Garret, will you please contact me?" I pocketed my phone and handed the elderly woman a business card from my bar.

Once out of ear shot, Bobby said, "I'm sorry. I just sort of took over."

I shrugged. "That doesn't bother me. I'm allergic to cats. I was just trying to breathe and keep my food down."

"I think she's telling the truth."

"Me too."

Another dead end. I pulled on my helmet and settled behind Bobby on his bike. Once on the highway, we headed east toward home. While Bobby handled the traffic, I thought about my case. True, I was no longer the primary suspect, but I didn't want this murder hanging over my head the rest of my life, either. What would be my next move? What had we learned about Lee Garret? He had scars on his wrists and possibly, probably, worked in the computer industry.

I tapped on Bobby's shoulder. Leaned my helmet against his. Shouted, "Let's swing by some software firms!"

He shook his head and tapped the side of his helmet. I motioned to the upcoming exit. He nodded and leaned the bike onto the ramp. At the top, we paused at the stop long enough for me to explain my idea. His only answer was a shrug. Which really could have meant anything. But, he turned left and took us into the industrial park, stopping on CityPlace Drive in front of a giant building that advertised six software firms.

I dismounted, removed my helmet, stretched, and shook out my hair. Bobby flipped up his visor and asked, "What's your plan?"

"I'm going to tell them I'm helping the police search for Garret."

He shook his head and pulled his helmet off. "They won't help you, because you're not police. And don't tell them you're a PI either. They'd like you even less. You have to give them a reason to want to help."

"Like?"

"I dunno. Like maybe he's your brother and you're supposed to meet him but lost the address. Or someone in his family has died. Or somethin' like that."

I handed him my helmet and walked toward the entrance, wondering again about Bobby's past. Aware that there was a whole mountain of things I didn't know about him. Why would he know this? In what scenario had he reason to do what I was going to do now? He was right though.

Despite the size of a building that promised a large lobby, it was cramped. Dark green carpet covered the floor and went halfway up the wall to a stained walnut chair rail. On either end were two companies with giant doors emblazoned with their names: Lukor Tech Solutions and SoftwareWorld. Chilled air brought up goosebumps on my arms. A woman in a trim uniform blazer sat behind a small desk, centered between the two firms.

She gave a dark red lipstick smile that revealed perfect teeth. "May I help you?"

I approached. "I'm supposed to meet Lee Garret."

"What's this concerning?"

"He told me he'd introduce me to his boss. Maybe I'd get hired."

She typed on her keypad. Shook her head. "There's no Lee Garret listed with any of the firms in this building."

I frowned. Pulled out my phone and showed her the picture. "This is him. He said to meet him here."

"I'm sorry. He doesn't look familiar."

"You're sure?"

The woman frowned at me and I noticed that she had a unibrow. Short hairs had sprouted since she'd last tweezed or waxed, pointing in all different directions. She said, "Maybe I should call someone to help you."

"No. That's all right." I shrugged and turned to go. Stopped and pulled up Blaisdale's photo. Turned back. "This guy was with him. They were friends. Does he work here? I really want that job."

With an exaggerated sigh, she leaned toward the phone. Shook her head. "No. He doesn't work here either." Her hand crept toward her phone.

"Maybe one of the other firms in a different building then. I know he said it was on this street. I was sure he said this building, though." I smiled and beat a hasty retreat.

We tried each building along CityPlace Drive. I used varying stories, but no one knew Garret or Blaisdale.

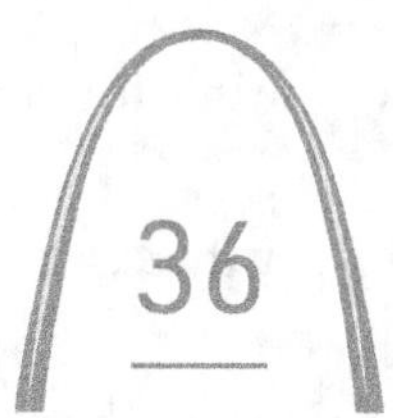

Bobby took me home. He came in with me to help check the rooms. Not that I believed anyone was there; the dogs were calm. But because I still felt uneasy. He said, "You had a good idea. But there are a lot of computer places around St. Louis. Not just software places."

"I have to start somewhere."

"The cops have more manpower. Let them do the scut work."

"Maybe."

Bobby turned to go. I gripped the front of his tee, pulled him close, and whispered, "Be careful."

He gave me a wicked smile, eyes sharp and twinkling. "Always." With a peck on the lips, he disappeared into the brilliant sunshine of the day.

I'd missed my Krav Maga class. When I called Marshall Teague and explained what had happened during the night, he insisted on another private session Thursday morning. Normally, I'd cynically suggest he only wanted the extra money, but the training was a good idea.

I called the cleaning service to come to my home next. As luck would have it, they still had the gap from my cancellation of the bar. They agreed to come right away

Karyn was next. I told her what had happened. She said, "Coming right over."

She hung up without waiting for my response. I called her right back.

"What? It'll wait until I get there," she said. I could almost see her frown.

"No. I'm okay. Really. See you at the tourney."

"Oh. Okay." She sounded deflated. Why was it something inside me said I had to make it up to her that she couldn't comfort me?

Confused, I disconnected. Googled 'Lee Garret' He'd said his home was in Alberta, so I added that to the search parameters. No one by that name in the whole province.

Leaning back in my seat, I closed my eyes and tried to picture the conversation we'd had at the bar. His voice had a touch of a southern twang, not heavy though, so probably not too far down. Probably not even Tennessee. But maybe lower Missouri. I changed the search parameters and pulled up plenty of Lees and Garrets, including a couple of brothers that had become famous high school football players a few years ago, but still no Lee Garret. I searched east and west from there and scored a few people with the right name, but the wrong profile picture.

The guy didn't exist.

Eccheli probably already knew all that. No point calling him.

The cleaning service came. While the house was getting a good once-over, I made myself lunch and joined my dogs on the patio for the duration.

As soon as the cleaning staff was finished, I took the pooches with me to the bar, where I discovered a police car in the back lot. Apparently Eccheli and Johnson considered me as still at risk. I left the dogs in the Jeep and walked to the back door. The only cop in the car got out and met me there. His nametag read Leach. He was tall, solid, and pretty in the face. He smiled, but I just nodded, too keyed up to really be interested in making friends. I unlocked the door, reached in, flicked on the lights, and turned off the alarm. Wordlessly, I handed him the storeroom key. Leach pulled his weapon and edged his imposing bulk into Smugglers.

Within five minutes he returned, once again smiling, and trying to catch my eye. "All clear. You're as safe as the Queen of Sheba in her palace."

He dropped the key into my palm with a flourish. Charisma wasn't in shortage with him. But I still wasn't biting. I said, "I have my dogs with me. You'll have to go to your car so I can get them."

Once he was safely ensconced in his vehicle, I fetched my pups and escorted them inside. They forgot they'd been there recently and treated it as a new place, therefore suspicious. While they traveled the floor, walls, and furniture with their noses, I called Aaron. Told him I had the dogs with me.

He gave a gruff, "Okay." Then hung up. Something had gathered his britches in a twist.

I put the dogs into the storeroom so I could set up for the tourney. It was nearing 3 PM and opening time, still a few hours before Karyn and Tom were scheduled to arrive. But, there was still plenty of time to investigate more. I decided to take a look at the football player brothers before I started loading bottles and mugs into the cooler. I settled on one of the stools in front of the bar and was typing the search back into Google, when Aaron called again.

He said, "Peaches is at the airport. Can you pick her up?"

"Excuse me?" Did he just say what I hoped he hadn't?

"Peaches flew into Lambert just a few minutes ago. I'm tied down here, so you need to go get her. I'll pick her up at the bar after work. And before you get all pissy with me, no, I didn't know she was coming either."

Dammit! Peaches was visiting, ostensibly to give comfort. It didn't thrill me. I loved her dearly, but it would add extra weight of being a tour guide. I didn't need that right then and Aaron didn't either. What I needed was answers, not comfort. Even though my aunt was in St. Louis for us, mostly me, she'd want to see the Arch, the Museums, Forest Park, the Grant Historical Site, Union Station, the Old Capital, everything. It would be exhausting.

With a deep sigh, I texted Karyn. *Can you come to work now?*

Yeah, sure. What's up?

Peaches just flew into Lambert.

WooHoo! She'd loved Peaches from the first second they'd met while we all still lived in Texas. Often, the two of them could be found shopping together. I had, in fact, been suspicious that Karyn, when she'd first proposed moving to St. Louis, was a spy for my smothering aunt. But nothing had come of it.

Karyn quickly followed her text with a dancing Carleton from the old Fresh Prince TV show. Followed by another fast text. *Why didn't you tell me?* Pouty face.

I was almost done typing my answer when another text came. *You didn't know, did you?*

I deleted my three lines of unfinished text. *Hell, no.*

On the way. GIF image of a jet flying across the screen.

Peaches was my next call.

She answered with, "Surprise!"

"What are you doing here?"

"Is that any way to greet me?"

"Sorry. Hi. How are you? What are you doing here?"

"Your brother called me this morning. He told me what happened. I turned right around to your uncle and told him to get used to eating his own cooking for a while. I was on a plane in an hour. My best girl needs me. I'm here. End of story."

Aaron. Figured. He may not have known she was coming, but he certainly had been the catalyst. I was miffed at him. But perhaps more miffed at myself for the bubble of happiness that swelled up because my aunt was there. I didn't bother to remind Peaches she had another 'best girl' at home: her daughter. "I'm waiting on Karyn to take over here, and then I'll be on the way."

"No rush. I still have my luggage to get. And there are lots of cute shops for souvenirs for the kids."

"Try not to buy too much; you can get the same gifts cheaper elsewhere. I'll call you when I arrive." We disconnected.

While waiting for Karyn, I took the dogs outside to do their business along the edge of the back parking lot. Officer Leach waved at me from the safety of his patrol car. I nodded coolly in return. My interest hadn't changed in the past few minutes.

Even though I was happy, my anxiety had ramped up with the news of the impending visit and wouldn't calm again. I closed my eyes and took a deep breath, slowly blowing out through pursed lips. Did this several times. My mind had just started to clear when Karyn's little black Nissan zipped into the back lot. She lived close enough to walk, but rarely did.

My friend frowned out the driver's side window at the dogs. I held up one hand to let her know to wait, and ushered the pooches back into the storeroom. Turned on the radio to confuse any noises they'd hear. Went back outside.

Karyn met me halfway across the lot. She jutted her chin at the police car. "He going to stay?"

"I think that's the plan." I didn't look that way, I didn't want to see him wave again. There was just something grating about him, though he'd done nothing to make me feel that way. Perhaps it was just the day.

She nodded, not interested in Officer Leach either. Focused on me. "Any notes?"

"Just babysit. Stay out of the storeroom. I'm coming straight back. We can set up for the tourney then."

She nodded. "Good luck with traffic." She turned for the bar.

I grimaced. Rush hour started at 3 PM, now, and lasted all the way to 7 PM. It was why Smugglers opened at three. Safe harbor and all. But it was bad timing for a round trip to the airport. I climbed into my Jeep and pulled out of the parking lot. Or rather, tried to. Vehicles of every shape and description lined Olive Street in both directions, and none were moving. It begged the question, how had my friend arrived to the bar so quickly? What would she have done?

I channeled my inner Karyn and stuck my hand out the window. Waved it frantically at the next car in line. Edged the cattle catcher on the bumper of my Jeep into the lane in front of a black SUV. The driver obediently stopped, albeit with a sour expression on her face, and my Jeep slid into the queue. Every time I had to change lanes, my hand went out the window, waving frantically. More than a few cars honked and I caught the single finger salute a couple times, but it felt good to be Karyn.

The best part of the drive was spent shaking my head, either at the idiot drivers in front of me, or at Peaches's arrival. But mostly at my aunt. What was I going to do with her? After the financial bath I'd just taken, money was tight. Aaron had his hot new job to protect; he wouldn't be any help. I decided my salvation would be Karyn. She could take my aunt shopping. I could send them to any number of shopping venues. Notably, Union Station and The Hill. And they could go sight-seeing at all the tourist stops, too. Perfect!

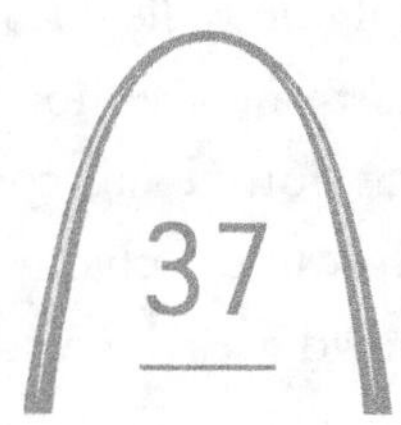

37

By the time the Karyn version of me reached Lambert International Airport, I was humming along with the radio. Short-term parking was jammed, but a red Camaro pulled out in time for me to zip in. I turned off the Jeep and hopped out. Called Peaches on the way to the terminal.

"Hi, Honey." Her Texas drawl filled the phone. "You here?"

"Just pulled in. Where are you?"

"I'm at Starbucks. My dogs are tired!"

"Which Starbucks?"

She paused. "The one at the airport."

"There are several Starbucks there. Which one?"

"I'm upstairs, if that helps."

It did, a little. "The one in the middle or all the way at the end?"

"Oh, I'm at the one at the end."

"Okay. I'm on my way. Stay put." I knew from experience that if I didn't add that last, she'd try to meet me halfway. That was nothing to attempt at Lambert during the busy hours. Once in the terminal, I snaked around groups of people and rode the escalator to the top floor where long heavy lines bulged into the main walkway from ticket counters with far too few overworked agents. People of every shape and color towed excited children or carryons in a sluggish river from the counters to the gates. They clustered in front of flight information monitors along the walls like farm animals at a feeding trough. The noise was catastrophic, echoing off the walls to double and triple itself. And it was hot. No air conditioner could compete with that many bodies. This time, I channeled my inner Bobby and shouldered through the crowd, weaving without slowing until reaching my destination, sweating buckets.

I looked around the Starbucks seating area for the familiar brassy blond hair and the ample bosom. But Peaches wasn't there.

I pulled out my phone to call her, turning to scan the crowd. For a split-second, the sea of people parted and exposed a dark-haired man standing by a central kiosk. He wore a beige oxford-type shirt and jeans. My mind automatically superimposed the killer's image over the man – as it had with every man I'd seen lately. Same jawline. Same body frame. Across the walkway, he looked at me with vivid blue eyes. Was that Lee Garret? Was he at the airport to fly back to Alberta?

The crowd surged again and he was lost from sight. I dropped my phone back into my pocket and pushed through the bulges of people only to reach the kiosk and find him gone. Bodies hemmed me out of the traffic lane, blocking my view down the walkway. A row of chairs lined a nearby wall and I pushed through the wall of bodies to them. Climbed onto the only empty one between a grandfatherly man and a woman holding a child. Judging by the narrowed-eye scrutiny from the woman, I'd usurped her child's seat. I smiled at her and said, "I'll just be one second. I was separated from someone."

It brought a cessation of the glare, but there was no return smile, nor words of encouragement. I sighed. Apparently someone else was having a harried day, too. I turned around in the chair, slowly scanning the sea of faces. Saw my mystery man disappear on the escalator to the lower level and the C concourse.

I jumped down and shoved into the mass of people, once again calling on my inner Bobby. The heat from the bodies was oppressive and by the time I reached the head of the escalator, my shirt was pitted in sweat. I watched the panorama below. Customers flowed in and out of shops with shopping bags, snacks, magazines, and suitcases. Most had that world-weary blank stare on their face as they milled about, looking for something to do while they waited for their flight. On the concourse, travelers added to the queue at the security gate. Garret was at the head of the line and stepped through as I watched.

Shaking my head at my luck, I pulled out my phone again, moving out of the flow of traffic. Surprisingly, the SLPD detective answered instead of letting it roll over to voice mail. I jumped in before he could even give his usual last name greeting. I said, "It's Sylvia Wilson. I'm at Lambert. Garret is here, heading down Concourse C toward the gates."

"Dammit!" He disconnected. No goodbye or anything. Detectives!

Within a few minutes, the security agents at the gate became more animated than usual. Several of them hustled down the concourse. It didn't take long before they were back, empty-handed. Either Garret had eluded them, or they'd left him at the gate. I called Eccheli back.

His answer was brief. "Security checked his tickets. He's headed back to Alberta. We don't have enough to arrest him, so we legally can't make him stay. My question is, what are you doing there? Are you following him?"

I really didn't like the way the conversation turned, so I put on my best wronged voice and said, "No. I'm not following him. I'm picking up my aunt. She just arrived. It's not my fault Garret is here too."

"Pick up your aunt. Go home." Disconnected again. Damn detectives!

I repocketed my phone and swam through the tide of travelers back to Starbucks, muttering to myself. Peaches stood in front of the vendor, with her arms folded across her large chest. Her scolding frown made me feel like a disobedient teen again. Brilliant green eyes that had known every secret this teenager could have had glittered at me from a weathered face normally filled with laugh wrinkles. She wore jeans and a jungle print v-neck shirt that hugged her curves all the way down to her trim waist. Top-heavy was a good description of her. My uncle had fallen for her the first time he'd seen her. So had most men.

She shook her finger at me. "Where have you been? You told me you'd be right here. You told me to stay put. Then you don't show?"

"I'm so sorry. I'll explain on the way to the bar." I kissed her on the cheek.

She, in turn, pinned me in a bone-crushing hug. "It's so good to see my girl!"

Again, I bit down on the urge to remind her that she called Stetson, her daughter, her girl too. And whichever of her friends she happened to be with. It was hardly exclusive.

Once I extricated myself and was able to give her a proper return hug, I said, "We're going straight back to the bar. I have to finish setting up for the tournament. Aaron will come get you to drop your suitcases at my house and will take you to supper."

She waved it off and took my hand. "Pooh! Anything that works for you. I'm here to help. Now tell me all about it."

"On the way. Right now, let's just concentrate on getting out of here."

I picked up her big suitcase while she grabbed her small one. We pushed into the turmoil of people and slowly, silently, edged toward the escalator, then through the baggage claim area, and out the exit. It was a short walk to the Jeep.

"Oh. You still have this old thing?" Peaches wrinkled her nose. She'd rescued me a time or two while I was learning the basics of car maintenance.

"It's not old." It wasn't easy to keep the petulant pout out of my voice, but my aunt was gearing up to something and this was no time to show weakness. I threw the luggage onto the back bench and we climbed into the twin bucket seats up front.

"I just thought you would have traded up, now that you own your own bar."

"This is my third bar." With a turn of the key, the motor roared to life. I faced her. "As you well know."

Her green eyes were calculating when she spoke. She was a very smart woman, though sometimes played dumb when it suited. "I just think you could own a bar anywhere. Even Texas."

"Aaron's job is here." Not sure what the location of my bar had to do with my choice of vehicle, I pulled the Jeep through the maze of ramps to the exit and paid for an hour's parking. She would either tie the two points of conversation together somewhere, or in typical Peaches fashion, she wouldn't.

"We always need police in Texas. What with those rowdy boys 'n all."

"Aaron likes St. Louis. So do I. We're staying."

"It's cheaper in Texas. You could afford a new car."

I nodded to myself. There it was. The tie-in. "We're happy here."

We lapsed into silence as we pulled onto the ramp for the highway. Most people were trying to get out of the downtown area at this hour, headed to their homes. Traffic was better headed into the city, as we were. But, it was still bad, because it was now a little after 4 PM, the beginning of the restaurant rush.

Once we were moving at a decent speed on the congested highway, Peaches said, "So, tell me all about it. Start at the very beginning, when you found the body. Don't skip anything."

I told her about the body. About Patty Degere. "The second time I visited her, we found a scrap of paper with part of a name and phone number at Blaisdale's apartment."

"You took that to the police?"

"Patty did. The receptionist at Blaisdale's place of employment told me that he had a second job and was planning on taking her on a trip. She went to the cops with that, too. It made me think that he'd been robbing other places, but Aaron couldn't find anything."

An idiot in a bright yellow Saturn swerved into our lane right in front of us, and I tapped the brakes to give him room. Peaches braced herself and swore. She said through tight lips, "I'll never get used to city driving."

I watched her out of the corner of my eye. When the wild-eyed tension left her face again, I said, "Bobby and I identified the guy we think is the killer. The cops interviewed him when he showed up at the bar again. His name is Lee Garett. The trouble is, his address is bogus and I haven't been able to find anything about him online."

"Not everyone is online, my dear."

"Not everyone is on social media. That's different than info being online. These days, there's usually something somewhere: a newspaper article or a listing. I can't find anything. I did, however, find when he broke in a couple weeks before the murder. Took that to Eccheli too. The lab is backed up with all the trace evidence from the initial murder, but they're rushing the analysis on the blood from my back door."

She gave a visible start, her eyes wide open. "Blood?"

Oops! I thought Aaron would have said something. It seemed he told her everything else. "The goon put a bloody handprint on my sliding glass door. It wasn't from the dogs, so we're just waiting for the lab. It's a priority. But Garret is why I was late picking you up. I saw him at the airport." I told her about the non-outcome of that.

"Well, I, for one, am glad he's gone. Good riddance, I say. Don't need to be distracted by worrying he's going to break in again. I'm here for you. Whatever you need. Two heads are better than one."

I stifled a groan. That was exactly what I'd feared. "Maybe you and Karyn can do a little shopping while you're here, too."

She dimpled. "Maybe."

38

We arrived at the bar a little before 5 PM. Officer Leach annoyed me by waving again as we entered. Karyn had done everything she could without going into the storeroom, leaving the rest for me. She slipped out the door to finish some errands soon after greeting Peaches. Aaron came over pronto-like after work and whisked my aunt away to drop her bags at my house, and then to take her to a meal. They'd promised to bring me something. I wasn't holding my breath.

Around 6 PM, I carted boxes of bottles from the back room and began stocking them into the cooler. There was still an hour before Karyn would be back and Tom was due to show. Because of the arrival of Peaches, I hadn't gone back to my phone search, but it was still in the plans.

Once the coolers were stocked and ready to go, I took out my phone and looked up the football brothers again. It was an old article, but it said they'd lived in Walent, a little town a couple hours south of St. Louis. No street address. I pulled up an online directory and found their address and phone number. Still in Walent. Entered it into my phone notes.

I considered my options. I could call them to ask if they had a brother. Or I could assume they were somehow connected to the killer, take a trip down there, and poke around a little. If there turned out to be no brother, somewhere in that town was another answer. I knew it. I could feel it. Tomorrow, then, I might take a trip.

Even though Garret had, in theory, flown out of the city, the squad car stayed parked outside the back door of the bar for most of the night. I took the dogs out back for a potty break. Leach was gone, thankfully. He'd been replaced by two others who nodded when I waved. Smugglers, of course, won the tourney round, jousting with a small bar just a few blocks down.

As soon as the last game was over, most people left. Only a few remained for the rest of the evening, watching the first of the Cardinals games against the Dodgers out on the west coast. It was a three game series, then we'd go on to play 2 games against the San Diego Padres. Finally, we'd come back home with a day off.

I told Karyn and Tom about the bonus I'd decided to give them, then sent them home. Tuesday nights were usually a bit slow anyway and I needed to unstress. But it felt a bit creepy in there and I was glad of the patrol car parked outside. As the night wore on, it felt like everyone was watching me, though every time I checked, every person in the bar was engrossed in something else. Not that there were a lot of people. Even the room itself seemed gloomy, sometimes even a bit sinister. The shadows thrown by the dim lights were long and reaching. Every odd noise made me pause and listen. My bar gun, the Ruger, was under the counter, out of sight on a hidden shelf, but within reach. I kept checking the booths and bathrooms for someone hidden.

Aaron and Peaches showed up about eleven-thirty, just as I finished washing mugs from the tourney crowd. Beside me on the bar was a half-eaten bag of chips: my supper. Apparently they'd been at the restaurant the whole time. And had brought no bag of food for me. Hence, I decided I'd been the topic of conversation. Dark bags were slung under my brother's eyes and his shoulders were slumped. It wasn't just from no sleep the night before, but also from the whole mess wearing him down. I imagined I didn't look much better. He peered around the room, saw only two patrons remaining, and said to me, "What about closing early until this whole thing is over?"

Peaches was on edge, twisting her small body to glance all around the room as if expecting someone to jump out of the shadows. If she could have rolled into a ball and hidden in the corner, I think she would have. Her face was grim, her eyes wide. All she said was, "Honey, we don't need to invite trouble."

I nodded. Truth was, I was exhausted. My thoughts had been running along the same track. And I couldn't have Aaron getting too tired by staying up until my regular closing time, either. His FBI assignment would suffer. But that didn't mean I liked shutting the doors early. "Not the weekend, though."

"'Course."

Peaches said nothing, just continued her surveillance of the shadows.

I was actually surprised my brother agreed so easily to the weekend hours; he'd never been crazy about my working in a bar. It was dangerous, he'd said when I first started. I now owned the bar I worked in, but his sentiments remained the same. Peaches, once a bartender herself, had gone to bat for me, so he'd learned to keep the comments to himself.

He made the necessary announcement to the two patrons, escorted them to the front door, and locked it behind them.

I cleared the register. Peaches fidgeted.

Aaron said, "Eccheli discovered how Garret got into your house." It seemed he wasn't completely frozen out.

I didn't look up. But, I stopped breathing. Lost count of the cash in my hand. "Oh? And how was that?"

"Apparently he breached Almera's firewall, copied the whole code for the alarm, inserted his own piece and pasted the whole thing back in. Probably took just a few seconds, but it took the IT guys a long time to find it."

Made sense. And pretty crafty too. All the code would have been suspect and each line would have had to be checked by the Almera techs. "And what about my dogs? Did anyone say why I wasn't notified about the police being called earlier in the night? I should have been because of the killer. Eccheli promised he'd find out, but I've heard nothing."

On the periphery of my vision, I saw him put his hands on his hips. He hung his head. "I've been checking into that. It seems the dogs were quiet when the patrol drove by. There was nothing out of the ordinary. The call to you just slipped through the cracks. I'm sorry."

Lightning should have cracked from my eyes when I looked at him. "Slipped through the cracks?"

He lifted his gaze and met mine. Had to give him credit there. "I gave them hell about it Syl. I really did. Took it all the way to Command. I was assured it wouldn't happen again."

"Damn well better not." I dropped my eyes. My insides felt like molten lava. Slipped through the cracks! My dogs could have been killed. I could have been killed.

I felt Peaches's cool hand on my arm. "Water under the bridge, Honey. Let it go. They'll do better if there's a next time."

They'd better. I asked Aaron, "What about the blood on the door? Whose was that?"

"Lab's backed way up. Even though it's a priority, it could be a while before we get an answer. As for your question about other bar robberies in the area, there haven't really been any."

Neither one of us said any more, but I was on a slow simmer. That molten lake of lava wasn't going to go away any time soon. Blaisdale had been murdered in my bar, not even in a robbery. Just cold blooded murder. And the slipup about my dogs was just plain unforgivable. I recounted the cash and put it in my bag to take home. I dropped my Ruger into the bag with the money. I felt safer carrying a gun. Did a quick clean. Then fetched the pooches. When I introduced them to Peaches, they gave her a full sniffing, seemed satisfied with what they found, and ignored her from then on. I set the alarm, and we left.

We all followed Aaron as he walked to the patrol car and leaned over the passenger's side window. He said, "If this guy's around the house when we get there, I want him caught. One of you keep an eye on the civilians and the other take the back door. I'll go in the front and clear."

Though Mendez, the cop on the passenger's side, had joined SLPD at the same time as Aaron, the other cop, Smithson, was several years senior. But for whatever reason, neither of them argued with the plan. Respect, I guess. I was Aaron's sister, ergo, this was his show. Or maybe word had filtered down about the screwup with the dogs.

They followed us in a mini parade on the highway: Aaron, the silent Peaches and me, and finally the patrol car. We traversed through the series of turns after leaving the highway until we reached my house. Aaron and I parked out front, but the cop car went past and circled through the alley to drop Mendez before it came back to park behind us. When Smithson was in place by my Jeep, Aaron stepped out of his truck, his service revolver low beside his leg. He watched the silent street and the neighbors' yards, then he started to the house.

I pulled out the Ruger and opened the door of the Jeep. Peaches grabbed at my arm to stop me, but it did no good. She should have known better. Aaron looked askance at me as I fell in beside him, but wisely didn't protest. He *did* know better.

I nodded to my brother that I was ready and we moved silently to the front door. I unlocked it and deactivated the alarm while Aaron covered the space beyond. When I reached for the light switch, he tapped my shoulder and shook his head.

We listened, heard nothing, and moved into the dark front room. My heart was thudding, and the sharp bite of adrenalin tightened my gaze in the dark. The furniture took on sinister meaning as hiding places for a malevolent monster. The island in the kitchen made a barrier from behind which someone could spring out at us.

We'd done this dozens of times when we were young in Iowa. Dad had often taken us to the law enforcement training site or an abandoned building to practice. His hope was that we'd both grow up to be cops like him. He'd said there was no higher calling. At least Aaron had followed in his footsteps. I sometimes wondered if Dad would have been disappointed in me if he'd known I'd be nothing but a bartender.

Aaron went right and I held left, my weapon pointed down the hall to the two bedrooms. My brother moved slowly, checking everything. Eventually, he came up behind me, reached around and placed his hand on my arm. I lowered the Ruger while he slipped around to the lead, then brought it up at an angle to the left while he angled his to the right.

There was nobody hiding in either dark bedroom. The beds looked ominously like flat table coffins. The bathroom was empty, too. I even pulled the ladder to the crawlspace down and took a look up there. Nobody. Aaron turned on the lights. Mendez came through the back of the house to escort me out to the Jeep for Peaches and the pooches, who took extreme vocal exception of somebody new with their mom. They quieted after only half the neighborhood woke, and we were all escorted back inside, where the dogs cleared every room again.

39

would have thought that with coming home and going to bed early, not to mention everything that had happened that day, I would have been wide awake all night. But it had been the Day From Hell. Despite getting the occasional good sleep, the restlessness of the recent nights took their toll, too, and I fell into a deep, unmoving sleep. When I woke at 7 AM, my body ached all over from lying like the dead in the same position all night.

The murmur of voices reached me from the front of the house. Aaron and Peaches. He was getting ready for work. And though Peaches had been a bartender for quite a while, she'd acclimated quickly to ranch life after she'd married my uncle. It seemed even at that early hour, I was the slugabed.

I rolled to my feet and wandered to the kitchen in my hot pink pajamas. Apparently my two guests had been speaking about me, because they both stopped dead when I made my appearance. Peaches even had her mouth open as if she were mid-sentence. I walked past her and grabbed my favorite mug. Poured coffee. Turned to them. "Must be pretty serious."

Peaches colored. "I was just telling Aaron it would be nice to have you come visit."

I turned my gaze his way. He wouldn't dare lie to me. He'd tried it only once and it had produced a devastating bruise on his arm when I found out.

He said, "It might be a good idea. Just until this thing blows over."

I nodded to myself. I'd figured that was the topic. "I will go visit *when* this has blown over. Right now, I'm going to get dressed. When I come out, I want you gone to work." I pointed at my brother.

My finger rounded toward my aunt. "Neither of you get to bring it up again. Understand?"

As one they both nodded, clearly not happy.

I walked down the hallway to my bedroom, blowing on my coffee. Dressed in a solid navy blue tee. It felt like a no nonsense day. After straightening my room, I returned to the kitchen. Peaches was alone in the front room. She cast her gaze everywhere but on me. I dropped a couple pieces of bread in the toaster. Refilled my coffee. When my toast was done, I took it to the couch and plopped down next to my Aunt. I said, "I'm thinking of taking a short trip a couple hours south of here. But first I had planned on going to a local gun range. Do you want to go with me?"

"I'd love to go on a trip with you. And as for the gun range, do you really need to ask?" Her face broke into a wide grin. No, I didn't need to ask.

I brought out all four guns from their new hiding places. Emptied and placed them in a sealed lock box with the Ruger from the bar, and we drove to the firing range on Gravois Road, both of us cursing at all the stop-and-go construction. The bright sunshine and moderate weather was wasted on me. I couldn't have cared less. But, Peaches's head swiveled from side to side as she tried to take in everything.

When we reached the gun range, it was just a bit after 9 and the place was mostly empty. The range manager sold us targets and new ammo for all five weapons and lit the furthest two lanes. Peaches took two of my pistols and I took the other three.

I placed my target, then realized it was a person's silhouette, whereas I normally chose the bullseye or a variation of the same.

It gave me pause.

I'd have no problems shooting a person, but could I actually kill someone, if necessary? My mind flittered, unbidden, to the memory of Blaisdale's body and the heavy pool of blood on the floor of the bar. Then, as always, the memory segued into that of my parents when I'd seen them dead at the funeral home. Could I take a life like theirs had been taken from Aaron and me?

Not on just a whim. That was for sure. Maybe that was a good thing. But what if it was a choice between my life or someone else's? Would the identity of the other person make a difference? If I killed someone, even someone who was trying to kill me, would that make me a murderer? Not in the eyes of the law, but in my own eyes?

Acutely aware that my thoughts bordered on cliché, I loaded my first weapon, the Dirty Harry, and took aim at the silhouette. My shot went way wide. Trying a few more times brought the same results. I emptied the ammo, set the gun aside. Beside me, Peaches was belting shots down the lane and obliterating her target. I went to fetch a bullseye.

My aim improved dramatically with the new target. Picturing Garret's face superimposed over the center of the target didn't have the same effect as the silhouette did. I finished with my three guns and swapped with Peaches. By the time we each finished with all five guns, the centers of both our targets were punched out. I considered the firing range fees money well-spent and decided to carry a gun on me for a while, just until this whole Lee Garret thing blew over.

We returned home via a different construction-free route. After cleaning all five guns, I picked up the Browning 1911-22, a sweet single-action piece that held 10 rounds in the clip, and slid it into an ankle holster. Peaches raised her eyebrows. "You gonna carry that?"

I nodded. She reached for the Ruger from the bar. "You got another ankle bracelet for me?"

"Just a shoulder holster."

"I have a jacket."

I handed her the holster and she fetched her jacket, a bright floral thing that hurt my eyes. It looked good on Peaches though.

On the trip, she told me everything that had happened with everyone in our Texas hometown for the eighteen months Aaron and I had been away. She talked nonstop on our southwest journey down I-44. Or rather, she shouted. Heat was quickly building with the ascent of the sun toward its zenith and we had the top off the Jeep to cool us down. The noise level was high. Just past Sullivan, we turned south and traveled until we reached our destination at a little after 12 noon.

Walent was indeed a small town. According to the welcome sign, it boasted 1,526 people and was the home of prize-winning barbe-cued beef. The road led straight into a downtown roundabout that had four main exits and four small alleys. The address I wanted was 134 East 2nd South, so I reasoned if I took the southern exit, I'd find myself on, or near, the right road.

Sure enough, the road I took was South Broad. I cut over two blocks to the east to what the sign said was East 2nd South. It quickly became a gravel access road that bordered an ancient railroad line. 134 was the second house in the 130 block. White ranch-style. Filthy siding. Trash in the yard.

Peaches, who'd stopped talking when we'd made the last turn, looked at me pensively. "Why are we here?"

I parked and said, "These people may know the guy who broke into my place."

I knew that wouldn't be enough of an answer for her, so I quickly climbed out of my Jeep hoping to forestall any further conversation. I said, "I won't be long."

"Oh, no. You're SO not going in there alone." She joined me on the edge of the road, patting her brazenly blond hair into place. "You'd just be inviting a whole passel of trouble."

Her use of the word 'passel' made me smile. Very Texas. Very Peaches. I nodded as solemnly as I could. Not that I was planning on a next time or anything. She huffed at me, which was her way of letting me off the hook, and led the way up the front walk. I rang the bell.

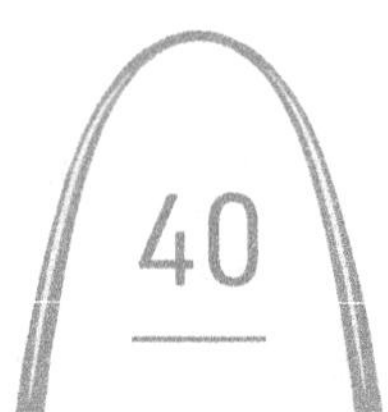

I rang the bell again. The house seemed to be as empty as the streets around us. I'd wasted a four-hour drive roundtrip and had no idea what to do next. I was just about to return to the Jeep when I heard movement.

The door flung open and a pot-bellied man in greasy tee and grey, baggy briefs stood at the entry. "Yeah. What is it?"

"Are you Lee or Garret Pike?"

"Garret. What do you want?"

"This may sound strange, but do you have a third brother?"

"Yeah." He scratched his balls.

Peaches could stand it no more. With a flaming face she said, "Boy, don't you have any manners? Get yourself inside and put some pants on!"

He shrugged. "This is my home. I live here. You're just visiting." But he turned to comply. We followed him inside.

Peaches looked askance at me with wide eyes. I motioned to one of the stained recliners. The place was devoid of any decoration. Bare paneled walls led the way down a hallway to three doorways. A small kitchen with refrigerator, stove, tiny table, and doorless cabinets opened off the living room. The place was warm already – no air conditioning I guess – and it smelled like old McDonalds. Like

Blaisdale's car. Garret came back into the room, dressed in crusty sweats. "Want a beer?"

I shook my head. Peaches scoffed. "It's just noon."

He headed into the kitchen and came back popping a can of Budweiser. "So. What's this about?"

I asked, "What's your brother's name? Do you have a picture?"

He looked around at the bare walls. "His name's Ray. Our house burned down a few years back. Took most of the pictures with it."

"Would it be possible for me to see his room?"

"He moved out. Doesn't have a room anymore." He shook his head. Took a step toward me, scowling. Stopped. Took a swig from the can. "Look lady, why the hell do you want to know about him so bad?"

I blinked and looked at Peaches. This had taken quite an unexpected turn. From down the hall, we heard a heavy groan and footsteps. I began to think about my gun.

Peaches rose from the chair where she'd perched. She placed her hand on my shoulder. Spoke quietly. "The fact is, your brother and my daughter were a couple. Now she finds out she's pregnant and she wants to talk to him."

Garret's eyebrows shot up. He turned and shouted down the hall-way. "Hey Lee! Get in here! RayRay's knocked up some girl."

The heat of embarrassment burned on my face. Lee, who could have been a twin, joined his brother and they both stared at my stomach.

Peaches said, "So, you understand why we need to find out as much as we can about … RayRay."

Lee gave a huge guffaw. "I always kinda thought he was gay." Garret nodded.

I assumed my role in the lie. "I assure you he isn't. Why would you think that?"

Garret shrugged. "Never saw him with a girl." Sat in the recliner recently abandoned by Peaches. Started to scratch his balls through the sweats, glanced at her, then apparently thought the better of it.

Lee chimed in, "Never saw him with anyone." He sat in the other recliner, thereby leaving us to stand.

So, Ray Pike had been a quiet child. An introvert in a houseful of extroverts. I could imagine he'd had quite a tough time of it. "When was the last time you saw him?"

After another swig of beer, Garret said, "He calls us from Minnesota sometimes, but he hasn't been back to visit. I guess, after our parents died in the fire, me and Lee aren't enough reason."

Minnesota? Parents died? What?

"Maybe we have the wrong person. What does your brother look like?"

"Skinny. Tall. Brown hair. Brown eyes." He shrugged.

"Blue eyes." Lee threw it over his shoulder at his brother.

While they argued about the color of his eyes, I glanced at Peaches and gave her a small nod. I raised my voice to be heard over the brothers. "That sounds like my Ray. You said your house burned down. How did the fire start?"

They both stopped. Glanced at each other. Shrugged. Lee finally said, "No one knows. Just one of those things. We weren't home or we would have burned up too."

Peaches asked, "Where were you?"

He frowned. "We got invited to a party a couple towns over. Ray drove us, even though he was underage. But when we got there, no one knew about any party. We came home to the fire."

Garret spoke up. "It was really weird. Lots of little things happened to our folks before the fire. You just knew something bad was coming."

"What kinds of little things?"

"The wheel came off Dad's truck when they took a drive to look at the fall leaves. A skunk got trapped in the garage – back then we had a nice house with a garage – ruined some of Mom's favorite clothes. Dad fell through the deck. Little stuff."

"Did anything happen to you or just your parents?"

"Oh no. It was like they had all the bad luck and we had all the good."

I had a bad feeling in the pit of my stomach. Maybe it was just the smell. Or it could have been a premonition. "How old were you when the fire happened?"

Lee shrugged. "Twelve?"

"So Ray would have been fourteen? Did he get along with your parents?"

"What the hell does that have to do with anything? I've just about had enough of you." Garret half rose out of his stained recliner, but settled back in when I placed my hand on my tummy.

I said, "I just want to find out if he's going to be a good father. If he had trouble with his parents it might tell me something."

He shrugged. "I dunno. They didn't talk much. I don't really remember."

Lee avoided my gaze. Seemed like he didn't remember either.

Peaches was gently pressing on my shoulder, giving me a cue that she wanted to leave. I ignored her. One last try. "Are you sure you don't have a picture of him? He told me your parents adored him. We really might have the wrong guy."

After a moment, when I'd just about given up, Lee stood. "Yeah. I think I've got one or two. They're old though."

At my nod, he lumbered down the hall to his room. Returned within seconds. The first photo was when the three brothers had still been in grade school. The two wore matching football jerseys and stood directly in front of their parents, who both looked athletic as well and had proud and loving hands on their shoulders. A taller, older Raymond stood to the side of his mother. He was leaning slightly away from her and even through the heavy glasses I could see the hurt of betrayal in his eyes.

The second photo was smudged and smelled a bit like smoke. It was much like the first, but the boys were all about junior high school age. Matching football jerseys on the two. Again, proud parents with possessive hands. Ray to the side of his mother. It had to have been just before they died. This time, though, young RayRay was turned in toward his parents. His hands were laid flat against his legs, as if he'd been coached to relax. Malice spilled through his glasses. A chill swept through me. I'd seen that look before.

I handed the photos back to Lee. "This is your brother? He doesn't look anything like my boyfriend. This isn't him. I'm sorry. Thank you for your time."

Peaches and I hustled out the door. In the brief time we'd been inside, the seats of the Jeep had turned into fried sheets of agony. We didn't say anything until we could finally sit and were rushing home. She looked over at me and asked, "That was him, wasn't it?"

I nodded. "Oh yeah. It was him."

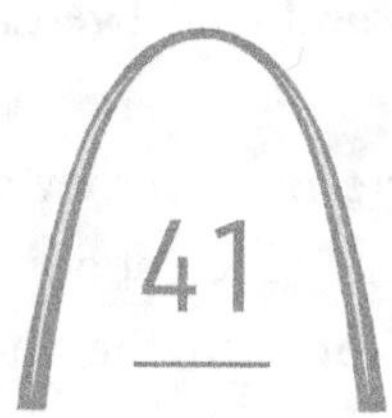

41

Peaches and I were about twenty minutes into our trip home before either of us spoke again. The center highway dashes were blipping by at an alarming rate, and try as I might, I couldn't take my shock-leaden foot off the gas. The Jeep top was still off because of the heat, and wind whipped our hair in every direction.

My aunt cleared her throat. Leaned into me. Asked, "You're sure it's him?"

I nodded. She apparently saw me, because her next comment was, "We should have taken pictures of the photos."

I nodded again. "That would have been a good idea, but I'm not sure how we could have worked that in, especially since I told them he wasn't the father of my make-believe baby."

We lapsed into silence again and she sat upright in her seat. The pavement growled beneath the heavy duty tires of my Jeep. We were traveling well over ninety, but Peaches, usually a backseat driver, said nothing. My mind kept jumping from the boy in the photos to the man in the bar, to Blaisdale dead on the floor, to Pike's dead parents, to the break-in at my house.

Peaches was again the one who broke the silence. "The fire doesn't seem like an accident. The boys were called away. Do you think RayRay killed his parents?"

"Don't you?" I glanced at her.

She gave a terse single nod, and I returned my attention to the road and our escape.

She said, "He was fourteen when they died. Like you."

Like me. I wasn't sure how I felt about that. Losing your parents at any age was hard, but at fourteen, the whole world was topsy-turvy anyway. You were just trying to figure out yourself. Parents would help sort everything. Aaron kinda already had figured himself out, but I'd had a hard time without them. Only Peaches's intervention had saved me. Raymond Pike had no one to save him but the two exceptional specimens of younger brothers, who looked like they still hadn't figured themselves out yet.

Pike had killed his parents. I had killed mine. Pike's crime had been one of meticulous planning and attention to detail. Mine had been of a troublesome teen and frustrated parents. I'd been in a fight at school. Kicked the ass of some boy I no longer remembered. Got detention. Again. My parents had decided to walk off their anger and discuss how to punish me. That's why they were on that back road where the drunk driver mowed them down.

Thank God for Peaches. She'd helped me screw my head back on right.

Odd that Pike had given his brothers a pass, saving them from the judgment of the fire. Did he consider them innocent in the family drama?

I said, "Did you see his eyes in the pictures? He looked at me that way the other night at the bar."

Peaches didn't say anything, and when I glanced at her, her lips were pressed tightly together. I knew that expression. She was angry. Back home in Texas, even the Sheriff got out of her way when she was like that.

I slowed our headlong assault on the highway and pulled over to the margin. Took out my phone and hit speed dial for Mr. Detective. Surprisingly, he answered with his usual, "Eccheli."

"It's Sylvia Wilson. Lee Garret is actually Raymond Pike. He's got two brothers in Walent: Lee and Garret. I saw photos of him. Apparently, their parents were killed in a suspicious house fire when Pike was a teen."

"How the hell do you know all this? Where are you?"

"Just out joy riding. My aunt's in town, you know. Showing her the sights."

"You took her to Walent? I told you to stay out of this."

"Did you know about this?"

There was silence at the other end. Then he reluctantly said, "We knew some of it."

"Well, there. Scut work done for you. Now you can do more official stuff."

I heard a frustrated growl come from his end. When he spoke, his voice was hard. "Stop investigating. Not only are you impeding our work, you are endangering yourself. Am I clear?"

"The quicker you catch him, the safer I am. My work wasn't impeding. It was a definite help. But, I'll stop. It's all yours. Now that you're on the right track." I disconnected before he could breathe another threat. Eased back onto the highway to continue our headlong escape back to the city.

An hour down the road, we passed an intersection with a fish-fry truck. The sign said, "Fresh Buffalo Fish Sandwich and Deep Fried Chips". We were on a state highway, not an interstate, so it was nothing for me to pull over, flip around, and drive back to park with the other vehicles visiting the truck. Fry stands like this popped up at some of the state highway crossroads during the summer. The vendors usually arrived in a pickup with a deep fryer and a cash table. Some, like this one, brought a picnic table and dealt the cash and condiments off the tailgate.

We climbed out of the Jeep and stepped behind the two customers waiting for their food. When it was our turn, I ordered two meals, complete with Diet Cokes. Peaches was sweating buckets in her jacket, so after we visited the condiments boxes on the tailgate, we went back to the Jeep instead of joining other customers at the picnic table. With a grateful smile, she pulled off her jacket and shoulder holster and tucked the pistol under her seat. She lifted her arms, airing her sweat-stained pits. "Whew! I was plum roasted."

Buffalo fish were bottom dwellers from the Mississippi. Dirty fish. But oh-so-tasty. Especially beer-batter fried with hot sauce, onion, and lemon on soft white potato rolls. The chips were good too, heavily salted and peppered, mimicking the accordion look of the fish fillet by being not quite cut all the way through the potato. Twice I climbed out of the Jeep to fetch more napkins.

When I finished my sandwich, I pulled out my phone and called Tom. "Can you open the bar today?"

"You bet. I'm saving money for a trip home for Christmas." Home for him had started out in Kansas, but had moved to Florida while he was in college and working for me. Not for the first time, I wondered about his family. Tom was soft-spoken and didn't feel the need to fill silence with his voice. He'd never told me much about his past or his people.

"A surprise visit?" Hoping he would expound on it a bit.

"Yeah."

"They'll be happy to see you." Still hoping.

"Yeah." He waited.

I gave up on family introspection for the moment and told him the alarm code for Smugglers. Disconnected.

Peaches swallowed a bite of potato fries, took a deep swig of soda, and spoke. "So, what does what we learned today mean? How does it fit in with what you told me yesterday?"

I cleared my throat. "Well, we now know who our bad guy really is, that the name Lee Garret is a pseudonym. We know he's not Canadian, as he asserted."

"He told his brothers he was working in Minnesota. That's close to Canada. Do you think there's a Canadian connection?"

"Maybe. But, that's for the detectives to figure out. Not us. We're done."

She tipped the rest of her sandwich into her mouth and chewed slowly. Wiped the corners of her lips. Then asked, "But he left for Canada, right? You saw him at the airport."

"That's what Eccheli said."

42

We stopped at another roadside stand for a small box of fall plums, eating those on the way. I drove straight home, picked up the dogs, then flew to Smugglers, arriving a little before 4. The dogs went into the storeroom. Peaches and I both tucked our weapons into the safe. Tom didn't comment, but watched us silently and paused from stocking beer bottles long enough to eat a plum, then washed the juice off his hands and chin before he went back to the bottles.

Karyn came in at 4:15 to steal Peaches for supper. While Tom finished the bottles, I worked in the storeroom, then turned to stocking mugs, relishing the silence. It calmed my nerves after the chaos of the past few days. After Walent. Aligning with my wishes, the bar stayed really quiet for a Wednesday afternoon. From experience, though, I knew that would change about tournament time.

It was nearing the early dinner hour when an extremely large man walked through the back door of Smugglers. He topped around 6'6" and 320 pounds. I knew him on sight; I'd seen him before, most recently ten days prior, when I'd found Blaisdale. Chief Medical Examiner, Gideon Hayes. Aaron had warned me about him. It seemed the chief medical examiner frequently delved into the sport of bare knuckles boxing. It was said that though he was fat, he was lightning quick, his fury often erupting into a blinding rage. Many had found themselves flat on the mat wondering how they'd gotten there. Aaron believed he was trying to exorcise demons from when he was in the army and sniper skinny. I'd overheard plenty of complaints about him from other cops. About how arrogant he was, even painting a line on the autopsy room floor, behind which the viewing officers were to stand until beckoned forward to be shown something.

I left the mugs and walked down the bar to him. "You're Gideon Hayes, right??"

His grey eyes flicked up to my face and then darted around the room and finally swept to the spot in front of the door. After a brief moment, he settled on a stool at the far end of the bar; the other patrons of the room were huddled in front of an early Yankees-Mets game on the big screen at the foot of the 'L', so he had the front all to himself.

He asked, "What do you have in stout?"

I took that initial eye flick as an affirmation of his identity. "I have one or two Bud Reserve Black. I also have AleSmith Speedway, Goose Island, and Founders."

"Goose Island," he grunted. His gaze pivoted to the TV above that end of the bar. It was on some game show, leftover from a previous customer.

"Mug?"

He shook his head, not moving his gaze from the screen.

I went to fetch his bottle, noting how the other patrons had discovered his presence. They leaned in to each other and spoke low, paying no attention to the game. On my way back to Hayes, I snatched up the remote for his TV and set it and the Goose Island in front of him.

He picked up both, one in each fight-scarred hand and flipped rapid-fire through the channels while he took a long pull from the bottle. I went back to my task, but watched him out the corner of my eye. The TV landed on a news broadcast and Hayes put down the remote. Eventually, the bottle settled beside it. Empty.

I moved back down the bar. "Another Goose?"

He nodded, eyes riveted to the East St. Louis mayoral campaign poll results. The man who had been considered the favorite was losing. No surprise there. He had promised to make St. Louis safe again, but then it had been discovered he'd bribed his way out of trouble in court. There was a committee or five checking into it.

I brought the beer. Hayes turned the depths of those grey eyes on me. "Got a menu?"

The news shifted to a recap of the murder in my bar. The photo I'd given Eccheli of Lee Garret – Raymond Pike – appeared with a phone number to call if anyone knew anything. When the news moved on to the next story, I wandered to the midpoint of the bar and fished out the takeout menus. When I slid them in front of him, he looked at me like I had three heads. "A bar menu."

"I don't serve food, other than snacks." I gave an offhand flick toward the tower of chips behind me.

He frowned. Didn't even glance at the chips. "That's not what I heard. I was told you had an amazing looking melon and prosciutto salad the other day."

I raised my eyebrows. Eccheli didn't seem the type to gossip about salad, no matter how delectable. Had to be Johnson. Seems she and the chief ME were chummy.

"That was my private lunch. But, if you're hungry, I'm thinking of ordering from 'The Ripe Tomato'." I shuffled through the menus and lifted the appropriate one, though truthfully, it didn't matter. If it meant bonding with Hayes, I'd eat from anywhere he wanted. I didn't really expect Hayes to gossip about my case; he didn't get all the way to Chief Medical Examiner by spilling sensitive information.

After much shuffling of menus and discarding options, we ordered from 'Atza Spaghetti'. Despite its cheesy name, they offered a to-die-for Chicken Parm. It was Tuesday; their best cook would be working. Tom had brought his supper, trying to save money, so he declined. He'd eat later, just before the tournament rush.

I busied myself wiping tables. When the food came, I brought a stool and sat across from Hayes with two fresh bottles of Goose. I was glad to sit. All the chaos of the day had finally caught up to me, leaving me spent. We ate quietly for a few minutes. The cook had outdone himself, and the ratio of pasta to breaded chicken and sauce was perfect. Finally, I asked, "You're ex-military, right?"

His gaze locked onto mine. "I can't talk about the case."

"I know you can't. I'm not asking. Just making conversation." Though, the fact he was in my bar and was talking to me spoke volumes about his beliefs of my innocence.

He nodded slowly. Shifted his gaze away and lifted his beer for a long pull. Said into the mouth of his bottle, "Marines."

"It shows. You carry yourself like you're more dangerous than anyone else in the room. Plus, there are the scars. I don't know anyone besides ex-military who likes that kind of fighting. Though, I'm sure there are some." I motioned to his knuckles.

He actually smiled and tipped his beer at me in a kind of salute.

We went back to our food. Silence once again became king. It seemed like I'd passed some kind of test, and the Chief Medical Examiner and I were going to be buds. My tournament players slowly wandered in a few at a time to practice. Tom served them beer while they sidled glances at Hayes. For his part, the ME focused on the weather channel. But when the clacking of pool balls got to be noisy, he heaved his bulk off the stool, nodded a goodnight to me, and walked out the back.

Immediately, the low ambient murmur of the room built in volume, gaps filled with bold laughter. It wasn't hard to figure who they were laughing about. Sudden images of the two jock brothers in Walent crammed my mind, how they'd been the favored of the family, how they'd looked down on their brother and probably every other person who wasn't athletic enough. A bad taste filled my mouth. I left Tom to eat his supper at the end of the bar vacated by Hayes.

I quietly waited on the tables until Karyn returned with Peaches. Then she took over the tables and Peaches kept company with me behind the bar.

My aunt asked, "What's with you?"

"Nothing. It's just been a long day." I knew she'd understand, I just didn't want to talk about how shitty people could become and the parallels between the brotherhood of the blue and the prize-winning boys in Walent.

She nodded, taking my words at face value. "You're telling me. I nearly dozed off on the car ride from the restaurant to here."

I studied her. Her eyes were squinty and glassy. Her face was somber. Though she hid it well, she wasn't the young woman who had taken in me and my brother all those years ago.

I said, "You could take a cab or uber home."

She patted my hand and smiled. "I'm okay, honey. I'll stick around and help out here. It'll wake me up. But, I can always call that brother of yours to come fetch me if needed. He needs to work on getting his boss in line anyway. What kind of man is that to make a boy Aaron's age work more than 12 hours a day?"

"It won't hurt Aaron and it'll look good on his file. Especially if he decides to go FBI some day."

The bar got busier as it came time for the tournament to start. Peaches did indeed perk up, as did I. My players won every match, shoving aside my earlier angst. The opposition, from a bar on the other side of I-40, didn't stick around afterward. My team didn't either, and with the players gone, the other patrons soon filtered down to just a few. I sent Tom and Karyn home after we cleaned up the place.

At 10, I turned on the second of the Cardinals-Dodgers games. The LA team took an early lead and kept piling it on. My team couldn't seem to get any traction.

By midnight, when Aaron showed, the seventh inning game was 8–1, Dodgers. I turned off the TV, chased the last patrons out, and we repeated the sequence of events from the previous night: patrol following, Aaron and I clearing rooms, Peaches and the dogs coming in last.

My aunt went directly to her room. Aaron stretched on the couch, barking at me to not turn on the TV. I had to be content to watch the remainder of the last inning on my phone, parked on my bed with my two pooches. There were no more runs for either team.

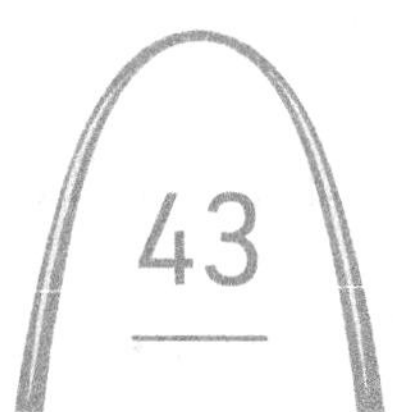

The following morning everything seemed difficult. I couldn't find my keys to the Jeep; I kept them on a separate ring from my house keys. Turns out, I'd left them in the ignition overnight. Luckily, my ride wasn't stolen. The dogs were finicky, didn't want to come in from the backyard when I pottied them. I'd forgotten to plug my phone into the charger before I went to bed, so it was dead and had to be charged.

I was still physically spent and the heat and mugginess of the morning bore down on me; I really didn't feel like putting forth any exertion. So I'd made coffee, but the pot had overflowed the basket; I was still picking grounds out of my teeth when I arrived at the training facility, late for my private 9 AM Krav Maga lesson. To top it all off, I'd left my pistol at home and I felt vulnerable and edgy.

When I entered the building, already dressed in black tights and a grey tee, there were grunts and shouts of a class in the big room. I poked my head around the corner to let Teague know I was there, but he beckoned to me. Eight sweaty students trained with kicks in the room, doubled in the mirror, to make the class look big.

"This is an intermediate class. I want you to work on your disarming skills with Julio." The man he indicated was a square scruffy fellow with a feral glint in his eyes. Just what the doctor ordered to remedy my crappy day. Every knee, every strike I tried to picture

Pike in front of me. The Pike I'd seen at the bar. Not the one in the family picture: the unloved and betrayed boy. I understood the boy. It couldn't have been easy growing up a quiet type in a house full of athletes. It looked as if his parents had given all their love to his brothers while virtually ignoring him.

The Pike I wanted to focus on was the sinister shadow creeping through my house, but it kept segueing to the boy. And it was infuriating me. The more I envisioned the boy, the more I tried to use the perpetual lava lake inside me to refocus on the monster.

After about fifteen minutes, Julio started giving nervous glances toward Teague. I caught the instructor's nod back and knew something was coming. Still, I was no match for the speed that was my sparring partner. The next strike, he was on me in a split second. I wrapped my legs around his, Judo-style, and threw his weight toward my shoulder, feinting to roll with him.

The class scattered to the walls.

Julio broke loose and we both came up like sumo wrestlers, shoulder to shoulder. He made to grab me, lunging hard. He may have known more about Krav Maga, but I was a black belt in Judo. Close quarters was my territory.

The molten lava lake within me erupted. I grabbed his hand and leaned back, bringing him with me and pushing my right knee into his chest. Up and over he went. A simple wrist lock and it was game over for him.

Teague applauded and said loudly for all the class, "This is what happens when you come up against someone better trained than you. Sylvia, here, is a black belt in Judo. Still, there were things Julio could have done. What were they?"

While the rest of the class threw out suggestions, I let loose of Julio and we both stood. I tried to catch his eye, to apologize, but he wouldn't look at me. It hadn't been my intention to humiliate him. I just wanted to work off some edge. To get a grip on who and what the real Pike was: the beast that threatened me. My crappy day just kept getting worse.

Apparently tired of the class discussion, Teague approached me with danger written all over his face, walking every bit like a tiger, despite his small stature. "Now try me."

I shook my head and stepped back. My lake of fury popped like a bubble and disappeared.

"That wasn't a suggestion."

Well, shit.

We got in the sumo position. And speaking of humiliation, I was flat on the mat before I even got a single move on him. I deserved it. He helped me up and turned to the class. "The only way to beat a better opponent is to be innovative, think quicker, and hit harder."

The class resumed their work, Julio waiting silently for instructions. Teague put his hand on my shoulder and looked in my eyes. "Anger isn't the answer."

I had no justification; I knew that. The slow burn of embarrassment heated my neck and face.

He gave my shoulder a shake. "What's the answer?"

"Preparation."

Another shake. "And what's your best weapon?"

"My brain."

He nodded. Let go. Beckoned to Julio again. "Let's teach her how to disarm someone with a gun."

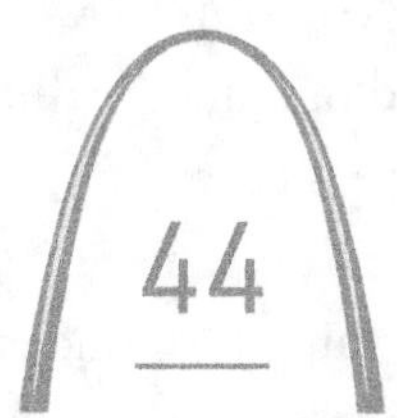

44

finished the Krav Maga lesson with more than my body bruised. Julio had taken great delight in embarrassing me in every step with the gun training. Not that he could be blamed. Teague didn't step in, but kept a close eye on us. I finally got the hang of what they were showing me, but still had a long way to go. Another lesson was scheduled for early tomorrow morning again. Teague seemed not to understand the hours bartenders kept, though I'd tried to explain.

"Nine is too early. I'll still be asleep."

He crossed his arms and waited.

"My bar usually closes at 3 AM." Though it would close earlier this evening. Still, I wanted to set the parameters. Get him out of this early morning mentality.

Nothing.

I gave in with a sigh. "Fine. I'll be here at nine."

He nodded. "You make time for what's important."

At that moment, it was a hard toss up as to which was more important to me, Smugglers or the self-defense lessons. As I left, I wondered if the early appointment was punishment for my anger.

My dusty Jeep sat at the curb in front of the facility, and I suddenly saw what Peaches had meant when she'd been talking about getting a new vehicle. The ragtop was faded and the plastic windows were hazy. A rip had started across the passenger's door. The top needed to be replaced. The body could use a wash and wax. Maybe some scuffs and scratches buffed out and repainted.

But a new car would be nice. Something with a solid roof. And a good heater. My first Midwestern winter had been brutal in the Jeep. But I didn't want anything … mundane. It had to be something special. It would take time, but eventually the right vehicle would come along. Until then, maybe I could buy a hard top for the winter.

I climbed into the Jeep, noting also the tiny crack in the dash. When had that happened? Didn't matter. It could, and would, be repaired right after the new top, which was added to a lengthening list of tasks to do as soon as my cash reserves had built again.

The street in front of me seemed dingy and grey. The whole city seemed that way to me now. All the sparkle was gone. My life since the murder was like that too. I felt trapped in a bubble of dark grime. Suffocated by it.

I didn't honestly know if my life could return to what it had been prior to the murder. The death of my parents had left scars, but they'd eventually smoothed out and blended into a new normal. Selling my prior two bars had brought about a change also. As had moving away from Texas. Hopefully, I'd find a new normal before I drown in this grungy bubble of decay.

What I needed was perspective.

Determined to put all things murdery out of my mind for the moment, I called Peaches. "How would you like to go see the Arch?"

"I've been wantin' to go."

"Great. I'll pick you up in about ten minutes."

"Ten minutes? Oh Lord!" She hung up. She'd still been sleeping when I left and I could imagine her now, scurrying around the spare room, throwing clothes on the bed to put on after her shower. Brushing and fluffing and starching her hair. Piling on makeup.

Unlike me, she didn't go anywhere without it. Maybe she'd grab a quick breakfast, too.

When I was a teen, we used to race to see who was ready first. Determined to make a clean break from the investigation, I concentrated on our game. My Jeep buzzed down the highway, weaving between the lanes to avoid slower cars, constantly shifting my gaze to spot any cops that might appear. Once off the highway, I took every possible shortcut. Parked the Jeep out front and bolted for the door. Only to open it just as Peaches appeared from the bedroom in her fringed denim jacket, purse swinging from her shoulder.

I narrowed my eyes and glared at her. She propped her hands on her hips and glared back.

"A tie, then?" I offered.

She gave a brief single nod, but it was probably because she was too out of breath to speak.

I glanced past her at the dogs' water dish. Full. "Let's go then."

After the alarm was set and the door was locked, we climbed into the Jeep and drove downtown. I went down Market so my aunt could see the city. Market was on the south side of a beautiful open park, Memorial Plaza, and Chestnut was on the north. Both one way streets. Fountains, benches, and statues adorned the park, as well as a small open-air amphitheater.

On the south of Market were such landmark buildings as the Enterprise Center, and the old City Hall. Much of downtown had been built to work in concert with the Arch and the old Courthouse to create a memorable beauty; high curved arches, stepped domes, and mirrored glass were everywhere. I pointed out Union Station to my aunt. It was a prime tourist shopping spot. Suggested Karyn might like to go there with her. Warned her to bring plenty of cash.

Market's east end culminated at the Arch and the Old Courthouse. Though nearly 11, it was still early enough that parking was easy, though it wouldn't be that way for long. We pulled into a slot and went on foot along the cement path. As we approached one shining triangle leg, Peaches looked 630 feet up, to the observation deck. Her step slowed and her face paled.

"Are you planning on going up?" Her voice was soft.

"Absolutely."

"I read somewhere it sways in the wind."

"Not much. Only a couple inches in a normal wind. The triangular structure makes it very safe." Seeing her still hesitate, I added, "You can see all downtown from one side and across the river into East St. Louis and Illinois from the other. Everybody should go up, at least once. If you don't, you'll kick yourself later."

She blinked and let her gaze roam the monument again. "I s'pose I will at that. All right then. Let's go."

We went inside and bought tickets for the ride. The tram was just loading, so we squeezed into one of the five-seater barrel-shaped pods with a young couple holding hands, all our knees pressed tightly together. As we rode up the Arch, the pod bumped and leveled in a step-type fashion. With each bump, Peaches's face grew more pale.

My mind started getting cluttered with images of the murder: Blaisdale's body, Pike as Lee Garret, Pike as an angry child, the bloody handprint on my sliding glass door, and more. I took a deep breath and focused on the trip to the top again. Concrete and steel and stairs showed through the glass on the door. No help. Studied the girl and boy, who both looked to be younger than I'd originally thought. Maybe juniors in high school. They had matching half-heart pendants around their necks. Their fingers were interlaced, and they leaned their heads together. Whispered.

They were dressed similar in jeans and tees. Though the boy's tee was a little frayed at the collar, and his thumb had a thick callus. His brown hair was naturally sun-bleached; hers came from a bottle. His shoes were grimy in the deep creases, whereas hers were fairly new.

Her tee was crisp white too. And she wore opal earrings. If he'd been a farm boy, he would have instead worn 'town clothes'. Although, he could have been from a poor family. She was obviously from a family that was well-off. I wondered if it was really true love, or if she was seeing him to spite her parents.

Either way, that boy had a rough road ahead of him. My heart hurt for him.

About halfway along the 4-minute ride, my aunt gripped my hand with vice-like strength and didn't let go until we stopped at the top. When we exited, she let go with a self-conscious laugh and wiped her hands on her jeans. "Don't know why I got so scared."

"Lots of people do. But it's safe. It was built to withstand earthquakes and 180 mile-per-hour winds."

She smiled and patted my arm. "For the record, details like that are essential earlier in the conversation."

We climbed the last few stairs to the 65 foot long observation deck.

"Oh!" Peaches said. The panic of just a few seconds before disappeared as she joined spectators gawking out the long thin windows on the west side. 7 feet away, I joined those leaning against the windows facing east.

Below me rolled the swirling eddies of Ol' Man River: the Mighty Mississippi. The drought had brought it low in its banks. Mud and silt islands had risen from the riverbottom. Long barges carefully navigated the deep currents, while fishing boats hunkered near the edge. The Spirit of St. Louis paddle boat churned water upstream. The flat river basin stretched beyond the water into Illinois, filled with trees, businesses, parking lots, and highways. It was said the whole Midwest long ago had been the Western Inland Seaway. Though it was only a narrow river now, comparatively, it still had all the climate of a massive body of water.

I stared down at the muddy water, trying to let my cares follow the barges all the way down to the ocean. To let them get swallowed whole, like a stick, by the roils in the river. Didn't work. With a sigh, I pushed myself upright and stepped across the deck, landing next to my aunt. "What do you think?"

"You're right. I'd have kicked myself. This is amazing."

"Yeah." The city stretched to meet the sky at the horizon, and 630 feet in the air made all the buildings seem tiny. Vehicles the size of aphids crawled the asphalt veins below. Microdots walked to their places of employment. I pinpointed all the famous landmarks for Peaches, telling her what few stories I remembered.

"Where was the fire of 1849?" She peered around the vista, as if she could see the remnants at this late date.

"It was on the waterfront." We moved to the other side. I pointed upriver just a bit. "A riverboat caught fire. When it burned through its moorings, it floated downriver, catching more boats on fire. Eventually, the flames jumped to dry land. When they eventually got it stopped, it had destroyed 430 buildings, 22 steamboats, and a bunch of smaller boats."

My aunt shook her head and leaned close to the window, looking down at the river. "Probably all small wooden buildings."

I nodded. "Building codes changed because of that."

We lapsed into silence. Eventually, I went back to the other side. There had to be some magic somewhere to put my life back in order. To make the traumas of the recent days feel small again. I put my hand on the window and stretched it across St. Louis, nothing stopped. Nothing changed. The city continued on. It would always continue on, no matter what happened within its borders. The burden on my heart and mind shrunk by comparison. I took a deep breath. Settled my forehead against the window and watched the aphids crawl.

I don't know how long I stood like that, thinking nothing, just staring out the window, but eventually I felt a hand rub my shoulderblades. My aunt moved in beside me again.

She said, "Karyn called. She wants to go shopping. Is that all right with you? I know you don't like to go, so I told her to pick me up here."

"That's fine. I have a few errands to run anyway." It wasn't true, but I'd never understood my aunt's love for shopping. She could and would spend hours roaming from store to store just looking. For me, it was a get-in-get-out affair. Aaron liked to compare prices, running from store to store to get the best deal and wasting any money he would have saved on gasoline and time spent. Our dad had been the same way.

I said, "I'll meet you at the bar."

She smiled and started humming. Until we started our return trip down.

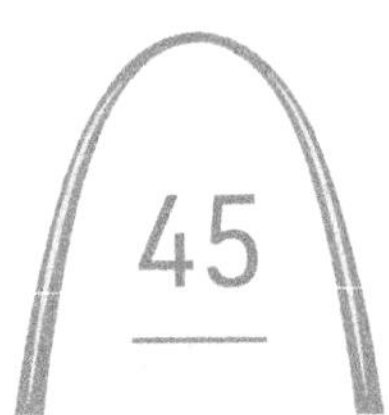

45

It was the noon hour as I walked back to my Jeep, sans Peaches. I called Aaron. "Hey, what are you doing? Want some lunch?"

"Can't get away. Sorry."

"I'll drop some by. What do you want?"

"You know, just some coffee would be good."

"Okay. Where are you?"

He gave me the address. I started up the Jeep and pulled into traffic. Coffee baristas were all over downtown and soon there were two steaming Kenya brews sitting in the cup holders of my Jeep. I drove to the small office Agent Dawes had taken for the bank task force. That the building also housed a couple software firms made me laugh. The irony. Investigation was in order. After coffee.

The closest parking space was two blocks down and around the corner. The city blocks were long, and the heat was overbearing with the humidity. By the time I reached the FBI office, the coffee was tepid, but I was hot and coated with sweat.

The building itself followed suit of other buildings in downtown St. Louis. Long thin arched windows. Arched doorway. Dark brown brick. Tall. The upper floor occupants could probably see the downtown St. Louis landmark itself. Maybe even the wide gleam of the river beyond.

Inside, there were columns of dark brick. Wide metal stairs. A bank of elevators. Cool fresh air that I drank in. And a directory board. FBI, 3rd floor. Enough walking; the coffees and I went up the elevators. The ride was very slow and there was some kind of strange techno-jazz piping in. I wasn't a fan.

Third floor was apparently all FBI. Right outside the elevators was a lobby guard with a tiny desk facing the elevators.

I smiled and announced myself. "I'm Sylvia Wilson. I'm here to see my brother, Aaron Wilson."

He just pointed to a plastic folding chair. I sat while he made a call. After a moment, the phone at the guard's desk rang. He answered, listened a quick moment, and buzzed open the only door.

With another smile at the guard, I entered the inner sanctum and admired the giant room. Admired the big white board that was layered with notes, photos, and scraps of paper. Liked the random scattering of desks with no partitions between. Liked how, even though most of the desks were empty, there was a quiet hum of busy energy that filled the room to bursting.

Aaron was sitting on the edge of a long table, staring at the white board. He turned, smiled, and rose to his feet. Came over and wrapped me in a giant hug. "You look like a dog that's been kicked too many times."

I nodded. Blinked back tears. Sometimes kicked dogs gave up. Sometimes they got mean. But they were never the same. I already mourned the old me.

He hugged me again. Pulled away and took one of the coffees. "Let's go to my desk."

"You have your own desk?"

He smiled over his shoulder at me. "We all do, here."

His desk turned out to be far from the windows and way back against the wall, in the corner, where the lighting was dim. Not very prestigious, but still, it was a desk of his own. He picked up a folder and glanced at it. Turned to me and pointed at the neighboring sta-tion, "You can pull over that chair."

I did as told. He finished reading what was in the folder and leaned down to his bottom drawer, but it wouldn't open. His chair had somehow gotten one leg jammed beneath it. He gave the chair a violent jerk and flung it behind him. Tugged open the drawer.

Like a coiled spring, and agitated by the violent movements and the sudden influx of light, a snake launched out of the drawer. It struck Aaron, leaving a searing set of punctures on his right arm, just above his wrist.

One of us must have shouted, because two agents suddenly appeared beside us. My brother pointed, dumbfounded, at the freed snake which disappeared under the next desk. His face flushed and he lurched. Somewhere in the recesses of my mind, I remembered another snake and a doctor telling us Aaron could go into shock and die if bitten again. I had been told to get him to an Emergency Room immediately.

I turned to the nearest agent. "You've got to help me get him to the closest hospital right away. My car's too far. We can't wait for an ambulance. There's no time."

He nodded and put his hand under Aaron's right arm, while I took the left. Guiding my brother to the door, I asked, "Did either of you see what kind of snake it was?"

Surprise lit the agent's face. "There was a snake?"

He shouted to the other men in the room, "Somebody catch the snake. Right now. Don't wait for animal control. This man's life depends on it. Call me when you get it."

Aaron shook his head. "I'm getting dizzy."

We nearly ran out of the room, Aaron's weight heavy on us. The other man pulled his cell phone. Made a call. "This is FBI agent Dan Busch. We're bringing in a wounded officer that was bitten by a snake and is going into anaphylactic shock. We're ten minutes out."

We passed the perplexed guard, his brows in a deep frown. Busch pointed at him and said, "Call Dawes, tell him to meet us at Barnes."

Busch repeatedly jabbed the elevator button. It finally arrived after precious seconds stretched into centuries. We rode down in silence and then walked Aaron into the muggy heat, right out into the street, stopping the first car that came. It was a navy blue, older model Chrysler sedan driven by an elderly woman with a teen boy in the passenger's seat. Busch held up his badge and said, "Medical emergency. Get us to Barnes as fast as you can. You're authorized to exceed the speed limit."

The senior woman pressed her lips together and nodded. Busch opened the back door. I climbed in and across the wide bench seat. From outside, he folded Aaron's 6'2" length and lowered him onto the seat sideways. The teen boy clambered out of the front and helped me pull until Aaron's head was in my lap. As the boy returned to the front, the agent took off his suit jacket and spread it over my brother's chest, then bent Aaron's knees and slid in under his feet. He closed the door, slapped the back of the driver's seat, and said, "We're in. Hurry! This man may be dying."

As the car sped toward the hospital, weaving around slower vehicles, Aaron's breath grew shallow. He closed his eyes. I nudged him. "Stay awake. Keep your eyes open. Tell me what's happening."

"I'm dizzy. Can't breathe. Cold."

"We're almost there."

His eyes shut again. A nudge didn't work, so I shook him. He opened his eyes briefly, mumbled something, but then drifted off. I shook him again. Hard. Got no response. Gave him a stinging slap that made Busch's eyes grow wide.

Aaron's eyes flew open, but there was no comprehension behind them. His voice came out like it was automated. "I'm all right."

No, he wasn't all right. I'd never seen him, or anyone, like that before. It was as if his soul had already left his body. It scared me silly. "Dammit! Keep your eyes open. Do you hear me? If you don't, I'll slap you into next week."

Again he came with that blank, "I'm all right."

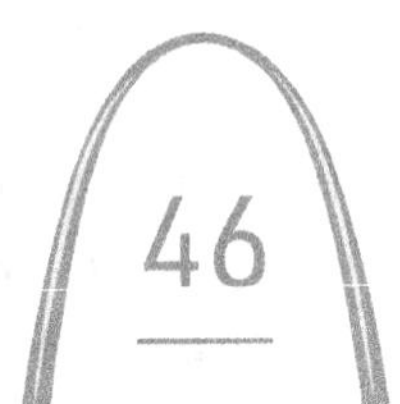

46

Within 7 minutes, the car carrying Aaron, Busch, and me turned off the highway onto hospital property. Barnes-Jewish Hospital was the bright shining star in the Midwest. Every intern fought to be placed there. They would take good care of Aaron. He would be okay. He just had to be.

When we arrived at the emergency room, we were met by three nurses, a gurney, and a surgical mask for both Busch and me. Even though most of the country was now back to normal, small pockets of Covid still popped up. Hospitals continued to require masks.

They lifted Aaron out of the car and propelled him past the ER reception to a prepared room. I followed closely. My brother's barely breathing form was put on a bed and an IV was hooked up to his undamaged arm. Busch, after he thanked the elderly woman and her grandson, joined us.

A man in scrubs and a white coat labeled Dr. Keely, came in immediately. Gave Aaron a shot of Epinephrine and examined the bite. Turned to Busch and me. Said something I couldn't quite make out through his mask. When I shook my head, he repeated it, louder. "What kind of snake?"

I shook my head, but Busch held up his finger. He took out his phone. After a quick second, he asked the person on the other end, "Yeah, did you catch it? … Describe it."

He relayed the information to the doctor. "Light brown. Dark brown hourglass stripes." Hung up.

"Sounds like a copperhead. They're not usually poisonous like this though. Usually they kill by infection. Has he been bitten by a snake before?"

I sucked in my breath. "When we were young. In Iowa."

"Do you remember what kind of snake it was?"

"A timber rattler."

The doctor nodded. "That explains why he went into shock. With most snakes, a person is able to build an immunity. However, because both Copperheads and Rattlesnakes belong to the pit viper family, the opposite is true; people become more sensitive to them the more they are bitten. When your brother was bitten by the copperhead today, it triggered an allergic reaction to the venom which sent him into shock. We're just lucky he was so close and could get here quickly."

Dr. Keely turned to a nurse. "Administer 8 vials CroFab AV with another 4 on standby. Constant monitoring. Keep me apprised of any changes either way."

Aaron. My world narrowed to a tiny dot as it had on that day our parents had died. I felt as I had then: so desperately alone. If it hadn't been for my brother, I wouldn't have made it through the funeral. Now, he was in serious trouble.

The doctor turned to me and placed his hand on my shoulder. "He'll be fine. We'll get him stabilized. But he's going to need to stay here overnight. A nurse will be in shortly with paperwork." His eyes cat-smiled at me over his mask, and he left.

Busch left for the waiting room and I called Peaches. "I'm at Barnes Hospital. Aaron's been bitten by a snake."

"A snake? Oh Lord! Karyn and I are on the way. Did you tell them about the rattler?"

"I did. The doctor seems optimistic."

"How'd he get bit?"

"I'll tell you everything when you get here." I disconnected and settled in a hard plastic chair to watch over my brother. He looked smaller somehow. Not the protector brother he'd always been. My mind was numb, just a blank space. I couldn't think, couldn't comprehend how he'd come to have one arm with an IV coming out of it and the other with a big wrap around his lower arm flexor muscles.

When he'd decided to be a cop, we'd known he could die on the job. But it hadn't seemed real. Not until an idiot had slipped a snake into his desk drawer. Of all the stupid things. This new feeling, this knife edge of pending doom, was something I was going to have to get used to. On top of everything else I was going through right now.

Nurses came in every couple minutes to check his vitals. Another came in after about 15 minutes with a thick clipboard of paperwork for me to fill out. I'd barely finished when Busch led a tall black man in a dark overcoat and blue mask to the door, nodded at me, then left. The new man, obviously from the FBI, stood just outside the room. I'd seen him before, at the police station, patting his leg and whistling for Aaron to follow like a puppy. He was so focused on my brother now, I didn't think he noticed I was there.

"Are you Agent Dawes?" I softly asked.

He nodded, but kept his gaze focused on my brother's pale, pale face. "I am."

I stood as my anger turned into a snake of its own and roped through me. My voice came out ice cold and flinty. "Who the hell put a snake in my brother's desk? What kind of office do you run?" My fists were clenched so hard the fingernails bit into the palms of my hands.

He turned his gaze on me. Softly he said through his mask, "It wasn't one of my men." Waited.

"Aaron told me your office is locked and guarded."

"It is."

"Then it had to be …." I stopped as another sickening possibility hit. Raymond Pike didn't leave town after all. I stared at Aaron's still form and my mouth dried. My brother had almost been killed because of me. I sank back into the chair. "The killer from my bar bypassed the alarm in my house pretty easily. He could have done the same at your facility. But why would he do that?"

When I finally looked at Dawes, his eyes were black diamonds boring into me. "It's a message to you."

"Message?"

He nodded. "He's showing how proficient he is. He's saying even the FBI can't stop him."

I gulped hard, trying to clear my heart out of my throat so I could breathe.

He gestured to my brother. "Why would he take to a snake bite so badly? Copperhead bites don't usually cause this kind of reaction."

I told him what the doctor had said. "Pike must have accessed my brother's medical records too. It's the only way he could have known. But I don't know why he didn't kill Aaron. He could have so easily. Same thing with my dogs when he broke into my house."

Dawes raised his eyebrows and looked over at the hospital bed. "As I understand it, your brother nearly *did* die."

I shook my head. "Pike had to know how fast Aaron could get to a hospital. It doesn't make sense."

Dawes looked off into an invisible distance. "Killers are odd in that sometimes they feed off the actual kill, but sometimes it's the victim's terror that thrills them. I'm not sure which kind your guy is, but these accidents were clearly warnings. I know you've been investigating on your own. He's telling you to back off."

Warnings. That would certainly fit what had been happening: glaring at me in the bar, breaking into my house, drugging my dogs, a snake in my brother's desk. "I want him stopped. My dad was a sheriff. He said that the only way to really stop someone is to put them in jail or kill them."

Dawes nodded, but further conversation was cut off as a nurse came in and told me Peaches had arrived. We went out to the waiting room. My aunt's face was ghostly white, her eyes wide open. Her breath came in short, shallow gasps. She shoved past the FBI agent and crushed me in a hug. Karyn stood at the reception desk, arms crossed as if hugging herself, her face puckered with worry.

Eventually, Peaches let loose. She still ignored Dawes, so I introduced the FBI agent to both her and Karyn. Explained what had happened and what the doctor had said.

We all lapsed into quiet. Peaches went to sit in the room with Aaron. I wondered if, like me, my aunt was thinking not only about my brother, but also of her own parents, both of whom had died within the past year. With most of my blood-relative grandparents already gone, they'd been like grandparents to me as well. Now, my paternal grandfather was the only grandparent I had left. He lived in his own house on the ranch where Peaches and my uncle made their home.

The waiting room of the hospital was crowded with pained and masked people. Busch was nowhere to be seen. He'd presumably gone back to the office. We searched for three chairs together, but were only able to find solo seats here and there. Instead, we moved outside into the muggy heat and settled on the edge of a planter, removing our masks.

After a moment, Dawes resumed the conversation we'd had before Peaches and Karyn arrived. "I'm not part of your case, but as I understand it, when Pike broke into the bar, he used a different method. Is this right?"

I nodded. "He did, but no one's sure what. The most likely theory is that he had a camera somewhere, but we haven't found any sign of it yet."

Karyn spoke up. "I don't understand. Why does it matter how he broke in?"

Dawes said, "Because it's an outlier. The other two break-ins use the same highly technical method. It says something about him."

I considered. "We've been thinking he wanted to mislead us in the hunt for him. We believe he works in the computer industry. Possibly writing software."

Karyn shook her head. "But he's giving it away now. Why would he do that?"

Dawes shrugged. "Could be he just doesn't care to hide himself anymore."

We paused for a screaming ambulance coming up the drive. Watched it quiet and unload.

Karyn sighed. Stood. Said to me, "I'll open the bar. Take your time coming in. And if you stay here all night, that's okay too."

"Tournament crowd should be heavy. You'll need me to be there."

She propped her hands on her hips. Put on her rebellious teen attitude and tucked her chin in mock surprise. "Who are you kidding? You don't do any work. It's always me and Tom who slave away while you play prima donna. We'll be fine without you."

She cupped her hand around her ear.

I said "279394."

She threw her head back like an evil genius. "Mwahaha! Now I control the world!"

With that she turned and walked toward the parking lot. I glanced at Dawes to find him watching me, his eyes now like shattered glass. "What your father said about stopping a man was true. But he was law enforcement. You're not. This Pike has proven he's dangerous and smart. You need to leave this to the authorities. You take care of your family. Concentrate on keeping them safe."

Dawes left, but not until he made sure there was a uniformed officer stationed at the door. Despite what the nurse had said about only one visitor, she didn't put up a fuss at my presence with Peaches as long as we stayed out of her way. My brother was moved to the ICU about an hour later, police guard and all, and we stayed there until the ICU nurse kicked all the visitors out. I debated going home to fetch the dogs before heading to the bar, but there was supposed to be a patrol stationed there.

Instead, Peaches and I went directly to Smugglers where a serious tournament crowd was above and beyond, even for a Thursday. Tom and Karyn rushed like bumper cars on a circular course, running into each other while they tried to keep up with the beer orders. The room was warm enough that Karyn's hair, normally a full-blown dandelion, looked more like a weeping willow. Tom was dripping splashed beer from the hem of his shirt. Customers lined the bar, waiting. Everything was sticky. And all four TVs played the same game: the early Cardinals – Dodgers game. I changed the channels on two, turned the A/C to a cooler temperature, and started serving tables. Peaches washed dirty mugs, saying it would stop her worrying, but every time I had a chance to glance at her face, her brow was furrowed and she was muttering to herself. I was too. Pike was still in the city. We were all in danger.

Even with the four of us, we barely managed to keep up with the demand of our patrons. To make it worse, our team lost the tourney that night for some unknown reason, dropping us below the cut-off line. If we didn't bounce back quickly, we would be eliminated from pairs competition. Singles would be starting soon, too.

I closed the bar early again, at midnight, and kept both Karyn and Tom to help with the cleanup. They took the tables and front area, while Peaches cleaned behind the bar. That left the bathrooms and back hall for me.

I was halfway through the second bathroom, the one furthest from the back entrance, when Tom came in. His fleshy face was a bit pale, but no more than usual. Most of his time was spent in his university room studying. When he wasn't tending bar, that is. He watched me wipe the sink for a moment, then said, "I guess I never asked if I could have time off for Christmas."

While we were both 22, there was a world of difference in our work experience. As far as I knew, Smugglers was Tom's first real job. I looked up at him in the mirror.

Froze.

In the reflection over his shoulder, I could easily see the alarm panel by the back door. During my earlier investigation for signs of Pike's camera mounting, I'd checked all direct-line-of-sight possibilities, including around the bathroom mirror. But I'd never considered that Pike might have used a reflection.

"Tom," I said, still staring at the back hall in the mirror. "We'll talk about Christmas in a minute. For now, I need you to go to the alarm panel and make as if you're putting in the code."

He frowned, but did as I asked. Plain as day, I could still see the number pad and the movement of his hand as he pointed to each number.

"That's good. Thanks." I slowly turned and viewed the other side of the small room. It was standard in bathrooms. There was a toilet on the outside wall, sideways of the sink where I stood. Beside the sink was the trashcan and paper towel dispenser. I'd also hung some typical bathroom artwork: skunks mostly. There also was, of course, the usual graffiti that came with bar bathrooms.

There was only one angle from which a camera could see the reflection of the alarm pad. Tom returned as I climbed on the toilet and checked the top of the framed skunk photo there. Nothing. I pulled it the off the wall and checked the back. Still nothing. Leaning close to the wall, I looked along the contour of it and spotted the adhesive where it had been hidden by the photo.

"Go get one of the police officers from outside, please, Tom."

While he was gone, I pulled out my phone and snapped pics of the adhesive and the angle the camera would have viewed. I sent the photos to Eccheli with the text "Found where Pike mounted the camera in my bar."

A text immediately shot back. "On the way. Don't touch it."

As if I would have wanted my fingerprints all over the only bit of evidence that proved I didn't collude with the killer. I climbed down as Tom returned with Officer Smithson, who I could now see, was older than I'd previously thought. Gray laced through his hair and mustache. Sun wrinkles lined his face. He immediately took my place on the stool and confirmed my finding.

He said, "That's adhesive all right."

"I texted Eccheli. He said he'd be right over." I didn't trust Smithson – anyone – with my redemptive piece of evidence. I wanted him to get down, but he stayed where he was, turning to speak to me from the height.

He nodded. "He'll need to get Crime Scene down here too. That might take time."

I tried to figure a clever way to get him down. Gave up. Said, "Would you please come down? You're making me nervous."

His eyebrows lifted in surprise and the corner of his mouth turned up, adding more wrinkles to those on his face. He looked on the verge of saying something, but then he shrugged and came down. "I'll have to stay here to keep it safe."

I pointed at the floor. "Down here."

He hesitated, then nodded. I still didn't trust him, so I spent the rest of the evening running up and down the hall checking on him. I tried to send Peaches home to Karyn's apartment – she looked ready to drop – but she wouldn't go.

She said, "If this killer is still in the area, then you're not going to stay at your house alone."

"I have the dogs. And I have a patrol car parked right outside."

"No. And that's final." She turned away, the matter obviously settled.

I realized I hadn't spoken about the Christmas matter with Tom yet. Told him and Karyn to just initial the dates on the calendar they wanted for vacation. Then I sent them home.

Eccheli's 'on the way' must have meant he was out of the country. Half an hour later, I was still watching Smithson fight the urge to get up on the now grimy toilet seat. I was tired and getting cranky. Decided to call Bobby to calm down a bit. Filled him in on the happenings of the last couple days.

He seemed duly impressed. "Never a dull moment with you, is there?"

"You've always known that."

"True." He hesitated a moment, then switched subjects. "I heard you dropped below the cut line."

Bad news traveled fast. "Sadly, yes. Still close enough to make a play, though."

He gave his usual, "We're gonna kick your ass. You know that, right?"

"Sounds like false bravado to me."

A loud long rumble of laughter filled the phone. Then there was that hesitation again. Finally, he said, "Well, I gotta go. Unlike yours, my team is still playing tonight and they're thirsty."

As I disconnected, I wondered about those hesitations. Had they been him trying to decide about coming over? Or waiting for me to ask? Or something else entirely? Ultimately, it didn't matter what they were. My aunt was staying with me. That ended all romantic liaisons right there. Not that she'd object to my sleeping with someone. But, it might make for an uncomfortable morning breakfast for Bobby. He preferred simple.

Nearly an hour after I'd called, and well past one in the morning, Eccheli breezed in with Johnson and a yawning crime scene tech in tow. His glare at me was deep and he opened his mouth to, I'm sure, berate me on investigating, but I beat him to the punch.

"I was just cleaning," I said. "Anyone who was here can verify that."

He crossed his arms and stared at me, wide-legged and dominant, the way men do. His dark eyes bored into me. He wore a black button down shirt open at the neck and black suit pants. No tie or jacket. Striking against his dark skin. Johnson stood behind him, being shown by Smithson where the adhesive was located and how the picture had hidden it. The crime scene guy was already snapping pics.

Eccheli said, "I'm not a bad guy. And I'm actually pretty damn good at my job. Most of these things you've brought us are things we knew already. I need you to stop investigating. Pike is dangerous."

"I already told you I'm done."

He slowly nodded and started to turn away, but then turned back, shaking his finger at me. "And despite what you think, it was your lawyer who got your bar released to you."

I bit my tongue to keep from asking him why, then, had he had released Smugglers to me after I'd pushed him on the phone, if the release had really been my lawyer's doing. But I figured discretion was the better part of valor and all that. Besides, I knew why: I'd threatened to make a stink in the upper offices, and with the lawyer pushing to reopen, the shit from the proverbial uphill would roll down pretty heavy on the good detective. Still, he could have let me have the credit.

As he focused on the crime scene guy's photography of the new-found evidence, Johnson caught my arm and pulled me to the front of the bar. Peaches was nodding off in a booth by the big TV that now was on a replay of the baseball talk show MLB Tonight. Her blond highlights were spiky from hairspray gotten sweaty.

The IAD detective sat me on a stool and pulled out a notebook and pen. She wore a sling-back dress, apparently having been out somewhere with her husband. She'd straightened her hair recently, and it flowed like a chocolate waterfall down her dark back. "Tell me about what else you know that you haven't told us."

Well, now I was just offended. "Nothing. I've told you everything I've found, every step of the way."

She took a deep breath. Maybe in disappointment. Maybe to calm herself because she wanted to choke me. "Talk to me about Walent. What happened there?"

I told her. Peaches woke well enough to chime in occasionally from her booth, though her voice was muted and Johnson had to keep asking her to repeat.

When we finished, Johnson nodded and scanned through her notes, saying as an aside, "Those two brothers weren't happy to be interviewed twice in one day. They weren't exactly forthcoming. Of course, I couldn't play the pregnancy card. Which was very clever, by the way."

She looked up at me, her eyes glinting. "We were half way down the highway when you called. Got there maybe 45 minutes after you left. Now, tell me about the scrap of paper Mrs. Degere brought in. How'd you find that?"

Gulp.

"I saw it pinned by the window frame when I stood by the window where Blaisdale dressed."

"It's inadmissible in court as evidence because of you, you know. You should have just called us, like you did tonight. This," she motioned toward the bathroom, "will be admissible, should we find something. That's another reason why you let us do the investigating: court and evidentiary rules. Clear?"

"Yes." I felt like a scolded puppy. Peaches's eyes were as big as basketballs, but she said nothing.

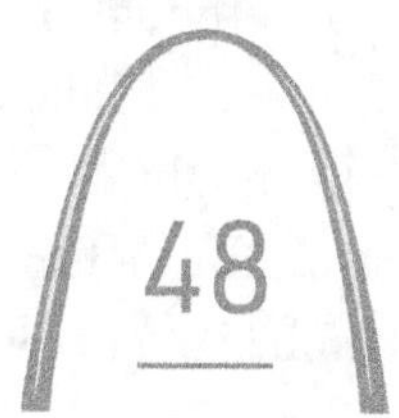

48

It took another hour for the detectives to finish their crime scene stuff. Peaches and I went home, escorted by Smithson and his partner, and spent the remaining dark hours in restless communion with the TV. By dawn, both of us were exhausted and crawled into our own respective beds. My alarm woke me a couple hours later and I lay there contemplating what I would tell Teague when cancelling my lesson. But, if I was going to keep Teague invested in helping me, now or any time in the future, then I needed to go. Even at the ungodly hour of 9 AM.

It took a bit to get me fully into the lesson, but after being dumped on the mat a few times, I finished my session in stellar form. My next appointment was with the Tuesday morning class.

I went out to my Jeep. Called the hospital. The nurses' desk phone was busy, so I called Peaches at home. She slurred in a sleep softened voice, "Hello?"

"It's me. When do you want to go to the hospital?"

"When's visiting hours start?"

"Not until two. But I'm willing to bet they'll let us slip in if we keep quiet."

"Let's try in a couple hours from now."

"Okay. Go back to sleep."

She disconnected without a goodbye. Now that I had some free time, I could investigate a bit. Though I had told Eccheli I would stop, I really couldn't. Not now that Pike had almost killed Aaron. He had to be stopped. My life might depend on it, too.

Google provided me with software firms near my location. Most within walking distance. I climbed out of my Jeep again and began my search for 'my friend who wanted me to meet his boss for a job'. The sky was clouding up, which was good and bad. Good because it might mean another desired rainfall, as the weather jockeys had predicted. Bad because it would make the air even more sticky and humid.

I worked in a circular pattern, setting off to the south first, into what had once been a magnificent shopping area, but was now mostly seedy shops and offices. The fourth place, a firm called Armstrong SRD, was in a renovated department store building. Unlike most of the software places, the lobby was huge and plush with newish dark grey carpeting and marble columns that stretched to an uber-high ceiling. There was a bank of polished steel elevators next to a giant, curved desk from which a Hispanic man in guard uniform watched me.

I approached, holding out my phone with Blaisdale's photo displayed. "I'm looking for my friend. He said he works here and would introduce me to his boss."

The young-looking guard, with a nametag of Ortiz, glanced at the photo and up at me. Nodded. Picked up his desk phone. "I'll call him."

"Just a moment." I held up one finger and backed away. Speed dialed Eccheli, who wasn't in. I was rerouted to the desk sergeant.

"Hi. This is Sylvia Wilson. Would you please have Detective Eccheli call me? It's urgent. Tell him I found the place of Blaisdale's second job." I disconnected and smiled at the guard, whose eyes never left me. He might be good at his job, always watching people who didn't belong. If Smugglers ever needed reason to have a guard, I wanted someone like him.

My cell buzzed after ten minutes of sitting in the lobby. Eccheli's voice was clipped. He sounded a bit peeved, but also excited. "You left a message that you found Blaisdale's second job site?"

"Armstrong SRD." I gave him the address. "I'm here now."

"Stay there." He disconnected, leaving me feeling suspiciously like Peaches when I'd told her to stay put at the Starbucks at the airport. It put a heavy pout in my mind and made me cringe at how I'd treated my aunt when she'd arrived. I vowed to do better.

Eighteen minutes of me watching the guard watch me went by before Eccheli and Johnson entered through the glass door, bright-eyed and almost breathless. They went straight to the desk, completely ignoring me. Why did they bother to tell me to stay? I rose and joined them.

Eccheli flashed his badge at the guard. He produced a glossy photo of Blaisdale and asked, "This man works here?"

Ortiz first glared at me, but then turned his attention to the detective and nodded. He again picked up the handset of his desk phone. "I can call him to meet you."

"I'd rather have your manager meet us."

While we waited, Eccheli turned to me. "You need to stop investigating. I mean it. I've already warned you. Next time, I'll take you in."

"I'm not obstructing. You're busy. I'm just doing some of your scut work. There's no evidentiary rules to worry about here." No way I was backing down. Not when the answers were so close. Somehow, though, I felt like a belligerent teenager trying to justify her actions.

He glared at me. Behind him, Johnson nearly smiled.

I said, "You know I didn't kill anyone. And I don't know how I would have been able to hire a killer who hated Blaisdale enough to cut him like that." I realized my mistake the moment I said it.

Johnson's face colored and her eyes bored into me. "Who told you?"

"I saw it myself at the bar." True, but I'd had no idea what it had meant until Aaron told me what he'd overheard the ME say.

Apparently satisfied with my answer, she sniffed and looked away as a medium-built, black man with a thick beard exited one of the elevators. He had slumped shoulders, and heavy bags under worried eyes. He held out his hand and shook with Eccheli. Nodded to Johnson and me. "Brian Armstrong. I'm the manager of Armstrong SRD. My brother is the owner."

Eccheli again held up Blaisdale's photo. "Does this man work here?"

Armstrong studied the pic. Shook his head. "He's not employed here."

We all turned to face the guard, Ortiz, who said, "I saw him leave here three mornings in a row last week."

Armstrong frowned and stepped behind the wide oak desk. I moved to the side of the desk to watch what he did. Johnson must have had the same thought because she moved to the other side at the same time. She noticed that I'd matched her and gave a tiny nod.

The desk was full of mostly empty cubby holes and niches and I wondered what reason they had to buy something so big that sat mostly empty. A security monitor showing 3 angles of the lobby sat beside a computer screen and keyboard. The manager tapped on the keys and the computer screen filled with more security videos. He found one of the mornings in question, located the man, and enlarged the video to his face. Definitely Blaisdale. Nodded. "He's been here all right. But I'm telling you, he's not an employee; I don't know why he was here. What's this about? And who is he?"

Eccheli said, "His name was Edward Blaisdale. We don't know yet why he was here. We're trying to find out as much as we can about him, pursuant to an investigation into his murder."

Armstrong sucked in his breath, and he looked straight at me, as if I could give him answers. "Murder? Do you think it's because of whatever he was doing here?"

Eccheli drew his attention back. "That's what we're trying to find out, sir. He may have been here to commit a crime. Do you mind if we look at those videos?"

"Not if it helps find out what he was doing here." He made room for us all to get behind the desk with him. Eccheli glanced at me and I thought he was going say something, but he pressed his lips thin and turned to focus on the computer screen.

"His badge will tell us which area he patrolled." Armstrong tightened the focus onto the uniform chest. The badge read, 'Mark Gagne', but the photo ID was Blaisdale. My mind flashed to the tiny scrap of paper from Blaisdale's apartment. It had read *–gne* with a *5*. Had that been about Mark Gagne? The manager shook his head. "No. That's not right. I know Gagne, and that's not him."

Johnson asked, "Would Gagne be a big square guy with a mustache? This man?" She held out a police sketch. Presumably it was the one Vonda had mentioned. The guy on it looked suspiciously like who she had told me about.

Armstrong nodded. "Yeah. You know him? Is he in trouble too?"

The two detectives exchanged meaningful glances. She said to Armstrong, "We need to speak with him. Is he here?"

"He isn't here now. He works night shift. In fact …." He minimized the video, typed in another password, and brought up a work schedule and picture ID of Gagne, along with his phone number and address. I made a mental note and also noticed that Gagne's phone number ended with a *5*. Mystery of the paper scrap solved. It was definitely about him.

Armstrong frowned and pointed at the screen. "He was scheduled to work those nights. It's my guess his friend here took his shifts for him."

Johnson asked, "Is that common practice here?"

"It certainly *isn't*."

Eccheli jumped back in. "So, you check IDs coming in, but not going out?"

Armstrong shook his head, his frown deepening. "We've never had to before. I guess this means we'll have to start."

He held up Garret's photo. "Have either of you have seen this man?"

Armstrong pursed his lips and slowly shook his head. "I'm not sure, but I don't think so."

Ortiz shook his head.

I waited for either detective to ask about Pike, but both seemed to be considering what to do next. I spoke up. "Do you have a Raymond Pike who works here?"

Eccheli flashed an annoyed frown my way, but stopped when Armstrong nodded and said, "Yes, we do."

Johnson asked, "Would you bring up his employee photo, please?"

"Certainly."

When the file opened on the screen, Johnson stabbed the picture with her finger. It was of a young white male of light frame, with brown hair, and blue eyes covered with thick lenses. He had a goofy smile and had looked somewhere to the left of the camera just as the picture was taken. Raymond Pike. He looked like the kid in the brothers' early photo, not the threatening one in the later picture, nor the killer at my bar.

Eccheli propped the photo of Garret next to the monitor. Pike's eyes were blue, but less so than Garret's, and hidden behind heavy brown frames. The jawline looked the same, but it was hard to tell because the man in the Garret photo had his chin tucked. The hair was definitely different. But maybe the same length? Mr. Detective turned to me with a guarded look in his eyes. "Do you think that's him?"

I nodded. "The jawline is similar. Same mouth shape, same eyebrows. He might walk with a hitch on his right side?" I saw that Pike's address was only a few blocks away. Doubtless the detectives would go there first. But while they were there, I could visit Gagne.

Ortiz spoke up. "He limps sometimes. Just a little." The security guard rose a little more in my estimation.

I nodded to Johnson. She motioned to Pike's picture on the screen. Said to Armstrong, "We need to speak to this man, right now. Would you take us to him, please?"

He shook his head. "He's been on vacation for the past couple weeks. Do you think they're all together in this … crime? Or whatever they're doing?"

She pressed her lips tight and jotted down the home addresses and phone numbers of both Pike and Gagne.

We hustled out of Armstrong SRD together: Mr. and Mrs. Detective, and me. Humidity filled in the spaces the heat of the day had missed. My tee soaked through with sweat almost immediately and looked more gold than yellow. Grey clouds scudded over the city from a horizon packed with them. It would be more than just rain; a storm was coming. The two detectives powwowed.

"We should split up. I'll take Pike; you take Gagne," Johnson said.

Eccheli raised his eyebrows. "Why do you get Pike?"

"I called it first."

He shook his head. "I think we should both hit Pike's address. He's dangerous."

"I'll wait for backup. We can't let Gagne get away just because we're busy with Pike."

"How about this: we call patrol for Gagne, and you and I visit Pike?"

Johnson gave a slow nod. "That would work."

No one had said anything to me, so I turned to walk back to my Jeep. Johnson immediately asked, "Where are you going?"

"Home to get my aunt so we can visit Aaron in the hospital." I shrugged. She didn't need to know I was headed to Gagne's address as soon as I got rolling again.

She nodded. "See that you do."

I didn't answer. They were detectives. They should have detected I wouldn't stop investigating.

One way or another, Raymond Pike had to be stopped. Mark Gagne might be able to provide some information that would help achieve that goal. And I didn't trust he would stay put while the detectives were at Pike's place.

Gagne lived in one of the multi-unit apartments south of Gravois Road on Loughborough Avenue. Parking wasn't an issue in the middle of the day, so it didn't take long to find a space close to one of the doors. I suspected Eccheli's requested patrol wasn't far behind me. I wasted no time bolting inside and up the stairs to the second floor. Warm muggy air followed me in and swirled around me. A couple loud TVs inside closed apartments vied with each other for ear time in the cramped hallway. The navy carpet was old and worn, threadbare in a few places, but clean and dry. I stopped at the door with #207 on it: Gagne's. Hesitation hit me. What was I going to say? "Excuse me, did you help Raymond Pike kill Edward Blaisdale?" Gagne probably wouldn't answer that.

I knocked. Waited. The room behind the door was quiet, except for the hum of something mechanical. Probably the A/C. I knocked again. And again.

Down the hall, one of the apartments with the loud TV opened the door, spilling the sound into the hallway. An ancient head poked out, looked both directions. Spied me and disappeared behind the closed door again.

I waited a beat. Took out a credit card. My dad taught us all sorts of escape tricks in case we were ever kidnapped, including how to pick assorted locks. He then beat our butts when he found us breaking into the neighbor's house. In truth, we were just practicing, but the lessons had ended there.

I braced my knee against the door and pushed with it at the same time I lifted the door handle. Then slid the credit card into the gap between the door jamb and the lock. With a loud 'snick', the door popped open. I sidled in backwards, watching the corridor. Carefully closed the door. Goosebumps immediately sprung up on my skin from the chilly air pumping into the room. There was a strong odor of pine too. Not real pine though. A bad feeling dropped into the pit of my stomach and I slowly turned and faced the room.

Directly across from me were four windows, three of which looked out over the street I'd just driven. The fourth window was completely blocked by an air conditioner that was cranked full blast, twirling a score of pine tree air fresheners overhead. Beneath the trees and in front of the windows was a green and yellow floral sofa that was about twenty years old. It was filled with a long plastic and duct-taped tube that was just about adult male size. The tube bulged in places, stretching the plastic but not the tape. And one taped seam hadn't sealed right and dripped some kind of pinkish fluid onto the sofa. There was a faint 'off' smell that mixed into the pine of the room.

"Well shit," I softly said and turned around to the door again. Opened it. Pulled the hem of my shirt up and wiped the door handles, both inside and out. Glanced around the floor nearby to make sure no stray hairs had fallen from my head. Then crept out into the hallway. I didn't close the door all the way so that the patrol officers would have exigent circumstances and could enter without waiting for a warrant or a landlord. Then I beat feet the hell out of there.

I opted to go out the back, through the door to the grass courtyard, instead of the front, where I could be spotted by any arriving police-types. Of course, if they were already there, then they'd seen the Jeep and I was in big trouble.

I paused at the corner of the building and peeked up and down the street. Not seeing anything cop-like, I put my head down and walked nonchalantly to my Jeep. Got in and drove home where a patrol was guarding out front with another officer on foot in back where I parked. My dogs greeted me like it had been years since I'd left. Peaches, tired of waiting, had left a note that she'd called a cab and had gone to the hospital. She'd meet me there.

I let the dogs out and called my aunt. "Sorry I'm late getting back. How's Aaron?"

Her voice was quiet, yet thick, when she spoke. She'd been crying. "He had a bad night. They had to give him more of that anti-venom stuff. But he's okay now. Recovering nicely, as the doctor says. They're keeping him another night. It scared the hell out of me." She blew a gust of air out.

I didn't know what to say. My brother was still in jeopardy. My hands started shaking. I worked to keep my voice on an even keel. "I'm on my way. Do you need anything?"

"My light jacket, is all. If you don't mind. I have my sweater, but it's still cold as blazes in here."

"You need a book? Or magazine?"

"I have lots of books on my phone. All I need is my jacket."

"Okay. I'm going to bring in the dogs, grab your jacket, and call Tom to open the bar. Then I'll head out."

"Maybe a sandwich would be nice. Even two or three in case Aaron wants a couple when he wakes."

"I'll make a few. See you soon." I stabbed off the phone, slid it onto the kitchen counter, and shoved my hands into my jeans pockets to stop the tremors. Then went outside to love on the pooches. Dog kisses always calmed me and they wiggled like pups, bowling me over again and again.

Eventually, I went back inside and discovered a message on my phone from Johnson. She said, "Pike's apartment was cleaned out. We found Gagne's door open, with him dead. A neighbor reports seeing someone like you about an hour ago. For your sake, I hope we don't find any of your DNA or prints."

I hoped not, too.

I called Tom. "My brother's still in the hospital. Would you please open?"

"You bet."

"Thanks."

We disconnected after I gave him the new alarm code. Then I changed into a soft turquoise shirt and went to fetch the required jacket, setting it by the door so it wouldn't be forgotten when I left. I checked the mail and found a rather hefty bill from my lawyer, Mr. Charlie Moore. The price tag made me blink, but I would happily pay it because he'd helped get my bar reopened.

Then it was sandwich time. Being from Texas, all three of us appreciated hearty food. I opted for a Cubano sandwich and checked the fridge for ingredients: ham, pork, beef, swiss, and dill pickle. I layered these on 4 stone-ground-mustard smeared hoagie rolls, buttered the outsides, and wedged them into a press. I also made a couple cold Cubanos – though technically since they were cold, they couldn't be called by that name – in case Aaron couldn't eat the butter-soaked ones. Put those fresh into a cloth grocery bag.

As soon as the sandwiches in the press were done, I layered them between sheets of parchment paper, slid them into their own bag, and wrapped the bag in a towel. Then dropped the whole thing in a second cloth bag. Brought the dogs in, tucked my Browning pistol into one of the bags, grabbed the jacket, and headed out the back to the Jeep, waving to the cop stationed there as I left.

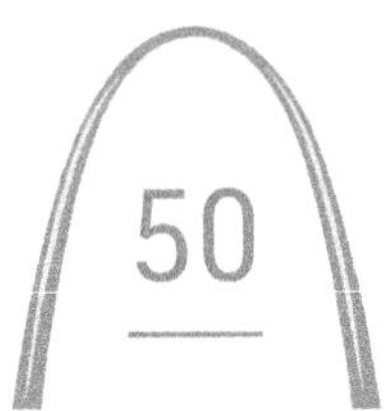

50

There was strangely very little traffic on the highway for noon hour on a Friday. I made it to Barnes with the sandwiches still hot and piping their aroma throughout the Jeep. My stomach rumbled unmercifully.

Though the highways weren't busy, the emergency parking lot was packed. The nearest space I could find was at the outside edge. The weekend was looming and nobody wanted to be in the ER for it, so they all came today. After collecting my mask, I stopped at the first vending machines inside the hospital, picking up three bottles of water and three bags of baked chips. Swiped some paper towels from a bathroom. Stowed them all in the bag with the cold sandwiches. Headed to the ICU.

The room where Aaron had been now held an ancient woman who stared at the ceiling with unmoving eyes and a barely rising chest. Tubes stuck out of her everywhere. I doubled back to the nurse's desk and spoke to a medium-built Hispanic woman with a nametag that read 'Dresden'. I said, "I'm looking for Aaron Wilson."

"We just moved him to a regular room." Her fingers flew over the keyboard. "Fifth floor, room #571."

"Thank you."

As I walked away, she said, "That smells good. Be careful you don't start a riot."

I stopped, turned around, and asked, "Would you like one? They're hot and melty."

"Thank you, but I'm vegan."

I squinted my eyes to smile. Returned to my intended path. While I understood the whole vegan/vegetarian thing, even envied those who chose that lifestyle, I loved the taste of meat too much to ever give it up. Carnivore all the way.

A different uniformed officer was guarding Aaron's door. My brother was asleep, but Peaches looked up when I entered the room. Her eyes immediately turned red and teared. My heart clutched. I could barely speak. My throat closed, my breath stopped, and my eyes flew immediately to the monitors hooked to my brother, as if I could magically decipher their meaning. Tremors returned under my skin. "What's happened?"

She shook her head and hugged me hard. Whispered in my ear, "Nothing. He's fine. I'm just glad you're here with me. They gave him some serious drugs, so he'll be sleeping a while."

I took deep breaths. Held onto Peaches a little extra long. Nothing had happened to Aaron. He was all right. My tremors subsided and I finally let go.

Peaches sniffed and dabbed her eyes. Patted her stiffened hair to make sure it was still in place. Took her jacket from where I'd threaded it through the crook of my arm.

I handed her the bag of hot sandwiches. "Cubano."

She opened the bag, lowered her mask, and dropped her nose into it like a mule with a feed bag. Its sides went concave as she took a deep intake. Then she lifted her head and smiled at me. Her eyes twinkled. "Mmmm."

"I made 4. And I've got two cold ones here, in case the hot ones are too rich for Aaron." I lifted the other bag.

She fanned her hand in denial. "Pish. He can handle anything with that cast-iron stomach of his."

It was true. Through the course of his lifetime, my brother had eaten plenty of questionable things, including a couple that would make most anyone else blanche. Back in Texas, he was famous at the local bars for some of the bets he'd take.

She handed me a hot sandwich, took another out for herself, removed her mask completely, and settled back into her chair, the bag on the floor beside her. I pulled the other chair, a sturdy wood-framed job, out of the far corner and across the room. Sat beside her. Pulled off my mask and took chips, napkins, and water out of my bag. Peaches took a water and napkin, but waved away the chips with a grimace. "Baked? I'll pass."

Other than that brief statement, we were silent while we ate. The Browning dug into my back from where I'd tucked it into my belt. I felt odd with a gun in a hospital. But I also felt safe. When my aunt finished with her sandwich, she rooted in the bag for a second, which she divided in half, grease from the melty cheese dripping onto the napkin beneath. Offered the other half to me, but I shook my head and opted for chips instead. While I didn't like baked chips any more than she did, there was only so much arterial gluing my body could stand at one time.

The heavy crunch of the chips seemed to echo against the linoleum floor and bare walls, so I only ate a couple, and then put the bag away. Put my mask back on and pulled out my phone. Opened the security videos in the cloud, looking for Gagne.

Why had Pike killed him too? What was the connection between those two and Blaisdale? I knew Pike had felt wronged by Blaisdale. Betrayed. Something that obviously involved Gagne. But what?

I went back to the first night, when Blaisdale had slid that envelope to Degere, then had gone to sit with someone else. Enlarged the video to the other man's face. Gagne. But Pike didn't seem to be anywhere in the room.

Backing the video further brought no other instance of the two together. While Aaron slept and Peaches read her eBook, I returned to the only instance they were together and compared faces and body types between all the videos. At the end of two hours, I could definitely say Pike wasn't there.

It wasn't until I was ready to shut off my phone that something caught my eye. I enlarged the video that showed the back hall so that it showed just the door. As it opened, the light from inside spilled out onto whoever was out there. Blaisdale came in, the door started to swing shut on an empty lot, but at the very edge of the light, there was a figure watching. I enlarged the image again. A shiver ran through me as I stared at Pike's malevolent glare.

Eccheli and Johnson had probably seen it. They'd probably seen Blaisdale sitting with Gagne, too. Besides, I was already in trouble with them. But, I stared at my phone, tapping the edge of it with my finger. Then decided not to chance them missing such a vital clue. Even if it got me burned.

I called and left a message, gulping panicked air like a beached fish afterward. Then I calmed. If they were going to arrest me for obstruction, they'd have done it at Armstrong, or after Gagne's apartment. Not after something as inconsequential as looking at my own videos.

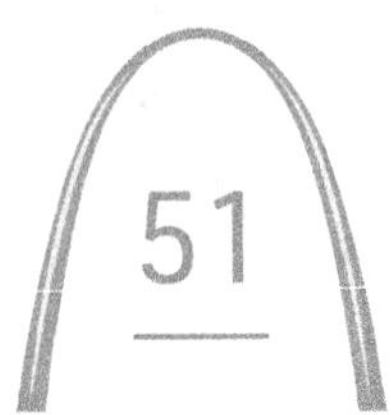

51

I dozed off. Something about the constant background voices of life-giving machines, the murmurs of nurses at their desk, the rhythmic tapping of Peaches's foot as she read, and the coolness of the room, put me into Nod Land. It also could have been the beyond-hectic days, the sleepless nights, the extreme physical exertion of the morning, and the stress of the whole mess.

It was probably all of it.

Anyway, I woke with a start when something brushed my arm. Peaches was standing beside me, her hand still on my wrist. I hadn't been dreaming, but for a few seconds, I had no idea where I was when I woke. The white walls and white linoleum gave me no answers. The grey sky outside the windows didn't help either. It wasn't until I saw Aaron smiling at me from the bed that I remembered.

"Welcome back to The Land of the Living." I rubbed my eyes with the heels of my hands and rose. Went over and leaned in for a hug. Squeezed him as tightly as I could with all the wires and hoses attached to him. Kissed his cheek. Dabbed away the relief from my eyes. Straightened.

"Good to be back." His eyes twinkled.

"For the record, you're never allowed to do that again."

"Deal."

The smell of meat and gravy came through the open door, accompanied by the rattle of wheels. I glanced at my phone. 4:50. There was an afternoon game against the Padres that started an hour ago. Plus I was late to the bar.

Peaches said to Aaron, "Your supper's coming. How about Sylvia and I go get some coffee while you eat?"

I hit the number on my phone for Smugglers to see how Tom was doing. See if he needed help. No answer. I called Karyn. Got no answer there either, but wasn't surprised. She usually responded best to texts. My quick message: *Can you go into the bar now? I'm at the hospital still. Will be there soon.*

Got a thumbs up emoji in return.

Peaches and I nodded to the uniformed officer when we left. We were silent as we walked to the elevators. But once in, and speeding from the fifth floor to the main lobby, she turned to me. "Where'd you go this morning?"

The elevator walls were smooth steel. Almost like a mirror, but a little fuzzy. My reflection was a stranger. My eyes were just as haunted as Peaches's, with black bags slung under them. My cheeks were gaunt and pale. A frown thickened my brow, and I honestly couldn't remember the last time I'd laughed. I actually thought I looked worse than my aunt.

"Sylvia?"

"I'm sorry I wasn't back in time to bring you here." I turned to face her.

Her brow furrowed. "It's not that. I don't care if I have to take a cab. Where'd you go when you called?"

I told her about finding Armstrong SRD and what happened there. By the time I finished, we were standing in line with our coffees. We paid a masked attendant. As we settled at Peaches's choice of table near a wide window, distanced from the others, I laid my phone beside my coffee, took off my mask, and shifted the story to that of Mark Gagne.

Then I showed her the video I found.

She put it together before I had a chance to tell her what it all meant. She said, "So, it's like a love triangle. People kill for that all the time."

"Well, I don't think anyone was in love. I think it was just a friendship thing."

She nodded, her eyes large. "He doesn't strike me as the kind of man that has lots of compadres. Maybe he only had these two and they left him out."

"I think that's it. Yeah." I let my gaze travel the room. Besides us, there were 7 other tables occupied. Most by singles or duos, but one table near the center of the room had a family of five seated at it. There was a mother and father, a sullen teen boy, a younger teen girl staring at her phone, and a toddler clamoring for attention. The mother was shaking with barely controlled sobs. The father's face was red and twisted with emotion too. They held hands across the table, their fingers white with pressure. If they were at the hospital for a parent/grandparent only one of the adults would be that distressed. The other would be somewhat distressed, but not as much as now. I wondered at the age gap between the teens and the small child and decided there was a child missing, probably the reason they were all gathered at the hospital. It didn't seem like it was going well for the child, either.

My heart was breaking for them. For me. For anyone and everyone who'd ever lost someone important to them. Tears burned my eyes and I pulled my gaze back to my own table. Peaches was halfway through her coffee, while I'd barely touched mine from talking so much. I took a drink from the cooling black sustenance. Concentrated on the bitterness. Bitter like tears.

I took a deep breath and contemplated taking a vacation when this was all over. I'd told Peaches I would go back to Texas for a visit, but knew I wouldn't. Nor would I take a vacation to catch up on my sleep. No one in my family was cut that way. Though, Peaches would enjoy more sightseeing. We could do that. Maybe a tour of the Budweiser brewery. That trip to the Arch had helped me get my life back in perspective. For an hour or so.

My phone buzzed with Karyn's number. Not a text. I snatched up the phone. Her voice came out frantic. "Something's wrong. I can't get into the bar and there's smoke coming from the windows. I called 911. What do I do? Tom isn't anywhere."

I lunged to my feet, bumping the table and spilling my coffee. Motioning to Peaches to leave the mess and come with me, I spoke to Karyn in a steady calm voice. "I'm on my way."

I turned off the call and said to Peaches, "Smugglers is on fire."

"Oh Lord!"

"Get up to Aaron's room right now. Alert the officer stationed at his door what's happened and to watch out for any strangers, including unknown hospital workers. I'm going to the bar."

"You think it's him – Pike – don't you?"

"I do."

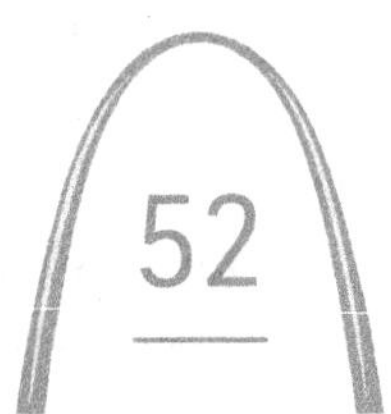

52

I fought through the rush-hour traffic all the way to Smugglers, my heart barely beating. Tom had been at the bar! Thick smoke rolled into the cloud-darkened evening, visible from a long way off. That would be the wood of the building burning; alcohol had no smoke. Damn! Tom just had to have made it out. He had to!

I cut over to Olive. The red strobes from the fire trucks bounced off the canyon of buildings broken only by empty lots. As I got closer, the red from the fire added itself to the light show. Flames poured out the broken windows and fire hoses stretched like engorged boa constrictors from the trucks and the hydrant across the street. The hoses from the trucks sprayed an alcohol resistant foam on the back of my bar. Those from the hydrant watered down the buildings next door and those parts of mine that were well away from the booze.

My Jeep screeched to a stop. I was out and running for the cordoned blockade. An officer stepped in front of me, arms wide. "I'm sorry, Ma'am. This is restricted access."

"It's my bar. I had an employee in there. Did he get out?"

"Wait here." He motioned another officer to stand with me while he walked toward a group of men.

I scanned the crowd, but I didn't see the face I wanted. No Tom. I pinned my hopes on the ambulance peering around one of the fire trucks.

The officer returned with a thick-set dour man I could only assume was the Fire Marshall. Hicks was on his name badge. He motioned for me to be let in, and I scrambled past my guard. Marshall Hicks asked, "Your name, Ma'am?"

"Sylvia Wilson. Did my employee make it out? Is he okay?"

"I need his name and a description."

"Tom Lawson. Medium height. A bit heavy. White. Brown hair. Glasses."

His lips pressed into a thin line as he wrote. When he looked up at me, his eyes were so, so sad. "I'm sorry to tell you, but we found a body. It was burnt so badly that identification will have to be made by the ME."

I couldn't talk. Couldn't breathe. I bent double, clutching my stomach. Clutching the hollow feeling that something, someone, had been ripped from my life again. Vaguely, I felt the Fire Marshall take me by the arm and lead me toward the ambulance. The heat from the alcohol fire was staggering. The singed air made it even harder to breathe. I coughed and cleared my throat again and again.

A gurney with a giant black bag was half-hidden behind the ambulance. Tom. First Aaron, now him. True, I didn't know Tom as well as I should – he was quiet and always busy with school – but he'd been part of my family circle. He'd eaten barbeque at my house. Shot pool with me. Happily run errands for me. I stopped and shook my head. "I can't go there."

I looked for Karyn and saw her standing by a police car. When she saw me, her face split into grief. A huge sob wracked her body and she half-ran, half-stumbled toward me. We held each other while tears washed from us. Our Tom was gone.

Eventually, I remembered what Dawes had said about Pike sending warnings. If that was true, he'd been watching me closely all along. Maybe was watching me now. I disengaged from Karyn, but held her with my arm around her waist. Scanned the myriad of faces watching the action, looking for either the man I'd seen in the bar, or the man in the photo I'd seen at Armstrong SRD. Neither was there. There was no one of that general face structure, either.

Lightning split the clouds above in muted strobes, buffered behind and within the grey tops. Low thunder rumbled no louder than a truck on the highway. A storm was building fast. It would break in a few hours. Eccheli pushed his way past the perimeter officers. He walked over. "I heard the call. Are you all right?"

"Is the patrol still watching my house and my dogs?" My voice was low and tight from inhaling the smoke.

"They are. I told them to make a visual check through a window too. We should hear back soon."

I nodded. "Dawes said this guy did this to warn me. If that's true, he should be here, but he's not."

A loud sizzle, then a ripping crash, came from the burning mess and flames belched out at the crowd. As one, the spectators stepped back, even though they were far enough away. Eccheli said, eyes still on the bar, "Doesn't mean anything. The way technology is these days, he's probably watching via camera."

"That doesn't seem like it would be satisfying enough for him. Seems like a step back."

"You two stay here, in the center of things. Don't wander off."

"I found something in the videos. I sent it to you. You probably already saw it, but I want to make sure. Way back, there's a scene where Blaisdale comes into the bar. Hands off some money to Degere, then goes to sit with Gagne. Pike was watching from outside the back door."

Eccheli nodded. "We saw that."

"Did you see the look on his face?"

"We did," he said quietly. Then, "Stay where we can see you."

He waited for my nod, then went to speak to Hicks.

Karyn and I watched the fire. In truth there wasn't much left to it. The flames were starting to suffocate under the foam, and the rest of the building was turning into a smoldering, soggy mess. The acrid odor of smoke had been added to by that of chemical. The heat, though, was still heavy. I couldn't think about Tom. Every time his face came to the forefront in my memory, I pushed it away. Thinking about Aaron didn't help either. It could just as easily have been him. Or Peaches. Or me. Maybe Pike had meant to kill Aaron like Dawes thought. It didn't sit right though.

I heard my name called from the crowd and turned to see Bobby towering over a perimeter guard. To the cop's credit, he didn't back down. Eccheli also turned from his conversation with Hicks and called to let my sometimes lover in. Bobby rushed to me and wrapped me in a big bear hug. He pulled Karyn in too. "You two okay?"

I blurted, "Tom didn't get out."

Shock lit across his face and his brow grew heavy. I could see that he thought we'd been in the bar and couldn't understand why one of us hadn't brought Tom out. I told them both everything that transpired that day, starting with my visit to Pike's workplace, through the visit to Gagne's apartment, Aaron's relapse from the snake attack, and ending with the fire.

Karyn sank to the pavement, her face blank with shock. In a monotone, she said, "Tom's grandmother is really sick. That's why he was planning on going home for Christmas. This is going to kill her."

Bobby lifted his gaze and slowly roamed the crowd. While he was doing that, Eccheli returned with news. "Your dogs are fine. Furious at the officers looking through the windows. The patrols will stay there all night."

I thanked him. At least that was one less thing I had to worry about.

As he walked away, Bobby finished his scrutiny. "So this guy, Raymond Pike, he's not here."

"That's what worries me. Why kill Tom, when he didn't kill my brother? It's backwards, you know?"

"Unless he meant to kill Aaron."

"Maybe." But I still had my doubts. Dawes's words haunted me. This could be a third warning.

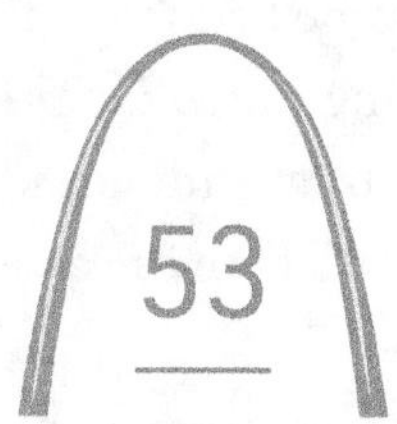

53

Around 7:30 PM, Olive Street was still closed from the fire. I'd called Peaches and found out Aaron was eating a Cubano. I told her about Tom. She started crying. I'd stayed on the phone with her as long as I could take it, but honestly, I was just barely hanging on.

Karyn had left an hour earlier, still tear-streaked. Bobby and I sat on the bumper of a fire truck across the street, staring at the black smudge that had been Smugglers. The whole place was completely gone. Cinders were all that was left. Both neighbors had taken a hell of a scorching, too. The street was slimy with foam and the air reeked of chemicals and sour wet ashes.

Lightning had moved from above the clouds to below, sparking across the night sky. A wind had kicked up. The air was still heavy with humidity though. If the storm was as bad as I thought it would be, the wind would have to get more serious.

Almost no one was on the street; the novelty of the fire was gone. The only people around were a couple patrolmen who were chatting with the few remaining fire fighters babysitting the embers. One of the cops was angled so he could glance at me every few minutes. The ambulance was long gone, snaking wet tracks down the road to the morgue. I had been told there would be an autopsy on Tom's body to learn why he hadn't come out of the bar. Most everyone assumed the fire killed him, but the consensus was he'd been tied up or unconscious at the time. I hoped he hadn't felt it.

Bobby asked, "You going to rebuild?" He'd been asking me odd questions here and there to take my mind off what had happened. Off the loss of my friend. Off the near death of my brother. Off everything.

The smoke hung in the air, trapped by the thick cloud cover. It raked at my lungs and I cleared my throat. I nodded. "It'll take a while for the insurance to settle. But after that." Maybe by then I'd be able to think about the bar without being haunted by everything that happened.

"The same bar? Smugglers?"

"Pretty much, yeah. But lately I've been toying with adding a kitchen. Nothing fancy, just sandwiches and burgers. Pizza." I cleared the smoke from my throat again and stood. I was sick of having cops watch over me. Sick of the whole thing. There was no way this was just another warning. This was much, much more. Where was he? Where was Pike? Again I scanned the crowd. He had to be there.

Bobby stood with me, overprotective that he was. "Kitchen's a lot of work. Higher overhead."

"Customers will stay longer, though." I walked the length of the fire truck, Bobby trailing. Stopped at the far corner and turned around. Scanned the remaining faces in the crowd yet again. Still no Pike.

The temperature dropped and the wind pushed against me. The preternatural dark sky was full of boiling clouds that constantly strobed from lighting. The storm had finally arrived.

My sometimes lover asked, "Want a job until you reopen?"

The cop glanced at me, then away.

I turned to tell Bobby how grateful I was and to suggest we hurry to find a place out of the oncoming storm, but he slowly fell sideways against me as red blossomed along the far edge of his teeshirt collar.

Before I could even react, there was a 'pop' and more than a million volts of electricity sang through my body.

Contrary to popular belief perpetrated by Hollywood, most people don't pass out from a normal stunning. Though, I certainly wished I would. My muscles clenched hard, pulling in opposite directions, until it felt sure my bones would snap. The agony was excruciating and all I could do was fall to the ground and moan. The sharp odor of urine filled the air around me as my bladder let loose. A dark form appeared above me. Brilliant blue eyes. Raymond Pike, dressed as the Lee Garret that had been in my bar, gripped me under the arms, and pulled me into the dark. He whispered, "I really enjoyed that. I hope you did, too."

The long stun gun wires sagged and scraped on the pavement. Every time they hooked, even on a tiny crack, they jerked the prongs in my chest, tearing my flesh. I wanted those wires to snag hard enough on something that they pulled the prongs right out. My Browning clattered out of my belt and onto the street. He scooped it up, jammed it in his own belt, and dragged me to a dark, ordinary looking sedan parked beyond the glow of the firetrucks.

He dropped me by the rear passenger's door. Right up on it, I could see the car was green. That great long drips marred the sides. That a hidden decal's edges stood out in sharp relief. Through the window, I saw the plastic cage divider between the front and back seats. A taxi. He pulled open the door and motioned me in. I struggled to my feet and complied. I couldn't have even managed to yell, much less fight. He snapped on some handcuffs and zip tied my feet. Then he cleaned out my pockets. Tossed my phone onto the street.

He'd been talking the whole time. "— to press this trigger to feed electricity to your body again. This stun gun holds two cartridges and I have more in my pocket, if you get the bright idea of ripping the probes out. If all else fails, I can use your gun and shoot you with a real bullet. However, I'd prefer to have you ambulatory, so behave yourself."

I nodded, though my head felt like a 70 ton boulder. Then the door slammed shut and he walked around to the driver's seat. I closed my eyes and tried not to think about Bobby's prone body bleeding out on the street.

Any second now, that cop was going to turn again.

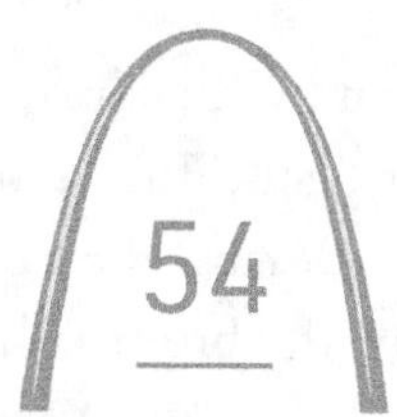

54

Once in the driver's seat, and pulling away from the fire scene, Pike said, "I have to confess, I halfway hope you try something. This stun gun is just too fun. That's something I didn't expect."

He made no attempt to hide where he was taking me. There was no blindfold, no twisting and turning. The heavens opened and dumped gallons of rain on St. Louis. He flipped on the wipers, then turned them to high. He might as well have not bothered, as heavy as the rain was coming. I kept hoping we'd have an accident so I could escape. Even if I died, it was still an escape. We slowed to a crawl.

During the lock training by my dad, he would let Aaron and me play with his cuffs. We got to be masters at slipping out of them just by putting a small pin or even a piece of paper in them when they were locked. No pin or paper in the backseat. But there was dried blood that had splashed onto the plastic divider. There were also splatters of it on the front dash and a smear of it on the steering wheel.

My abductor half turned in the front seat, speaking to me over his shoulder. "I warned you twice to stop. You should have listened. Did you think my brothers wouldn't call me? Your boyfriend would still be alive. So would your bartender. I even pretended to leave the country. You should have taken the hints. Instead, you betrayed everyone by thinking only of what you wanted. It's all on you."

I stared at the back of his head, starting to understand, remembering my video and the expression on Pike's dim face in the shadows outside my bar. Blaisdale and Gagne had been friends. Maybe even excluding Pike from their plans. They'd been punished, like Pike's parents had been punished. Because the parents only wanted the two athletic younger boys. But the brothers had been left untouched. Had Pike considered them innocent? Was that why he hadn't killed Aaron or my dogs? Because he'd considered them innocent too? What about Bobby, who was dying at that very moment? Why wasn't he considered an innocent? But I knew that answer: because he'd helped me identify Pike.

Somewhere in my bar, Pike had set up a second, or maybe even a third, camera.

One to focus on the big screen TV. One pointed at where he murdered Blaisdale. Maybe somewhere near my own cameras. They would have been micro cameras, too. But I hadn't seen any remnants of their mountings when I moved the positions of mine. Neither had the cleaning crew when they were working. Most likely they'd been behind the photos there too.

I asked, "Why did you kill Tom? He wasn't involved in this. He did nothing to help me."

Pike shrugged. "Right place. Right time."

The bitterness of that statement filled my mouth and settled into my stomach. Tom had been killed for no reason at all. He hadn't helped me. The only reason for his death was that I'd sent him to work the bar. Images flooded me: Tom's big frame and gentle voice. Eating plums. Shooting pool. Stabbing a steak off the grill. Asking for time off to go home to see his ailing grandmother at Christmas.

Pike had to be stopped. No matter what the cost.

From Highway 40, he turned north on 14th. We passed the abandoned and derelict Carr School and I remembered the killings that had taken place there a few years before. Some nut had taken a hammer to four homeless people. I shuddered. I knew where Pike was taking me.

He turned the car left on Biddle, then pulled into the first apartment complex and parked in the central lot. He got out into the buckets of rain and came around to my door and opened it. He was already soaked through. His hair was plastered to his head and rain ran in a river from his nose. He shot me with the stun gun. "In case you've forgotten what it feels like."

Electricity scored through my body, turning my muscles into iron-bending machines. The agony forced tears down my cheeks, and all I could do was lie there, taking it. It seemed like forever before he let off the trigger.

"There won't be any trouble from you, will there?" Rain sprayed from his mouth with the force of his words.

I shook my head. In truth, I never wanted to feel that kind of pain again. I'd take a million regular bullets first.

Pike tossed a pocket knife onto the seat beside me. "Cut your feet loose. Then close the knife and toss it to the ground in front of me."

I did as he told me, though very slowly; I just couldn't get my muscles to cooperate well. For a brief second, I contemplated turning the knife on my captor, but one glance at his squint-eyed vigilance over the sights of the stun gun and I knew better. I'd be too slow and fumbly. It would gain me nothing but more pain. I tossed the closed knife to his feet, where he scooped it up without even glancing at it.

He ejected the spent cartridge, his face an impassive mask. Except his eyes. Those shot blue darts of lightning at me. "Pull out all the prongs. We don't want the noise from the wires scraping the ground."

I worked the barbs out of my flesh with my cuffed hands, dabbing at the blood that snaked from the wounds.

"I think that's the least of your worries. Come on. Stand up. Let's get moving. Remember, keep your mouth shut." He jerked me into the onslaught of rain, not quite hiding the twist of disgust on his mouth.

From the parking lot, we went on foot though the buildings, stun gun trained on my back. Though I'd promised to behave, I couldn't keep from searching for an escape. In the dark alleyway between buildings, there were no bushes, nothing to hide behind. I'd be shot before I took three steps. Especially as slow as I'd be.

Coming out the other side, the unlit Carr School stared at us like a menacing monster in the dark. To the left was another derelict building, the Elkay Manufacturing building, still in the property of Elkay. Again, there were no hiding places, no way to avoid the stun gun. I'd have to wait.

Carr Elementary School had been built in 1908, in a 90 degree angle, the two arms reaching out to embrace the children in the central playground. From memory, I knew colorful mosaics of playing children adorned the outer walls, but I couldn't see them through the dark wall of rain.

It had been shut down in 1978. Every few years, the city lobbied to have it torn down, but The Carr Square Tenants' Association owned it and fought to renovate it into apartments for the elderly. But there had been no renovations and the building crumbled more and more each year. At this late point, it would take a complete gutting to make it usable again.

We went close enough to see the graffiti that marred the front doors, and we passed a lion's head fountain, now filled with concrete. We went to the far end of the left arm, where Pike motioned to a large piece of plywood nestled beside a graffiti tag. "Pull it to the side, but do it slowly." He wagged the stun gun at me to show me exactly what he was talking about.

I gripped the board on the far edge and pulled. It was waterlogged and heavy. The wrist cuffs clanking against each other sounded loud in the dark. The board slowly crawled through the city grime and decayed bits. I considered my options. From here, my only avenue of escape was into the building. It was dark in there, despite the fallen sections of roof. I also didn't have any idea of the condition of the floor I would be running on. Not ideal for an escape, but it could be done. And there would be plenty of places to hide.

My captor motioned me inside, down the stairs directly in front, leaving the plywood open behind us. Rain fell through the gaps in the roof, in constant waterfalls. We turned the corner at the landing and dropped further into the depths. The dark sucked us in.

I couldn't see.

But that also meant Pike couldn't either.

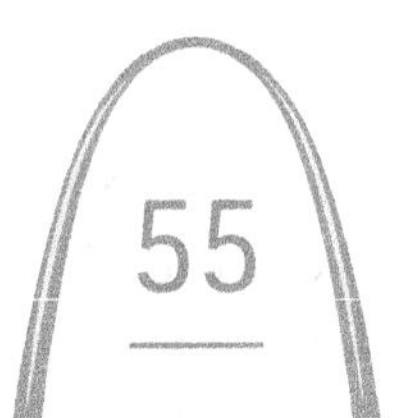

55

We reached the bottom floor and stopped. My captor flicked on a camping lantern waiting for him on the last step. He motioned me through a heavy steel door frame directly in front of us. The lamp cast shadows that bounced and swayed with each step. We passed through decrepit classrooms into those in even worse shape as we walked deeper into the old school's basement. I smelled campfires and heard the murmur of voices. My own shadow blocked most of the path ahead, but jumbles of crap were piled everywhere. One of these, then, would be my chance. If I could just get away, I could run to one of those fires where people would surely help me.

Thunder cracked above and the torrent of rain beat mercilessly on the ancient school. Even in the basement, water found its way down the walls. Formed a river that coursed down the center of the hallway we now walked. I slowed incrementally as we approached a pile of debris, to bring Pike closer. I even threw in a tiny fake stumble, but when I glanced back, he had stopped dead.

"Careful," he said.

"Something on the floor there." I made a motion behind me to a non-existent bump and began walking again. Much slower now.

Despite himself, Pike closed some of the gap between us.

Reaching the pile of trash, I was dismayed to spot no hard object to use on my captor. Rain had filled in a low spot there, soaking the crap. Smelling sour and gross. It didn't matter, I could do this. I had to. I would drop to the floor. Roll backwards toward Pike at the same time. Sweep my feet in an effort to knock him down. Push off with my cuffed hands, and disarm him like Teague had shown me. Then I'd be the one with the power.

I took a deep breath and fake stumbled again. Crumpled to the floor. Rolled backward. Swept my feet. Pushed off with my hands, prelude to standing.

And came face to face with the muzzle of the stun gun.

Every thought of what I learned in Krav Maga class left me then. Judo too. There were no moves, no stances, nothing. I was at the mercy of this monster. Pike's hot breath bathed my cheek and his voice was low and menacing. "Have you ever seen what happens to an eyeball when subjected to this much electricity? I have. Must be the worst pain in the world. Don't test me."

We held motionless like that for what seemed forever. Then he backed away, shifted his hand to the right and pulled the trigger. Two barbed prongs buried deep into my shoulder and I collapsed as hundreds of thousands of volts of electricity snapped through my body, pulling my muscles to the tearing point. I couldn't think. I couldn't breathe. I could only lie there, in that horrible agony, twitching and praying it would end soon. The barbs had gone deep, the pain they produced made my stomach lurch. Seconds stretched to eons.

Finally, he let off.

I felt wrung out like I'd hauled a tanker down the Mississippi by lead line on foot. Like I'd climbed to the top of Long's Peak in one hour. Like I'd swum the Atlantic until it met the Pacific, and across it until it became the Atlantic again. Like I'd crawled to the moon.

My stomach rebelled and bile rushed up my throat. I had no time to move. Vomit spewed over my turquoise shirt, the warm wet soaking through to my already drowned skin.

Pike said something, but my head was in a fog and I couldn't follow his words. I noted, however, that he'd moved back from me to a safe distance. I struggled to my feet, but my muscles didn't want to work like they should. My legs refused to hold my weight. It took several tries before I stood on shaky legs. My tormentor motioned with his stun gun for me to start walking down the hallway again.

My brain registered that my left hand had been hurting ever since my roll in the debris, and I saw now that a piece of broken glass was wedged into the back of it. A dark spot of blood welled from my wound when I pulled the wedge out. The shard was too big to use on the handcuffs, and too small to make an effective weapon against Pike. Still, it might come in handy. I snuck it into my pocket. That tiny piece of glass gave me hope. Somehow, I'd get out of this. I just had to figure out how.

My brain stumbled through this thought process, and added a couple more. First, I couldn't take any more of those shocks. I just couldn't. I didn't know how many it would take before my heart would give out, but it felt like it was close. Second, my time left on this earth was very limited now. I had to do something quickly. I had to remember what I'd learned. I had to try again. My weak legs seemed to trip over air molecules and my arms were quivering. But, I could do something. After the next blast of thunder, I put my hands to my forehead. "I don't feel good."

Pike didn't answer. We reached another set of stairs that went only up. Opposite them was a closed steel door. The hallway ahead made a sharp hook to the right. We were in the center of the building. He prodded me toward the door. I pushed it ajar and entered a dark, moldy room with big pipes that hooked out of the wall and attached to giant rusted boilers. Desks piled from floor to ceiling against a grime encrusted blackboard on the opposite side. Here, at least, the rain hadn't breached the walls yet. However, I could almost picture a giant lake over my head, building weight to break through the floor.

I let myself stagger a little bit.

"Careful!" he growled from behind.

"I don't feel well," I repeated over my shoulder, letting myself slur just a little bit.

In truth, I didn't feel well. But, it might have been a bit of an exaggeration. I leaned over and retched, hoping it sounded convincing.

As I stepped down onto the lower level where the massive boilers were located, I stepped short, coming down stiff legged, stopped, and then took a deep breath. Off to the left lay a hulking body in an olive military coat. The man's face was toward me, and I saw the barb buried deep in a mushroomed eye. I thought he was still breathing, but I couldn't be sure. Another of Pike's innocents?

Without any prodding, I continued toward what I assumed was to be my final destination.

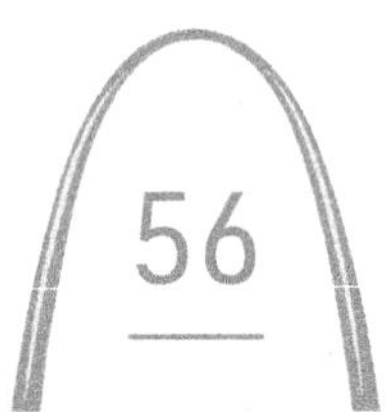

56

Pike motioned toward the ground near a fat cast-iron pipe. Hard rust covered it completely and holes filled the lower part of it like Swiss cheese. Rat feces, shredded papers, building debris, and chunks of plastic littered the floor. There was a circular burn mark where someone had made a fire at one time. The heavy odor of mold filled my nose. The thunder outside settled into a constant cacophony. The rain was so hard, I heard it all the way in the basement room.

"Sit," he raised his voice to be heard over the roar of the storm.

I sat.

He tossed another zip tie toward me. "Feet!"

I nodded and did as requested, fumbling with my fingers over the plastic. Once fastened, I tugged on it to show him I'd done it right. Not that it made any difference; I now had a use for the little piece of glass.

Pike reached into his shirt pocket and pulled out a handcuff key. He held it up so I could see it, and then tossed it to land by my feet. Shouted, "Unlock one hand, then relock it on the other side of the pipe!"

I unlocked my left hand and tossed the key back to him. It landed a couple feet short. He sidled closer and used his toe to pull the key toward him. Snatched it up and jammed it into his pocket. I wrapped my arms around the pipe to relock my cuffs. The pipe was about eight inches in diameter and came directly out from the tank horizontally for a couple feet, then turned ninety degrees and ran up through the ceiling. I gave it a gentle nudge and found it to be securely fastened.

Pike didn't seem to notice. The man before me was animated, pacing back and forth. He stopped and stared at me a moment, then between rumbles of thunder said, "You had to stick your nose where it didn't belong. This is your fault. You should have minded your own business like any other bartender!"

I shook my head. Crash came the thunder. "You're wrong. It's your fault. Everything is on you."

I was pretty sure he didn't hear everything I said, but he didn't seem to care. He frowned and resumed his pacing, but just a bit closer. He jerked his gaze over to me again. Shouted, "No one's coming!"

I didn't fall into his manipulation. I slumped, and letting my head loll, watching him closely. The storm somehow seemed to be on my side. Again the thunder let out a boom a split-second after I started speaking. "I don't feel good."

Pike appeared not to have noticed. His speech was slower now, his eyes dark blue, almost smoky. All the while, his march back and forth in front of me edged in closer. He continued his shout to be heard. "Your brother is lying in the hospital after being bitten by the snake I put in his desk! Your boyfriend's dead in front of your bar, where your friend burned! And your two detectives have a new murder to occupy them! No one's thinking about you!"

I slowly shifted my hands to wrap around the upturned part of the pipe. When the thunder quieted, I lowered my voice a bit more, my head still wobbly. "I don't need anyone to rescue me."

He stopped and stared at me again. Took a half-step closer. "And why is that?"

"I'm smart."

"Apparently not smart enough. You're trapped in a basement, chained to a pipe. About to die."

I took time answering, waiting out the thunder burst. Letting my words drift a lot. "I'm smarter than you."

Shock lit across his face. Took another half-step. I needed just one more step from him for my plan to work. My hands were in position, I was braced to go, even though I tried to look ill.

He waved his arms, the stun gun pointing in any and all directions. "I have a 193 IQ. You're not smarter than me."

I barked a laugh, then broke into a coughing fit that I hoped sounded real. I spoke even softer, nearly a whisper, slurring. The storm played its part in the drama and drowned out my words again. "Numbers mean nothing on the street."

He frowned and took the fated step toward me, leaning forward, and half turning his head to listen. "What?"

I pulled against my hands and shoved my feet right into his ankles. Attacked my attacker, Marshall Teague had told me.

With Pike's feet pushed backward and his center of gravity toward me, he fell in my direction, flailing to grab the pipe as he went.

I might not remember my Krav Maga, but I'd studied Judo for years. It was ingrained into me. I shoved my knees against his falling chest. His hand missed the pipe and he fell heavily onto his right side, still holding the taser. Another fast punch with my knees put him on his back and, while he was still unbalanced, I crashed my knees down on his throat, pinning him to the floor.

His hand came up with the stun gun, rearing back to shoot me anywhere he could reach. When it came close to my face, I bit, closing on the thumb. I held on, biting deeper and deeper, the warm salt of his blood filling my mouth. With a final crunch, his thumb separated from his hand and the stun gun fell to the floor with a clatter. The scream Pike let out was inhuman. It sounded like a wild animal.

I spit out the thumb and adjusted my grip on the pipe.

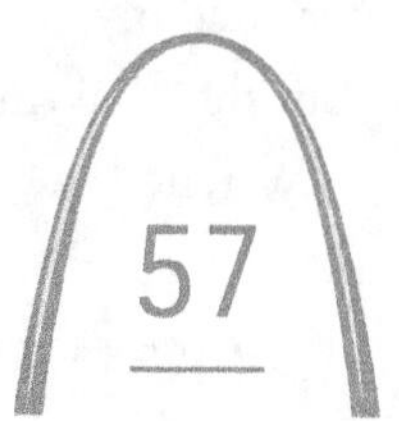

57

Another thing that's not true in the movies: a person is choked until they go limp in death. It takes very little time on the screen. They don't show the long, long moments while the frantic victim tries to tear himself out of your grasp, punching and clawing. They don't show his eyes begging for life and then reaching that moment of understanding he will die. And they don't show the reality that when the person did go limp, he was just unconscious.

I didn't need Pike able to wake at any indeterminate moment; I had no idea how long it would take me to get free. So, I stayed on his throat. His struggles grew weak and discoordinated. His face purpled with each passing second. The rasping of his breath weakened.

Through the storm, the piercing wail of a police siren reached the basement chamber. Like a volcano, Pike galvanized and thrashed until he worked his head out from beneath me. He scrambled to his feet, breathing deep harsh breaths, staring at the stun gun by my hip. When I shot my foot out to trip him up again, he staggered shakily out of range. With a final glare at me, he fled, leaving the taser behind.

Cursing, I moved my hips in close to my hands, diving into my jeans pocket for the tiny shard of glass. The cuffs impeded the depths I could reach, so I worked with my right hand on the outside of my pocket, squeezing the piece of glass up the material to my left hand.

The theory was easier than the practice. The shard stabbed me through the fabric. Twice, it evaded my grasp and slipped back down into the depths of the lint. But the final time, I prevailed and pulled out the chip. Through it all, I watched the darkness beyond the door for signs of movement.

The glass took a half-bite of the plastic zip tie at my feet and crumbled.

I growled until it became an open-mouthed, unintelligible scream at the man who'd terrorized me. I felt savage and above all, denied. Then I was done. Not because I wanted to be, but because between screams I'd heard approaching voices. I moved back onto my haunches and waited.

Within seconds, two young police officers swept into the room, one of them Jacobs. Their guns were at the ready, checking every possible hiding place, raincoats breezing behind them. The one I didn't know approached me, staring like I was a demon. He even crossed himself. Jacobs got a look at me and fell back a step. "Jesus!"

For a split-second, I couldn't figure out what the problem was, then I remembered the thumb. There was probably blood all over me, especially my mouth. There was still wet vomit on my shirt, too. I probably looked like I'd walked straight out of 'The Exorcist'. And there was no obvious reason for any of it. That could explain their reticence. Not to mention their religious references.

"Do you have any news on Bobby?" I asked the first cop, whose name badge read Charles, as he bent over my feet and cut them free. He smelled like he'd been locked in a car with chili dogs or nachos. Rain dripped from him onto my legs.

He shook his head. "I don't know anything about that, but I'll find out."

Once my feet were loose, he turned his attention to my handcuffs. Jacobs finished clearing the basement and turned to check the body of the blinded veteran.

The cuffs clinked to the ancient concrete floor. Officer Charles helped me to my feet. "Why don't we go out to the squad car while I try to find out about your friend." I knew what he was doing: he was managing me until my emotions diffused.

I hesitated. I really wanted to know about Bobby and Aaron. And I really just wanted tonight to be over. But Pike couldn't get away, not after everything he'd done. He'd drugged my dogs. He'd probably killed Bobby. He'd killed Tom, burnt down my bar, and nearly killed Aaron. And I didn't think he'd be done with me until I was dead, too.

I turned toward the door and sprinted after the killer. The two cops obviously hadn't seen him on their way down, so Pike had probably hidden in one of the nearby abandoned rooms. It was anybody's guess whether he was still hiding there or had taken advantage of the cops being preoccupied with me to escape the building. But I was betting on the latter. I couldn't be far behind him.

With both cops hollering at me to stop, I bolted up the stairs, two and three at a time, then raced down the hall and out through the squeeze space into the curtain of rain. A pair of headlights swept the courtyard as backup arrived, and I saw a slim shadow dart around the corner of the school. It had to be Pike. He wasn't running for the obvious choice of his car. I hurried after him.

Over the sound of the rain hitting the hard-packed dirt, Johnson's voice called my name. As I ran, I glanced over at the newly arrived car and pointed to where Pike had been. Shouted, "It's Pike!"

Then I rounded the corner just as she shouted back for me to wait.

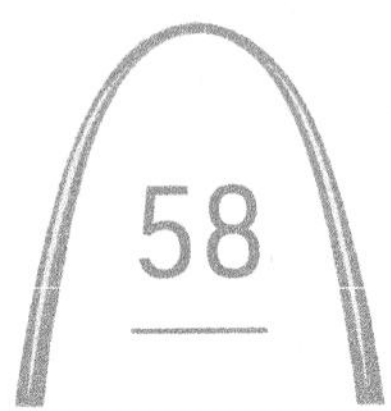

58

flattened against the dilapidated hulk of Carr School and waited. Not for Johnson, but for Pike to move again. Lightning crackled across the sky and the rain drove to the ground with punishing vengeance. The rain slewed sideways. The wind picked up even more and whipped the vegetation from side to side, but nothing else moved.

I wiped my nose. Rain always made my sinuses act up. It would be a miracle if I didn't catch pneumonia from this whole thing.

On the north side of Carr was a fence that separated it from a long, single-story warehouse-type building flanked by dense brush with hidey holes for vagrants. I'd heard it was owned by some ministry. They usually kept the lawn semi-mowed. Beyond that was an open, empty field filled with high, high weeds. The Elkay Manufacturing building stood at the eastern edge of that field. I couldn't see through the pitch of rain, so either could be Pike's destination. Or he could turn and cross Tucker to get lost in the maze of small buildings by the tracks.

Johnson slid up beside me on the wall. Through the growl of the wind, I heard her shout, "Where?"

I shook my head and wiped my nose. Nothing was creeping through the night. Had I imagined it? What if the shadow I'd seen was some displaced guy looking for a place to wait out the storm? What if Pike was still in the school? The rain became a wall between us and the far end of the mission building. It slid down the wall behind me and puddled where my shoulder blades met brick. Where my butt met wall. My beautiful turquoise shirt was a stained, sopping mess and stuck to every curve that I had. With the exception of the stains, Johnson wasn't much better. Water poured off the bridge of her nose, and she kept her head canted downward to keep the rain out of her eyes. I yelled back. "I'm pretty sure it's him. But he hasn't moved since I turned the corner."

She shook her head and cupped her ear. I raised my voice. "I think he's here, but I don't know where! He's got my Browning."

She looked me up and down looking at the mess, probably wondering how traumatized I was. She leaned in to me and yelled, "If I give you my backup, do you promise to aim to injure, not kill?"

At my quick nod, she leaned down and pulled a Glock 43 from her ankle holster. Handed it to me. She looked me in the eye. Shouted. A bright bolt of lightning shot the sky directly above us. Not even a second later thunder exploded the air. The only words I heard of Johnson's were, "—your promise."

The pistol felt good in my hand. Cool. Strong. Solid. Any indecisions I'd had about chasing Pike disappeared. He had been the shadow. I knew it. I pointed in the direction I'd last seen him, heading toward the length of the mission building. She jutted her chin toward a skinny path that traveled along the back of Carr and hooked across the fence toward the far side of the mission building. By that I took it to mean I was to search over there. She stepped away from Carr in the opposite direction and crept along the line of the fence and crossed through a break. I lost sight of her in the torrent of rain after that.

I turned away and followed the path along the back of the school. The ground was baked hard by the heat and sun of the past few weeks, and the rain hadn't been able to penetrate it yet. Water pooled on the bare earth, sloshing into my running shoes. When the path hooked into a dense growth of brush, I pushed through and scaled the fence, landing with a haphazard slide in the wet cut lawn on the other side. Moving in close to the line of shrubs along the mission building, I paused and took a good look around. During flashes of lightning, I could see there was nothing and no one between me and the next road. Otherwise, it was pitch black.

I couldn't see anything. The rain bit at my skin. I was soaked all the way through. My breath came out in a fog. My nose was a faucet.

Ambivalence filled me about Pike. Realistically, I expected him to be on Johnson's side of the building, but I hoped he was on mine. I may have promised not to kill him, but I still had a score to settle. I gritted my teeth and sidled up the length of the building, startling a shaggy homeless woman shivering beneath a wildly flapping tarp. She stared at the gun, panic wide in her eyes. I pointed the Glock away, nodded my apology, and moved on.

I was nearing the far end of the building when lightning bolted across the sky and I saw a lean shadow bulge against the shrubs and then merge into them. I held my breath. Pike or Johnson? Would Johnson have gotten there that quickly? I ducked low and crept along the side. I was nearly on the shadow person when lightning cracked across the night, turning it into a strobe theater. Thunder rumbled, as if from a heavy engine. Rain drove to the earth like a million sparkling arrows sprung from the heavens.

The shadow turned into a man's profile just a few feet in front of me. Pike!

And he was holding my Browning close to his body, facing the corner. The corner which Johnson would be coming around any second. Adrenaline spiked through me. I could end this nightmare forever. Make sure Pike never hurt anyone again. Screw the promise I'd made to Johnson. There wasn't a court that would convict me, after what I'd been through. At the worst, I'd get committed to a psychiatric ward for a little while.

But then I remembered the little boy, the two brothers, and their parents. Anyone like Pike who'd grown up in a place like that was bound to be not quite right. I closed the gap. Pressed the muzzle of the Glock hard against the base of his skull and yelled over the downpour, "Drop that gun!"

I didn't really think he knew any type of self-defense tactics. It would have shown when we scrapped in the school. I wasn't worried about that. But I *was* worried that he would try to shoot Johnson as she rounded the corner. Trapped animal and all. For a split-second, he didn't move. Then he half-turned toward me. Lightning played across the clouds like crazed pottery, and his eyes sparked. I could almost see him calculating the possibilities.

I pushed harder on the Glock, right in that soft little hollow under his skull. My heart beat like tribal drums in my ears and sweet adrenalin coated my mouth.

He lifted the Browning higher.

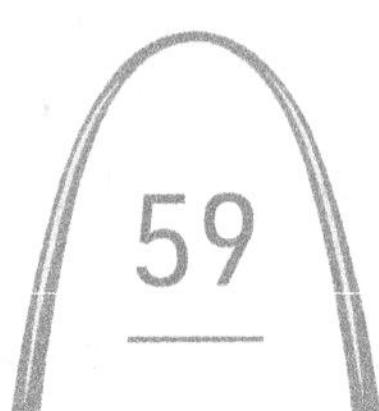

59

I tightened my finger on the trigger. Even though the pistol rocked back in my hand when it shot, the sound was lost in the storm. Pike dropped like a stone as Johnson rounded the corner.

She joined me at Pike's body. I barely saw her face in the dark. The weight of the rain made a sheer haze between us, even though she was right on the other side of Pike from me. I couldn't see if she was worried or relieved or anything. She reached down and took my Browning from Pike's still hand, then took her Glock from me.

Jacobs appeared out of the wall of rain. Johnson explained what was what. She handed off the crime scene. As we ran back to the vehicles, I asked her about Bobby and she held up her hand and took out her phone. The light from the screen momentarily lit her heavy frown.

She stopped by the car and hit speed dial. Spoke to someone I assumed was her husband. "We got Pike…. Yes, at Carr….Dead… She looks fine.….Any news on Crow?…I'll call them."

Disconnected. Hit speed dial again. Got routed through the hospital phone system. Spoke to a nurse. Then disconnected.

"He's alive. In surgery. The nurse I spoke to thinks his chances are good. Nick will take over here; he's on his way. I'm going to take you the hospital." She nodded. "Okay?"

"Thank you." Wiped my nose. All the terror of the past two weeks swept in on me and deep tremors started in my limbs. My teeth chattered.

Johnson propelled me to her car. "Bobby's alive. You're alive. Pike is dead. It's over." As if I was a child, she buckled me in and patted my shoulder. Water dripped from my hair and my ruined clothes to puddle on the seat beneath me.

An ambulance arrived then, strobing brilliant lights, and Johnson pointed the EMS workers toward the mission building, and then toward the plywood opening where Officer Charles waited. The attendants and Charles disappeared inside Carr.

When Johnson settled into the driver's seat, I asked, "How'd you find me?"

"We found a dead cabbie, but the cab was missing. Nick went to the taxi company. The dead driver's cab was there, but another was missing. The GPS was disabled. Then a homeless guy called about intruders at Carr." She shrugged as if it was obvious. And maybe it was. I felt guilty that I was glad the homeless were still so paranoid about what had happened at the school a few years ago.

"He put cameras in my bar. Besides the one that caught the alarm code."

"Makes sense."

"But then he had to know about my micro camera."

"Depends on where his were focused."

"I guess." Maybe Pike had removed his by the time I put in mine. I doubted the cops had set the alarm during the time they had the bar closed. He could have gone in any time.

"Will your cameras have shown what happened tonight?"

I shook my head, thankful to not be able to see Tom's death. "They load up to the cloud at five in the morning. So, no. There will be nothing."

We stopped talking after that. She drove me to Barnes emergency room. Got me checked in with the receptionist, who immediately handed her a mask. I didn't get one this time; patients didn't wear them. Upon seeing my shaking, the receptionist immediately had me taken to a curtained exam table where I was wrapped in a hot blanket and given coffee. Then she disappeared. The coffee should have warmed me, but it didn't. Slowly, I came to realize my chill was from the trauma of the night. Shock. I gulped the coffee like I was a writer on a deadline. Nurses came to check on me every few minutes. Every time my coffee was low, they refilled it. When my blanket cooled, one of them brought another.

Johnson was gone for nearly an hour, and when she returned, she had a big smile. "They say your boyfriend's going to be fine. Your brother's causing trouble; he wants to come down here to see you. The nurses won't let him. Your dogs are fine too."

I nodded. I'd completely forgotten about my pooches. Some mom I was. There was going to be some major sucking up when I got home.

She hesitated and then said, "I'm impressed. I really am."

I didn't know what to say. Was this a trick? Or was she serious?

She continued, "It isn't easy being the target of a killer, but you kept your wits about you. You did well."

She shook my hand and left. Eccheli was still out in the storm and needed assistance wrapping up things at the crime scene.

After a few hours, long after Johnson left, the nurse came to tell me Bobby was in recovery. The surgery had been a success. I had trouble stifling my yawns, so I gathered my blanket, left the emergency room, and wandered to where my sometimes lover lay asleep under a light-weight blanket. I watched his chest rise and fall with each breath. Somehow he didn't look so big, lying in that bed. Small, like Aaron had.

He woke briefly around the 45 minute mark, saw me and announced, "I'm gonna kick your ass."

Startled, I jumped to my feet, frowning. I leaned in close. "What?"

"Gonna kick your ass in the tourney." Then he was asleep again. Apparently he'd forgotten about the fire. I envied him. I wished I could forget about the loss of the bar too, but it had taken someone very dear to me with it. I rehashed the events that had led me there, cold and wet, waiting for Bobby to wake.

Pike had killed Blaisdale, Gagne, and Tom. He'd almost killed Bobby, Aaron, and me. He was a bad man. I was glad he was gone. No doubt about that. But I felt guilty, somehow. Was it just because I'd killed someone? Or was it more?

I wasn't ready for that answer yet, so shied away from that train of thought. I needed to call Tom's family. That was one phone call I didn't want to make. They probably knew about his death already, courtesy of the ME office, or cops, or someone. But as his friend and employer, I needed to speak to them too.

When Bobby's snoring deepened, I went looking for my brother. Even though still wet from the rain, I wasn't leaving puddles everywhere anymore. I dropped my blanket on an empty wheelchair in one of the halls and tore off my hospital ID band. I found two uniformed officers guarding my brother's room, and Aaron sitting up in bed, buttoning his shirt, having an animated conversation with Peaches, who was still in her blue health mask. They quieted the moment they saw me. I could only imagine the sight. Not to mention the smell.

I went to Aaron, and he held me in a bear hug for a long time. When finally pulling away, his eyes were rimmed with red. He wasn't the only one choked up. My eyes were burning from sudden tears too.

Peaches leaned in for a gentle hug and said, "That police detective told us what happened. I went to look for you, but you weren't in the ER anymore. No one knew where you'd gone."

When she pulled away, Aaron butted in with, "She was with Bobby. How is he?"

Was he actually asking about my boyfriend? "He'll be fine. Still sleeping from the surgery."

Aaron nodded. Seemed relieved. I made a mental note to mention it to Bobby. He'd get a laugh. Rain stung the window like a zillion furious bumble bees. The night sky was a constant cacophony of lights behind the clouds. Here and there, a zigzag bolt of white darted into view. I shivered, though not because I was still damp and the air in the hospital was cool. But from all that had transpired over the past couple weeks. The repercussions of Blaisdale's murder had taken over my life like a lightning storm, scarring and destroying everything, and nearly everyone, in its path.

A heavy clap of thunder shook the hospital and was quickly followed by a second and third. The lights flickered. As one, we all looked up at the ceiling for a few seconds, then when nothing further happened and the lights stayed on, we all returned our attention to the room.

An awkward silence followed, finally broken when a masked nurse rushed in. She landed a stack of paperwork on the bed table and glared at both Aaron and me. "There are a few papers to sign before you two go. Since it's obvious you're planning on leaving. You can't just walk away."

Her words mocked me, building my guilt. I should have walked away from the murder. Let the police sort the whole thing out. Eccheli would have eventually figured out I wasn't involved in the murder. Bobby and Aaron wouldn't be in the hospital. And Tom wouldn't be dead.

The room suddenly felt tight. The air, stale. I needed to get out of there, out of that hospital. I raged through my paperwork and signed my name to the final page of the documents, ripping through the paper with the point of my pen.

I brushed a kiss on my brother's cheek, then whispered in his ear, "I'm sorry."

Then I pulled away and asked, "You're staying with us after you get out, right?"

His eyes were open wide from my apology and it took him a moment to get his bearings. Finally, he nodded. "No arguments from me."

"Okay. See you there. I have a few things to do, first." I hugged Peaches. She gave a curious tilt of her head, probably suspecting something wasn't right with me. Wisely, she chose to look away.

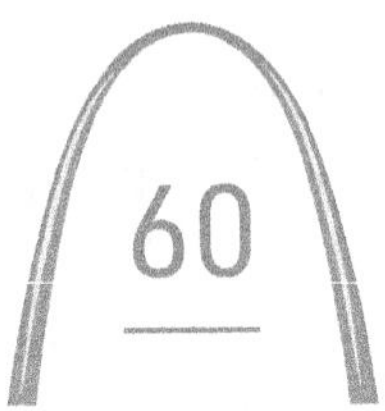

60

I returned to the recovery room where Bobby lay, his body dormant as death except for the heaves of his chest. I placed my hand over his heart and watched it rise and fall with the rhythm of his breaths. The blinding bright lights echoed back from the white floors and white walls. Slurred murmurs and medicine-dulled snores seeped through the blue curtains that flanked either side of him. I went to fetch the rolly chair that I'd sat in before, usurping it from beside a sleeping patient four beds away. I'd give it back if it turned out he had a visitor waiting for him. Probably.

I placed my chair and sat quietly, trying not to think about anything in particular. Trying to blank out the events that had just occurred. Trying to ignore the chill that crept through my still damp clothes. Shivers turned into teeth-shattering tremors. When I couldn't stand it anymore, I rose and went to the nurse's station. "May I have another blanket for my boyfriend?"

She cat-smiled over her mask and handed me a thin white one out of a warmer of some kind. I held it close to my chest until I was out of her sight, then cocooned myself in it. I even pulled it over my head and listened to the rain smacking against the window. Lightning still dashed across the sky, followed by the thunder. Slowly the constant shivers subsided to occasional. I told myself that I'd hand over the blanket to Bobby as soon as he woke. But for now it was all mine.

The ripsaw of Bobby's snores eventually stopped. His eyes fluttered awake, staring at the ceiling. As he got his bearings, he slowly looked around the room. His face flushed when he saw me, and his eyes moistened. He cleared his throat. "I wasn't sure …."

I spread my somewhat cooler stolen blanket across him, though it was now damp, sat on the edge of his bed, leaned in, and gave him a lingering kiss. I wanted him to know how important he was to me. How worried I'd been. How devastated I'd be if he'd died. When we finally came up for air, he fingered the wrap on his throat and asked, "What the hell happened?"

"Pike cut your throat because he didn't want to alert the cops with the sound of a gunshot. You're lucky to be alive."

He nodded. "And you?"

"He used a stun gun on me. Forced me into a stolen cab." I told him all that transpired at Carr School and the subsequent shooting. I showed him my disgusting clothes as proof of what had transpired, pointing out the appropriate stains on the turquoise shirt at different parts of the story.

He listened quietly and shook his head when I finished. "I get that Pike killed Blaisdale and the other guy for what he considered betrayal of their friendship, but I still don't understand why it happened in your bar."

The guy in the bed on the other side of the curtain coughed until he gagged. A nurse buzzed past to assist him. The sound of her soothing voice floated through to us, but not her words. The coughing stopped.

I returned to our conversation. "As near as I can tell, Blaisdale betrayed Pike's friendship with Gagne at Smugglers. Pike must have figured it was a fitting place. He decided to use robbing it as an excuse to get Blaisdale alone. It could have been anywhere at all."

"Huh." He got a far off look, and then he gazed around the room. At the nurse who glanced in at us as she returned to the nurse's station.

"Me. Tom. Aaron. The fire. All this because Blaisdale and a buddy stopped for a drink at your bar."

I ran my thumb down his cheek. "I'm sorry for what happened to you." I hoped he could see how much I meant it.

"What? It's not your fault." His voice was soft and he frowned.

"It actually is. Pike came after all of us because I stuck my nose in his business. He told me that. I should have left it alone. Let the cops handle it."

"All you did was identify the guy for your detective. Everything that happened after isn't on you."

"I went to see his family. That's on me."

"Pike's?"

I nodded. "And I identified him at his work place."

"Last I checked, none of that merits a death sentence. Not even from a nutcase."

I couldn't argue with that. I smiled and nodded. "By the way, Aaron was asking after your well-being."

That evoked another, "Huh."

"He'll probably deny it if you say anything."

"No doubt. Might have to start bein' nice to him, though. So, you comin' to work for me?" His eyes fastened to mine, hope brimming in the unwavering gaze.

I hesitated. I didn't really want to burst his bubble after everything I'd put him through. "There will be Tom's funeral. And I have to deal with the insurance. Make plans for the new bar. Get contractor bids. Give Ginger Jefferson her interview. And I'm going to sleep for a week. These past few days have been over the top busy and stressful. Then I'll start thinking about the job. My tournament players need a home, though."

"I'll see what I can do. Sounds like you'll be busy for a while. But the job'll be open for you whenever you're ready. Hey, who won the baseball game today?"

I shrugged. "I missed it completely."

"Slacker." Drugs couldn't hide the way his eyes sparkled when he grinned. He lifted his hand. Stroked my cheek, sending tendrils of heat deep into my belly. I forgot any chills I'd had.

He cupped my neck and pulled me in for another kiss. The sound of the storm moved away.

THE END